THE
GOBLIN
KING

THE GOBLIN KING

SHONA HUSK

sourcebooks
casablanca

Published by Sourcebooks Casablanca, an imprint of Sourcebooks, Inc.
P.O. Box 4410, Naperville, Illinois 60567-4410
(630) 961-3900
Fax: (630) 961-2168
www.sourcebooks.com

Printed and bound in the United States of America.
RRD 10 9 8 7 6

For Jon, for believing in my dreams

Chapter 1

THE SUMMONS PULLED AT EVERY CELL IN HIS BODY, TEARING the bonds that held him together and dragging him from the Shadowlands. He fought the compulsion to answer, as he did every time. And lost. As he did every time. The urge to obey his summoner's orders he'd tamped down long ago. Yet he attended, as he did every time.

The beads in his hair jangled and chimed, lifted on the breeze created as he moved from one world to the next, like golden music in his ears. He moved into the Fixed Realm wrapped in shadows to hide from the eyes of his would-be commander. Then he paused and looked around.

A bedroom. Not the first he'd been summoned to. The only light spilled from the nearby bathroom. His nose wrinkled at the smell of wet dog and wine. He frowned. No summoner stood before him, demanding an audience with the Goblin King. The human who'd called him from the Shadowlands and sought to control him lay on the floor at the foot of the bed. Immobile. Wounded. Female.

The goblin kept his hand on his sword and stepped forward. As he did, the shadows sloughed off him and slid away to the corners of the bedroom. The tension in his skin eased as the compulsion to obey faded. He'd attended. He could leave. Yet he couldn't look away.

The woman breathed, her breasts lifting with each inhalation. Her black silk dress clung to each curve, hiding and revealing without ever moving. His fingers rubbed together as if feeling the glide of silk on skin.

His concentration was broken by a knock on the door. The handle turned slightly. He raised one hand and metal jammed, securing the room. The door would hold until he was done.

"Eliza, you have to come down." A man's voice came from the other side of the door, the words just shy of an order. The handle jiggled, then a fist pounded on the door as the man tried to get into the bedroom. Could he sense the darkness creeping under the door, leaking from the goblin?

The goblin squatted and studied the woman the man had called Eliza. *Eliza.* Her name echoed in his ears as if he should know her. Her head was bleeding, the dark blood seeping into the darker carpet. He reached out to touch her, drawn to her beauty the same way he was drawn to the gold hanging from her ears. The light from the bathroom cut across his mottled gray skin. He jerked his hand back as if he'd been burned. It was this body the woman would see if she woke now. A body not even he could bear to see. He should unlock the door and leave. Let the man who kept knocking tend her cut feet and bruised head.

He hesitated. Eliza had called the Goblin King.

"Open up, Eliza." The knocking became more urgent. The tone less caring. "You look like a fool hiding from your own birthday."

Charming. *She is unconscious, you fool. And drunk.*

Something was amiss. He rocked back on his heels as he assessed the woman and the bedroom. Glass and wine covered the bathroom floor. Eliza lay unmoving.

Yet the man demanding her presence knew none of this. He shook his head and the beads rattled. This wasn't his problem. The gods knew he had enough of his own.

But Eliza had wished. Wished to be taken away. And he wanted to obey. Her words pulsed in the air and shook in his presence. The goblin let her wish settle around him like a cloak made of the darkest dreams—where hers ended and his began. He forced out a breath. No good would come of this.

The door vibrated under a fresh onslaught of hits this time accompanied by muttered swearing. His fingers brushed over the ends of her blond hair. There was something disturbingly familiar about her. Her face, the curve of her lips. Where had he seen her? Had she summoned him before? There was something about the magic, her words…His eyes narrowed and he glanced back at the door. He couldn't think through the thousands of summons he'd answered with that incessant noise. Couldn't the man give him some peace?

"What am I supposed to tell the guests?" The man's silence seethed with fear. "Fine, have it your way. We'll talk tomorrow." He gave the door a final slap before his footsteps faded away. No fight to be had.

The goblin smiled. Eliza was his.

He scooped up her limp body. Her fair skin was scented like summer blossoms. It had been so long since he'd felt the summer sun on his skin. So long since he'd been able to touch a flower without killing the bloom. So long since he'd had company, female company.

Her head lolled against his arm. He cradled her closer and murmured against her hair.

"You should be careful what you wish for, Eliza."

Her name rolled easily off his thick tongue. "For I am all too happy to oblige," he said with a laugh that held no joy.

The shadows closed around the Goblin King, drawing him, and his prize, home to the Shadowlands.

Eliza was warm against him. She glowed as if lit from within, a radiance not usually seen in the Shadowlands. He hesitated, not wanting to lay her down and lose contact. He liked her weight in his arms and the touch of her skin against his. If she woke now, in the Shadowlands, he would look human with a face he had no qualms about Eliza seeing. He inhaled her delicate female scent once more. His body responded as any man's would, and the lust for something other than gold burned through him as unfamiliar as it was pleasant.

Soon enough. He preferred women who participated, eagerly.

He placed her on his bed, and her dress rode up over her thighs, revealing long, smooth, creamy white legs. He ran his thumb over the scar on her inner knee. Like dew on a spiderweb, it accentuated the perfection of her body. He brushed the scar again. Years he chose not to count had passed since any woman had called the Goblin King, and he intended to make full use of the summons.

Who was he to disobey her command?

He fanned her hair over the sheets on his bed, an old four-poster taken from a palace. The posts were cleverly carved with a hunt, the prey forever chased by the hunter. He doubted the French king who'd originally had it noticed its disappearance.

He'd gathered beautiful objects from all over the world to fill his caves. Authentic Persian carpets, Ming vases, silk drapes, gold statues, gold mirrors, gold coins. Yet…something was always missing. So he followed his goblin nature—when in doubt add more gold. It was an easy way to decorate.

But an empty way to live.

Now he had another beautiful object to entertain him while he wasted eternity. His knuckle traced her cheek. Eliza didn't flinch and her eyes remained stubbornly closed. She would look upon the king she'd called and have her audience on her knees.

He tore his gaze away and stared at the cavern's ceiling. The beads in his hair hit his back like hail as they resettled. He was hard, ready. He fisted his hand, fighting the urge to possess the woman he had taken, and drew in three deep breaths. They did nothing to settle the rough lust riding in his blood.

Did he want her with the need of goblin, or the desire of a man?

Did it matter anymore?

Yes.

He still had a human soul, if only barely. If he were truly goblin, he would already be buried to the hilt, enjoying his first root in a couple of centuries.

His nails broke the skin on his palm. The pain grounded him and gave him something else to think about besides his daily battle with the curse. He uncurled his pale fingers. Scarred knuckles, callused palm. His hands. Warrior's hands. Not the gray, gnarled hands of the monster he was cursed to be. He ran the palm of one of those hands over his groin as he got up. The jagged need didn't slacken, but he wouldn't be the monster today. He didn't need to be.

She would awaken soon enough and realize what she'd summoned.

He pulled back the gold, embroidered silk curtain and found his subjects waiting for him on the other side. He truly never got any peace. His brother, Dai, and Anfri stood, arms crossed, in the hallway. They would've known the second he'd returned.

"She's mine." It was all he needed to say. He had been their king in life, and he was their king in curse. They were all who were left. The others had been granted the mercy of death, except the one who had faded to goblin.

He glared at Dai, then at Anfri. Anfri held his gaze for just a moment too long before looking past his shoulder to Eliza.

"A woman, Roan?" Dai acted as if they had never brought women to the Shadowlands before.

They hadn't. Not like this. In the past they had parted with gold, then silver, for a woman's company. Now they would rather keep the coin. A reminder of how far they'd come from being men who'd fight and drink and fuck, to becoming misfits so almost goblin they'd rather the glittering lure of gold.

"Only one." Anfri moved for a better look at Eliza.

Roan blocked his view. He placed a hand on Anfri's arm. "The woman is mine."

Anfri's face contorted as his eyes yellowed and bulged. The gold heart in Roan's chest ached in response. He could no longer ignore the change in Anfri.

He knew the signs too well and it was happening again. Anfri was fading.

"Roan, this isn't wise," Dai said. "What about—"

"This is different." Roan glared at him.

"Yes, brother, you kidnapped her." Dai pressed one hand against Roan's chest where his heart should've beaten. Concern deepened the lines in the younger man's face. Dai should have been the older sibling—he was always watching, making sure Roan didn't slide into the curse without noticing. His men's lives would have been so different if he had died that day on the battlefield.

Roan removed Dai's hand. "She asked."

"She didn't know what she asked."

"Too late." Too bad. Eliza was his. A prize fit for a king.

"She is injured," Anfri said, stopping Dai's arguments.

Roan turned away, not wanting to see the judgment on his brother's face. Instead he focused on the cuts on her feet, where blood stained her soles and spread to his sheets. His gut tightened as the magic of the Shadowlands ran through him, begging for use, urging his surrender. He hissed. He didn't want anyone else touching Eliza, but her wounds weren't life threatening, so no magic was required. He had to let Anfri tend to Eliza. He was the closest thing to a doctor they had, patching their injuries hundreds of times over the centuries.

"Get your kit," he said to Anfri before turning to his brother. "I didn't do it." He knew exactly what his brother was thinking, the same way Dai knew his thoughts too well. "I'm not that close to succumbing."

Dai nodded. They both knew. Not this time. Maybe not next time. But soon.

⚜

Milk dropped into Steven's coffee like a turd. It splashed onto his hand and the cuff of his shirt. He swore and tipped the foul brew down the sink. Then he pulled out another carton, the low-fat, high-calcium crap Eliza liked, and gave it a trial sniff. He gagged. Every drop of milk in the house had soured overnight. It would have to be black coffee, the perfect end to the perfect night spent in the guest room after Eliza's little temper tantrum.

He drank the coffee fast even though his stomach complained, still struggling with the after-effects of last night's alcohol. Last night, what a nightmare that had turned out to be. He'd made excuses for her not being there to cut her cake. A migraine. His knuckles whitened. She was giving him a fucking migraine.

Steven left the cup in the sink and stalked upstairs. He'd break the door down to get in if he had to. He should've hauled her out last night. He shook his head. No. Better she acted the fool in private. In public they were perfect, the soon-to-be Mr. and Mrs. Slade, heirs to the Coulter legacy.

He twisted their bedroom door handle. The metal groaned and opened. Last night the handle hadn't budged. He shrugged off the faint sense of unease gathering around him like whispered accusations. She must have jammed the door and then felt repentant this morning. Pity he wasn't in the mood to forgive.

He stepped into the room, then reared back at the appalling stench. His bedroom smelled like a party of drunken rats had drowned and then dried under a relentless sun.

"Jesus." It was worse than the milk.

His wardrobe door hung open. The rails where his suits and shirts had hung were gappy and grinning like an old man missing teeth.

"What the hell?" His face twisted with rage. Every suit was gone.

Steven turned. The bed was empty and un-slept in. Where was she? He spun. She wasn't in the bathroom but the bath was full. Every one of his suits was stuffed into the tub.

"Fuck, no."

The stink was wet Italian wool and wine. And was that wine or blood on the white tiles, pooling in the grout?

Steven snatched up the phone from his side of the bed and dialed Eliza's cell phone. This little stunt was too much. She had no right to do this, after everything he'd done...

A chirp answered his call. Anger congealed into a sharp-edged brick that wedged in his gut. He stomped around the bed and flung open her wardrobe door, knowing what he'd find. Her handbag. He pulled the little black bag down from the shelf. Her phone lit up the interior. Keys. Wallet. Sunglasses. All still inside. His rage exploded. The phone slid out of his fingers and bounced in the soft burgundy carpet.

It could have been the hangover, or the smell of his ruined suits, or that Eliza was gone and he would have to involve the police. His stomach heaved and acid coffee scratched his throat. Steven ran for the bathroom, stepping on the smashed wine glass and slicing his foot. He didn't have time to curse. He barely made it to the toilet.

If she ruined his plans, he'd kill her, he swore as he threw up.

Chapter 2

ELIZA'S HANDBAG SAT ON THE TABLE, SMALL AND NEAT AND expensive. But then he'd bought it for her, and it perfectly suited his tastes. Steven had brought it downstairs and placed it in the cloakroom for the police to find. She may be missing, but he didn't want the police in the bedroom. Not until he'd finished cleaning up. Partners were always the first suspect. Given the spat last night, a giant novelty neon-yellow sports finger was pointed his way, declaring him guilty of a crime he hadn't committed.

He didn't need the police uncovering the ones he had.

"So you had a fight at eleven," the cop read from his notes.

"Approximately." Steven folded his hands. He stopped short of wringing them; that would be too much.

"Then Ms. Coulter disappeared."

Steven nodded. "I thought she'd gone upstairs to tidy up."

"Tidy up?" The cop raised his eyebrow.

"Fix her makeup. She was upset."

"Give her twenty-four hours." The cop closed his notebook. "She's probably at a friend's."

Which friend? He knew all her friends and none of them would hide her from him…except the bitch sister-in-law, but she wouldn't involve her precious brat. Eliza should've been in the bedroom. How had she left the party without being seen by anyone? Without taking her car, or cell, or purse? Yet she'd vanished, leaving everything behind, but taking everything she knew about him and his business dealings. For all he knew she was having a chat with the Major Fraud Squad now. His throat constricted.

"I'm worried." What if she'd planned this and faked her own disappearance just to get the police involved? "She's never done anything like this before."

And wouldn't again, once he got his hands on her. His mind raced. If she didn't turn up, maybe he could still use it to his advantage. The paperwork pointed at her…that alone gave her motive to vanish with the cash.

"It happens more often than you'd like to think." The cop made to leave, then turned. "What was the fight about?"

Steven hid his frustration at the cop for lingering. Who cared what they fought about? He fabricated a lie around enough truth that it was plausible.

"She saw me talking to another woman. Got jealous. Women on their birthdays—they just don't like getting older." Steven walked toward the door.

He didn't want to seem overly eager to get the cop out, but if the constable looked hard enough, there would be something that would earn a more detailed investigation of the house. He couldn't afford that. He was working a balancing act. He wanted Eliza found *and* he wanted his privacy.

Did he want too much?

"She'll be back by dinner," the cop assured him.

She'd better be. But already he was making a contingency plan. Eliza wouldn't catch him with his pants down twice.

Steven opened the front door and winced. There was

probably glass embedded in his hand. It had been everywhere else—in the bath, in his suits, on the floor. One glass in a hundred pieces.

The cop had noticed and paused. "What did you do to your hand?"

Steven held it up for inspection. "Broke a glass while I was cleaning up the lounge room."

"Looks like you've got more to go."

"I've got cleaners coming in to help." He'd left enough mess to make sure he looked like the anxious fiancé. The bedroom he was going to have to finish himself. It was too much of a crime scene. Like Eliza was trying to frame him and make sure the police would search the house and office. Was she hoping they would find what she couldn't?

Whatever Eliza was trying to pull would fail. He'd already bagged his suits and put bicarb on the stained grout. Getting rid of the stink was going to be harder. But by the time he was done, there would be no reason for the police to suspect him of any wrongdoing at home, or at work.

If she came back, he would be teaching her a lesson. He needed to pull her into line. And fast. A performance like this at the wedding wouldn't fly. It would ruin his reputation.

Steven held the front door open. "Look, don't take this the wrong way, but I don't want to see you again."

If Eliza didn't come back, he would have to file a missing persons report just to look the part. A flicker of doubt surfaced. What if she were really missing? He pushed the thought aside. Who abducted a woman from her own birthday party?

Roan watched the rise and fall of Eliza's chest. Her lashes lay against her cheeks as if she were a doll waiting for life to return and reanimate her body. A purple bruise and patterned graze marred her forehead, and her feet were bandaged. Anfri had worked under his supervision, touching only where told, yet still it had been too much.

Now he waited, stretched out on the bed next to her. Over the span of two thousand years Roan had become very good at waiting. And watching.

Her black dress tightened then eased with each breath. Women hadn't changed that much over his long and unnatural lifetime. The clothes, the jewelry, the makeup— of which she wore too much—were all irrelevant. And he was sure the blond of her hair was false. He smiled and ran his hand up her thigh, nudging the dress a little higher. He was looking forward to finding out.

He pushed the soft silk until it just covered her underwear. The beads in his hair whispered in his ear as he moved. Would she fight or submit?

Over time he'd learned how to avoid being commanded by his summoner; after answering their initial call, he simply left. Some tried again. Most laughed and had another drink. Yet, ignoring their demands hadn't always been so easy. He wore the scars of being called by history's worst—weak-willed commanders, paranoid rulers, men who didn't deserve respect. He had committed atrocities in their names.

Decades had passed since anyone had offered him anything of value other than gold. The last summoner to give him something had been a child wanting to be a young woman. In helping her, he had remembered what it was like to be human again, something that happened far too rarely these days. For a while she'd thought of him, he'd felt her dreams on his skin, not quite a summons, more of a hope of seeing him again. He'd never responded. It was better to avoid temptation than fall headlong into something he knew he couldn't resist.

He glanced at the woman in his bed. For a moment he almost considered taking her back to the Fixed Realm. But taking her back wouldn't return his humanity. He might as well enjoy what he had left. She'd wished to be taken away. The words of the wish tugged at his soul like a half-forgotten dream. He pushed them aside. Her wish was granted and his would be too. Roan ran his palm down the woman's leg; the touch of human skin warmed his hand but didn't reach his heart.

"Silly, silly girl," he murmured, wanting to hold on to the moment before she woke and the fantasy shattered.

Her eyelids flickered.

Expectation tightened every one of Roan's nerves to battle ready. Starved for too long, he refused to rush. Anticipation was half the delight, half the torture.

Her eyes opened. She blinked and turned her head. Her eyes widened in fear when she saw him.

Roan placed a finger over her lips. He didn't want to hear her scream. Not until he was deep in her, her legs around his shoulders. "I've been waiting, Eliza."

Her lips parted for speech. Or was it a kiss? He took the latter, leaning over to brush his mouth against the red of her lips. She shoved away, denying him a taste in her scramble to escape. Power thumped through his body and his skin tingled.

A fighter. Always more entertaining than a simpering miss who'd cave to his every request.

Roan snapped into action, catching and trapping her beneath him. Eliza kicked her legs, trying to throw him off. One knee connected with his back. Roan grunted and shifted to sit on her thighs so she couldn't repeat the blow. She bucked and wriggled, all without a sound, then she struck out with her nails. He leaned back, dodging the cat scratch, and grabbed her wrists. He pulled her hands to his chest.

Eliza became as still as a corpse. Realization spread over her face, stretching her features. She knew she was his for the taking.

Roan kissed her hand. He didn't want fear. Without warning she lifted her hips, trying to throw him off. He hooked his feet around her legs and spread them. Her hands were trapped beneath his on the bed. Body to body. Hip to hip. The gold and amber beads in his hair danced above her skin. The clothing between them could be gone at his will, but he waited. What were minutes in the face of centuries?

The torment of being unable to taste her skin filled his thoughts. An eternity, that's what it was. An eternity of flesh-hardening agony with no release. And he no longer had an eternity to wait.

Beneath him her heart raced, and the echo resonated in his body and reminded him of what he wasn't. That he only pretended to be a man when it suited him. But he wouldn't inflict the curse, or the goblin, on any woman.

"I'm not going to hurt you," Roan promised as his thumb stroked her skin. He lowered his head to take a kiss.

She turned her head away, the only movement his

body allowed her. His gaze followed hers to her imprisoned hand. He froze.

Around her wrist was a plain gold bangle. On the bangle was a bead.

One amber bead.

Identical to the hundreds in his hair, the carved pattern was unmistakable.

If he'd had a beating heart, it would've stilled. He'd removed a bead only once and given it to the young woman who'd called on him for help. He glanced at the face of the woman beneath him. Her eyes gleamed golden-hazel. The same eyes that had gazed at him when he'd taken the girl to the Summerland so she could see him as a warrior and not a goblin.

Surely so many years couldn't have passed?

Time had no correlation between the Shadowlands and the Fixed Realm, but still this woman couldn't be the same girl. Eliza lay acquiescent beneath him, his hips hard against hers. No. It wasn't possible. He'd warned her not to summon him again. There had to be another explanation.

His fingers gripped the bangle. He tried to tug it off, but it was tight, too small to work over her hand. As if it had been put on before she'd finished growing. Her eyes, his amber bead. Why did it have to be her? Of all the women in the world who could have summoned him, it was the one he knew he would be helpless to resist and powerless to release. After all these years she was finally his. Cold crawled through his veins, smothering the heat of lust.

"Where did you get this?" He forced calm into his voice, but he felt like a strand of wire pulled too tight, his control held by the flimsiest thread.

She pressed her lips together and refused to meet his gaze as if she was a queen refusing to entertain the pleas of a servant.

His grip tightened. White bloomed on her skin under his fingers. "Where?" He knew the answer. Wished he didn't. He'd left it for her, a token to a child he shouldn't have bothered to help.

"I was given it." Her voice broke, but no tears glassed her eyes. She lifted her chin and met his gaze without blinking, her gold-flecked eyes glinting like polished stone.

"By who?" He shook her hand, holding the gold bangle, wishing he could tear it off and forget the child so he could enjoy the woman in his bed.

Her eyes flicked from his face to his shoulders and then back to meet his gaze. She shrank into the bed away from him. Her eyebrows drew together in puzzlement.

"It's yours." The words hung in the air. Her gaze darted around the cave masquerading as a bedroom. "Where am I?"

"Where you wanted to be." He released the gold bangle, but he couldn't pull away.

Eliza lay still, her breathing shallow, but she made no effort to escape. If she had, he may have let her leave the Shadowlands.

Her frown deepened and her eyes lost their focus. "I...I called..." She looked back at him as if seeing him for the first time and realizing who he was. "You're him...but you don't...don't look like a goblin." Her voice steadied as she tried to rationalize his existence.

"Looks are deceiving." He should have recognized her straight away. Maybe if her eyes had been open, he would have…or maybe he would've been sucked in the golden gleam and taken her anyway. Eliza was no longer a child who didn't know what she was asking. She was a woman who should know better.

"You're the Goblin King." Disbelief tainted her voice. She could have been calling him the tooth fairy.

Roan moved his hips against hers. "At your service."

———✳———

Eliza drew in a breath, and her tongue stuck to the roof of her mouth. She needed a drink. She needed to get him off her. She needed to keep the crazy man talking long enough to get away.

"Where did you get my bead?" The nutcase who thought he was the Goblin King lay over her, speaking through clenched teeth as if he was the one being inconvenienced.

Eliza had never told anyone about the night she'd called the Goblin King. Yet beaded-crazy-man knew, and she was just as crazy for wanting to believe in childish nonsense. Goblins. The indulgence of a terrified child. Yet her heart refused to believe her head.

There was something about this man, something just beyond her memory, trapped in a dream she'd never forgotten but couldn't quite remember. Summer skies and the warrior who'd helped her. No matter how hard she'd tried to hold on to what he looked like, his image had faded so only the outline remained. Was this really the same man? Where was the smiling warrior who'd handed her the bead and fixed her torn top?

She twisted her wrist, trying to free her hand without success. Her body was expertly pinned down by a man who looked like a cross between a Special Forces operative and a rock star. Dreadlocks filled with gold and amber beads that glinted in the candlelight and rustled musically with each movement. The sound was so distinctive and so familiar—heard only once and then repeated ever after in her dreams—that she shivered.

The man who called himself the Goblin King waited for an answer.

Keep him talking, make a bond, and he'll be less likely to kill me.

She swallowed and played along with his delusion, not wanting this man to be the kind warrior she could barely remember from a dream brought on by too much beer. Her mother had given warnings about being greedy and ending up like the man who'd longed for gold and been given a heart of gold instead. Cursed to be a goblin, he was compelled to answer other people's wishes.

Nine years ago she'd tested the story and summoned the Goblin King.

Eliza stared into his eyes. Aching blue. How could she forget? "You gave it to me when I was a teenager."

His face went blank. Her heart skipped, then raced. The unchecked lust was less terrifying than this new, unreadable expression. At least she'd known what he wanted. Now...

She let the words spill out before he could shut her up for good. "I called you, you broke up the party. Do you remember? You sent the boys running." The lights had gone out and goblin howls had filled the house. For a few minutes she'd lived in a nightmare full of screams and darkness. She'd never told her brother it was she who'd called the monsters. She'd never told him why, or what his friend had done.

"You protected me. I put the leftover beer outside to thank you. Do you remember?"

She remembered him. The faded dream grew stronger and the features of the man who'd saved her nine years ago became the features of the man above her. The full lips, straight nose, and blue eyes that would always be hungry. This man was the Goblin King.

"You took me to the Summerland and gave me the bead." He'd given her the bead to make sure she didn't forget. Had he? "Do you remember?" She willed him to remember.

The man didn't blink. His eyes burned into her soul as if he was searching for a lie that didn't exist. She'd gone to the Summerland many times in her dreams as a teenager waiting to see if she'd see him again. Not sure if she'd dreamed him into existence, but too scared to directly summon him and find out.

Eliza sucked in a breath but couldn't release it. Panic swelled until her chest hurt. "This is a dream."

It had to be a dream, but he had never been in her dreams no matter how much she thought of him. If not for his bead, it would have been easier to think she'd imagined the whole thing. But he hadn't allowed her that illusion. And she hadn't been able to let go of the memory. Now the warrior she'd dreamed of was made flesh.

"Why did you call me?" he demanded.

She squeezed her eyes shut. Steve. The party. The woman. The suits. The wine. Oh God. She had called him. She had called the Goblin King.

Again.

"Why?" He released her hands but still caged her

body. He was a prison made of flesh, and he demanded answers like a lawyer cross-examining a witness. "I warned you."

She hadn't thought of his warning at the time, but the words echoed through her mind now: *Next time I may not return you.*

She looked up at the man she'd often thought of before life had gotten in the way and she'd given up on childish fantasies and fairy tales. His gaze was hot, the lust simmering behind the frown that scarred his brow.

"I wanted to escape." It was the only answer she had. Living with Steve and his lies was like suffocating—it was only a matter of time until she died.

"Then you got your wish." His mouth closed hard over hers, stealing the air from her lungs.

She pushed against him, fighting the kiss. The first time she'd called him, he'd protected her. That's what she longed for—someone to make her feel safe, to care about her and listen to her. Not another man to use her for whatever he wanted. She hiccupped on a strangled sob. How could she have messed this up so much?

He jerked away as if her tears burned his skin. Freed, she lurched to her feet and ran. Ran because the memories couldn't be real, ran because she wanted to wake up, ran not caring where she went. Her memories didn't mesh with reality. Her warrior had been caring, where this man was harsh and dangerous. Eliza passed another man in black and gray camo. He reached for her and she twisted away.

"Let her go," the king called out, his voice ringing down the rock halls.

She ran through candlelit tunnels. Her lungs ached,

her head pounded, but then she saw the cave opening and ran faster. This was just another crazy dream, the dangerous imaginings of a desperate woman.

Fifteen feet beyond the cave Eliza stopped. He hadn't brought her to the Summerland. This place was empty. There was no sun. No stars. No moon. Just a gray twilight that was both oppressive and endless. Twisted trees grew out of gray dust, their limbs a tangle of blackened fingers. An oily river snaked into the distance. She squinted. Did it move, or was that an illusion?

As she stood there staring at the bleak scenery, her feet and legs became heavy and cold, as if the ground was sucking the warmth from her body and making her muscles sluggish. She looked down. The gray dust that was the ground stained the white bandages on her feet. Someone had tended to her, yet she couldn't remember hurting herself.

Eliza turned around. The entrance to the cave was nothing more than a crack in the face of a sheer cliff that rose with no end. There were no clouds to hide its harsh lines and no plants to soften the angles. Her beaded captor leaned against the rock, his arms folded, as impassive as the rock he had made his home.

"What is this place?" Her voice echoed in the empty world.

"The Shadowlands." His voice didn't echo. It dropped like a weight and was absorbed into the ground as if he were part of the strange landscape.

The Shadowlands. The name should mean something to her. She shook her head, unable to find the thought.

"This is a dream." It had to be. She would wake up with a hangover at home with Steve.

"No." His lips turned into a smile that cut her to the bone. "A nightmare."

Eliza's breath slid from her body and threatened to never return. She did know this place. So alien, yet so familiar. Every nightmare she'd ever had was created here, sired by goblins. The screeching and yells that had broken up the party had haunted her sleep, but it was a nightmare she'd thought she'd grown out of, the same way she'd put aside her dreams.

She glanced at the Goblin King. The first time she'd called him, someone had died. Her brother's friend Ben, the boy she'd been so desperate to escape, had fled the party in fright. He ended up wrapping his car around a tree on the way home. Whether it was the Goblin King directly, booze, or just reckless driving, she couldn't help feeling that her wish had caused his death.

Without sound or warning, the dust beneath her feet bubbled and swelled and grew. Eliza stumbled backward. Out of the blister burst Ben.

"You killed me," Ben accused.

Eliza stepped back again. "This isn't real." Yet he looked real. The same as he had on the night of the party—leering and drunk. "None of this is real. It's a nightmare."

All she had to do was wake up and all of this would be gone...including the Goblin King. She'd forgotten about him once before. Could she do it again?

She glanced at the warrior leaning against the rock. The memory of his touch lingered on her skin, cool and firm.

Ben moved closer as if he was stalking her once again.

Eliza covered her mouth and shook her head. No. No. No. Not possible. This was a nightmare created by the

Shadowlands to torment her. To awaken the guilt she'd thought long buried over Ben's death.

"It was a car accident. It wasn't my fault." She'd never believed those words before, even though she'd wanted to. The old guilt hadn't gone. It had grown stronger with time.

Ben reached out, almost close enough to touch her. His hands ready to paw at her the way he once had.

She forced out a breath and tried to be calm. None of this existed. It was just a nightmare more vivid than any other she'd ever had. But not real. Ben's chant closed in around her.

"You called. He came. He killed. For you." Ben pointed at her, his eyes lit with malice.

Had the Goblin King killed for her, to keep her safe? Or had it been for payment? It was a question she'd never gotten the chance to ask. One she wasn't sure she wanted to have answered.

Eliza pinched her arm, twisting the skin into a bleached white peak. She didn't wake.

Two other men joined the watching warrior as Ben drew closer, circling, closing in. There was nowhere for her to go…except back into the rock spire and the embrace of the Goblin King.

"Make it stop." She twisted away, not wanting Ben to touch her.

The goblin-man shrugged. "Maybe I could, if I were real. If I'm not, then I can't. If I'm a dream, you should have power over me. If I exist, then I have the power to make every day a living nightmare." He uncrossed his arms with the grace of a warrior readying for battle. "So, Eliza, do I exist?"

Her lips moved without sound. Did she really want to know what had happened that night? Would she be able to look the man who'd saved her in the eye, knowing he'd killed for her?

She glanced at the man who looked nothing like a goblin and stared into his unforgiving blue eyes, daring him to admit the truth.

"Did you kill Ben?" Was it her fault he had died?

"No," he answered without pausing for thought.

"Swear you didn't kill him."

"If you don't believe I exist, what do I swear by?"

Ben reached for her hand, the same way he had when she was sixteen. She knew what would happen next. The first kiss had been fun, the next not really. The scent of beer on breath still made her stomach turn.

"You win. You exist." *Goblins exist.* "Just make it stop."

Ben disintegrated into nothing more than dust settling on the flat barren landscape.

"I didn't kill Ben. And I didn't bring you back to the Shadowlands that night because you didn't know what you were wishing. But I warned you. You should've known better this time." His words were soft as he picked up a handful of dust. "Listen carefully, Eliza. Everything here is real. And everything here can kill you." He blew the dust into her face.

Her muscles went lax.

His hands caught her.

"Everything."

Chapter 3

THE WORDS HAD BARELY LEFT HER LIPS WHEN THE HOUSE WAS silenced. The next moment a howl of laughter rang off the walls and through Eliza's bones, curdling the marrow at their core. She clamped her hands over her ears and squeezed her eyes shut. The bitter beer in her stomach threatened to escape out her mouth. The room tilted and turned as if she was trapped in a spinning top.

She tried to make herself smaller in her torn shirt, as if she could be invisible against the locked bathroom door where she'd hidden from Matt's friend Ben. He'd laughed when she'd said no. Laughed as she'd run. Then followed. Not as old as she looked, she was just a scared child with no fairy tale prince to ride to her rescue. Ben calling her name, searching for her, had forced the words. She wanted to be anywhere but here. So she'd wished for him. The Goblin King.

And her wish had been answered. Now the house shuddered with the footsteps of the goblins she'd called. A click above her head made her lift her chin. Holding her breath, she watched the handle turn. It was him on the other side. The Goblin King. But she hadn't meant it. She'd just wanted the party to be over. Wanted the boys to leave.

"Please don't take me." The words were silent. Her voice had been stolen along with the party music. Tears tracked down her cheeks, spoiling the makeup she usually never wore.

From the other side of the door came the faintest chiming, a scattering of notes breaking up the dark. For a heartbeat she thought she saw someone with her in the bathroom in the shadows. Then for a moment she'd been somewhere else. A field with a black-clad warrior.

She'd woken with an amber bead in her hand and Matt calling her name. She didn't tell him what she'd done. She wasn't sure what had happened and no one would believe her, a sixteen-year-old made up to look older, more drunk than tipsy, and ranting about goblins.

Eliza sniffed and lay still, holding back the tears. Her head ached as if she had a hangover. It had been a long time since she'd relived that night. Her brother's first and last party without their parents being home had ended in disaster.

Ben's car accident, the police, the questions. The party was forgotten until Ben was buried. At the funeral, with Matt's eyes on her and her new gold bangle with the amber bead shining in the sun, the guilt had first risen. Matt had touched the gold around her wrist and said four words.

What have you done?

Her belief in the stories told by their mother had always been a source of teasing. Now her brother was serious and distant as if he blamed her for the strange magic that had ended his party. Had he seen the goblins tear through the house, terrifying his friends?

The amber bead was the only evidence of what had happened. Evidence that the Goblin King had been in her home and that she wasn't crazy and hadn't dreamed the whole thing.

Her fingers traced the familiar grooves in the amber. The bead was both a comfort and a reminder of the terror, as well as a warning never to try her luck again with the Goblin King, no matter how dark the day.

Eliza rolled over and tried to return to sleep. The sheets were cool and smooth against her cheek and the mattress soft. She eased into it, then stilled. Her body stiffened as consciousness gripped her, and she shook off the dream. This wasn't her mattress. It was too soft. She forced slow breaths. Her fingers brushed the sheets. Not cotton.

What she'd thought was music became voices. Male voices in a language she couldn't understand. *Goblinese.* She was still here. Sleep hadn't sent her home. Her waking nightmare was still running, demanding her presence.

Cautiously, she opened her eyes, half expecting the warrior to be lying in wait again. The bed was empty. A small mercy. And she was dressed. A second mercy. She ran her hand over her hips and felt the reassuring line of her panties. Fully dressed and unharmed. A thankful sigh escaped. How long she would be safe from his interest was anyone's guess, since his intent had been clear.

The need for water prevented her from swallowing. She reached for a glass on the bedside table. The glass was cold, the water clear. She brought it to her lips, then paused, unable to drink. It could be drugged. Had she already been drugged? Why else would she have slept? She pressed the glass to her lips and inhaled the fresh mineral scent as if it could quench her thirst. Then Eliza forced her hand to place the glass back. She couldn't chance drinking and falling back asleep.

How long had she slept for?

The hands on her watch twirled as if a madman played with the cogs. The long hand ran forward, minutes streaming past like seconds; the other plodded backward, counting hours like minutes. The second hand was frozen. Eliza tapped the face, frowning. The watch was new, a birthday present. She listened for a reassuring tick, but the timepiece was silent, giving no clue as to its malfunction.

How long had she been in the Shadowlands?

Her bladder cramped, demanding attention. She needed a toilet and fresh water. Food too. If she didn't take care of herself, she wouldn't have any chance of escape. She shivered, remembering the empty sky and tortured landscape. She wouldn't be able to get home on her own. Somehow she'd have to convince the Goblin King to return her to her world.

She slid out of the bed and left the bedroom. In niches carved into the tunnel wall, candles burned without melting. Their smokeless green-tinged flames were in an endless struggle to repel the dark. Shadows stretched toward her, to claim her, to make her join them forever. She fisted and flexed her fingers as she fought for calm.

Eliza looked right and then left—to the voices or away? She pressed her legs together. She didn't have the luxury of trial and error, and the quickest way to find the bathroom was to ask. Maybe she could just ask to go home. She straightened her back and lifted her chin, ready to face her captor again.

The same men she'd already seen sat around a round table talking and gesturing. The Goblin King rubbed a dreadlock between his fingers as he spoke. He turned, beads and dreads swaying like glittering snakes, aware of her presence before he had seen her. The one with his long black hair tied back looked at her with curiosity, and the other—his beard threaded with gold—with empty eyes. All three wore torques like Celtic warriors of old, but only the Goblin King's was gold.

They waited for her to speak. Her request to be taken home became one word under their stares. "Bathroom?"

"Second cavern on the left," the king said in perfect English. He said something else in Goblinese to the others.

Long Hair nodded and tossed a silver coin across the table to the Goblin King. Empty Eyes stared at her. The nothing in his gaze seared and chilled her as if an ice shard was lodged in her stomach. The man was already dead. He just didn't know it.

Eliza backed down the tunnel. Going home would have to wait until she had a moment alone with the king. Her heart hiccupped and her whirling thoughts spun out another set of problems. Could she face him alone? The memory of his weight over her, holding her down, was imprinted on her body.

He'd let her go once. Would he be so generous a second time?

The bathroom had a door but no lock. Eliza blinked at the décor—*Vogue* meets Stone Age. Pristine white fitting with gold taps and trim sat on a rock floor. Toilet, bath, shower, sink. The human-like goblins obviously needed to wash. The sink appeared to have plumbing, its pipes vanishing into the rock wall. Thick white towels were folded on a shelf, and toilet paper hung ready for use with the end folded into a hotel-style point. Eliza sat, grateful for some semblance of normalcy.

When she finished she flushed and watched black oily water swirl, froth, and drain away.

Normal wasn't even skin deep here.

Her gaze caught her reflection in an ornate gold-framed mirror. She paused and studied herself. Crumpled and bruised. Messy. There was a cut near her hairline, but green spread to her eyebrow in a garish addition to her smudged mascara. The grunge hostage look was sure to be a hit this summer. She examined the bump under the bruise but had no idea how it got there.

She'd danced on the suits in the bath, tipped wine from a bottle on them as she'd cursed Steve. Her eyebrows drew together as she tried to force the rest of the memory to surface. But whatever had happened was lost. She turned on the tap to wash her hands, hopeful that the water would be clean and clear. It wasn't.

Even though she knew she should have expected the dark liquid that came out, she couldn't help the stifled scream or the tears of frustration that pooled in her eyes. She would die in this cold corner of hell.

The door opened.

"I can't wash in this."

The king walked in and scooped up some black water in one hand. In his palm it became clear. "Take some."

She hesitated. Once her hand was coated in the stuff how would it get clean? How did they wash in this ooze? How could the bathroom be so pristine, so white, so…new?

Gritting her teeth, she cupped her hands together. Warm and slimy, the water stuck to her skin, thicker than oil. Yet in his hands it had become clear.

"Do you believe the water is brackish and toxic or that it is clean and pure?" he asked.

Eliza looked at the foul liquid in her hands. "It looks toxic."

"Mine isn't." To prove the point, he drank the water from his large calloused hand. "Your turn."

Her stomach heaved, but she was so thirsty she was crazy enough to go along with his trickery.

So she imagined clean, fresh spring water. The water began to chill her palms. When she glanced down, her hands cupped clear water.

"Now drink." His words weren't an invitation.

As she brought the water to her lips, it darkened. She threw it into the sink. "Goblin magic."

What was real and what was false?

"The stuff nightmares are made of."

She lifted her chin to look him in the eye. "Do you actually look like that, or is that another illusion?"

He pulled her to him. "Do I feel like an illusion?"

No, he felt real, and very much a man.

In the pale, clear, desert blue of his eyes, she watched his hair-trigger control tighten. He was seeking an excuse to snap. He could twist reality to his will, make water drinkable and nightmares real. Whatever he was, he was dangerous.

Dangerous and something more…something that made her feel like a teenager again, caught in his spell, fascinated by the man with a heart made of gold… something she had no intention of exploring.

What mattered was that she was alive because he wanted her alive, nothing else. She was trapped until he said otherwise since, as king, his word was law. In his domain she was just another subject.

The king released her as quickly as he'd grabbed her. "Dinner is almost ready," he said. Then he stalked out of the bathroom as if he didn't care if she followed.

Eliza turned off the tap. She rested her hands on the sink and tried to stop the shaking that coursed through her muscles and threatened to send her sprawling to the floor.

Whatever it took, she had to get home.

She smoothed her hair as best she could, after wiping her greasy hands on a towel in preparation for dinner. She wouldn't let him see any fear in her eyes. But the leashed power in his made her shiver. She didn't want to see him when he let his control slide.

When Eliza entered the cavern set out as a dining room, she was calm, poised, and everything she should've been at her birthday. She could fake like nothing was amiss, and dine with men who called themselves goblins.

Anything to wake up and leave this crazy kingdom.

A chandelier of candles was chained to the rock ceiling. Candelabras rose from the floor, every candle forever burning without ever being spent. Even they were not permitted to sputter and die and thus be free of the Shadowlands. Three large swords hung from the wall pointing down like a cross. The round table with seats for six was only set for four. Golden cutlery, plates, and goblets.

The tension in her shoulders eased. At least they ate like men. But where were they?

A water cooler sat against one wall with *Evian* plastered across the extra large bottle. Relief washed through her at the sight of something safe and familiar. While no one was watching, she walked over and took a plastic cup and drank, filling her stomach with clear spring water until it cramped. Cold fisted her gut and left her breathless. Her stomach twisted, breaking the ice and forcing it up. She brought her hand to her mouth. The water could be another goblin trick.

"It's safe." The shadows parted and the king appeared, leaning in his chair.

More goblin magic. She was starting to think of him as goblin. Breathing the air of the Shadowlands was making her crazy.

"I bet getting a repairman out here is a pain in the ass," she said, remembering she was supposed to be fearless.

He grunted and his lips twisted in an almost smile. "Fixed Realm objects are unaffected by Shadowlands magic."

"Huh? Fixed Realm?" The question came out before she could think twice about engaging him in conversation. She didn't want to be a part of this—she wanted to go home.

Empty Eyes appeared out of the shadows and dropped a platter of roast lamb and vegetables on the table. The scent of the food coiled around her, teasing her waterlogged stomach.

Long Hair dropped into a seat. "The cooler was pinched from an office in London. It's clean for the moment."

Eliza saw the look, which should have withered flesh, that the king gave him. Long Hair acted like he didn't notice. For kidnappers they were being very civil. Their behavior was unsettling—almost like she was a guest and not a hostage. She forced a weak smile and sat at the only other set place. They all looked at her like she'd sprouted wings and a halo.

"Wrong seat?" She half stood. Maybe she wasn't supposed to eat with them.

"It's fine." The king sliced the roast. He served her first, then the others in silence.

Eliza poked the meat with her fork. It didn't change or try to run away. It lay there like a good roast should, yet she couldn't bring herself to put some in her mouth.

The memory of the foul water was still too fresh. She knew she would have to eat sooner or later or die, but for the moment she could survive without eating.

The men ate without conversation or enjoyment. Empty Eyes watched her. His pale eyes glazed in the candle light. She cut up some meat and moved it around the plate, feigning interest in her dinner. His eyes tracked the movement of her knife. She laid the cutlery down and his eyes followed. He didn't want her here anymore than she wanted to be here.

She picked up the goblet, the gold rim was delicately carved in an endless knot, then she grasped the jug hoping for wine. Maybe if she got drunk again, she'd wake up at home. It held more water.

"Can't you turn water into wine?"

"I'm a goblin. Not Jesus." He held out his hand. A wine bottle formed out of the shadow in his palm. He set it on the table and ran his fingers around the neck. The cork plopped onto the table. "There you go."

Eliza closed her mouth. She shouldn't be shocked by his open display of the impossible. She poured the ten-year-old cabernet into her goblet but couldn't drink the wine. It couldn't be real. It had appeared out of nothing. No, not nothing, out of shadows. The Goblin King commanded the darkness she had always feared. She didn't belong here with him.

Eliza looked at the king. "I want to go home."

The words froze the room, even the candles held their breath, not daring to flicker as they waited for the king's answer.

"No." He spoke without glancing at her, his attention consumed by the food on his plate.

She pressed her lips together. He had no right to keep her here. "I command you to take me home."

Long Hair winced.

The king put down his fork. Then his knife. His blue eyes held her still. "You command no one."

"I have a life, a fiancé. I summoned *you*." She stood, knocking the chair over. The floor seemed to move as if she'd drunk too much wine. She put her hand on the table. She was giddy like she'd stepped off an amusement ride or spun around too many times.

The king looked up at her and shook his head. Beads bounced around his biceps. "No, you didn't. You wished yourself away. A wish I was happy to fulfill."

What had she said?

Her mind raced in pointless circles as if it could avoid the truth. The answer was to awful to voice. The words were the same as she had used nine years ago. The wish that was supposed to help her escape had instead handed her to the Goblin King.

I wish the Goblin King would get me away from here.

The rock floor rippled beneath her feet. Eliza swayed and gripped the table more firmly. "What was so different this time?"

His eyes narrowed a fraction as he assessed her, his captive. The dry desert heat touched her skin and pushed deeper. A fireball in her belly. Last time she had been barely sixteen, wanting to grow up too fast. Now…now she was an adult. Her lips parted in a silent *oh*. Obviously he had some standards.

A small smile passed over his lips. "You got what you wanted."

"This isn't what I wanted."

"No? It's the second time you called to me with the exact same words. Yes, Eliza." The king stood. "I remember."

Eliza stepped back and nearly fell over the chair legs. "I wish to go home. I wish the Goblin King would take me home." At home she knew what she was getting. She knew Steve and understood his unquenchable need for power and money. Once his drive had been attractive, but by the time it had become all-consuming it was too late. She was trapped in his fraud. Here nothing was as it was supposed to be.

The other two goblin-men looked at their king. He folded his arms in a stance that was both casual and threatening. His face was tight as if she'd wounded the creature.

"Looks like I'm done granting wishes." The tight control that held him back seemed ready to snap. "How about you grant one of mine?"

The heat of lust in his summer blue eyes made her step backwards. Without taking her eyes off him Eliza inched away. One wrong move and she was the next item on the menu. A dessert fit for a king. Her heart pounded so loud it echoed in her ears. The king watched her retreat yet made no move to chase. She didn't breathe until the wall of the tunnel hid her from view. But out of sight didn't mean out of mind. She knew he would hunt her at his leisure and there would be no escape.

—⁓—

The druid's summon filled the rock, resonating at a frequency only Roan could hear. Roan's hand dropped to the hilt of his sword as he watched Eliza flee down the hallway. His fingers tightened, but he resisted the urge to follow her the same way he ignored the druid's call to arms. Fighting the druid would take more of his soul than he was prepared to use. Chasing Eliza would not change the way she looked at him. Part fear, part uncertainty. He should never have taken her. What had he been thinking?

That he wanted her, and he'd been unable to help himself. But she wasn't a gold coin to be collected. She was a woman. The young woman he'd met once had grown up and stopped believing in goblins. In him.

To her he was a creature to be feared. Maybe she was right. He should stop playing human and get on with dying or giving into the curse.

A tremor ran through the floor of the cave system. He ignored the vibrations shaking the rock and the way the Shadowlands magic pulled at his body as if to draw him outside piece by piece. At least here he wasn't compelled to answer.

Dai spoke when the rock had finished grumbling. "You should've taken the opportunity."

Their ancient language rolled lightly around the room. A language assumed dead, now spoken only by three damned men. It was because of his brother he still clung onto his soul like a drowning man to a piece of wood, hoping someone would throw him a lifeline.

"I didn't want a cold meal." Roan sat and ate without tasting to reinforce the point. He didn't need to eat and they both knew he could've been to the Fixed Realm and back in less than a breath.

His brother was right, keeping Eliza here was wrong. But she'd asked, and he couldn't bring himself to take her back. Not to the man who'd let her be taken. He knew darkness when it bled into the soul. That man was born with it lining his veins and thickening his blood. Protective custody.

Eliza was here for her own good.

"What are you proving by keeping her here?" The wine bottle danced as the table shook to the druid's call. Dai lifted up the bottle before it could spill and poured himself a goblet. "Nice choice."

Roan couldn't tell Dai that he was so close to giving into the burn for gold that he would trade his soul for more. That with every breath he fought the curse, and that every time his drew on the power of the Shadowlands he paid with a piece of his soul. Sliding between realms on people's nightmares was the one thing he could do without cost, and it kept him sane. Escaping to the Fixed Realm wasn't a solution, but it was all he had to keep him going. If he faded, then Anfri and Dai faded with him. He couldn't condemn them to an eternity of being soulless goblins.

"That I'm a nice goblin and a terrible human." Fighting the lust for a woman was good. It meant he still had enough of a soul to want something other than gold. Keeping her was keeping him human.

Eliza was here for his good.

Dai sighed and flicked his gaze at Anfri. "A terrible human is still human."

Anfri admired the sheen of candlelight on his gold knife. Mesmerized by the play of the flames, the gold reflected in his eyes. Was his skin duller? His finger joints more swollen? His ears a little longer?

Roan checked his own hands for signs of becoming goblin. They were all running out of time. Unable to find a cure for the curse, their only choices were now death or fading. He knew he would have to take Eliza home before he reached that point. He let a smile form. Until then he would enjoy her company.

Chapter 4

ELIZA KNELT ON THE FLOOR OF THE CAVE THAT SERVED AS his bedroom. In front of her was the old cardboard box that she'd pulled out from under his bed. Roan watched as her fingers traced the letters scrawled in black marker on the flap. He curled his hand. His fingers had traced the same path, those same eight letters countless times. *Thank you.*

In nearly two thousand years only one person had ever thanked him for answering a summon. He'd defeated armies, killed princes, stolen treasure, yet his greatest achievement had been breaking up a teenager's out-of-control party and saving Eliza from unwanted attention. In that night he had been more human than he'd been in five hundred years. It wasn't the words of her wish that had drawn him, but the desperation in the young woman's voice to do something. That girl, now grown, turned.

Eliza jumped up. "That night really happened."

Roan looked at the box, the bedsheets pulled back and the open chest. Only his clothing in the drawers remained untouched by her hand. She'd been through his things, pawed through his personal belongings like a scavenger looking for scraps on a carcass.

"You always knew it happened. You never wanted to believe." He kicked the box back under the bed. The two bronze torques inside clanged together with the hollow ring of his failure to save the men who'd worn them.

Roan slid his hand between the mattress and the headboard. He held up a sheathed, short, double-bladed sword. "This what you're looking for?"

He tossed the sword to Eliza. Weapons were the first thing he'd looked for when he'd woken up in the Shadowlands.

She caught the sword and held it awkwardly. "I was hoping for a gun."

He pressed his lips together to hide the smile. He doubted she could use either weapon, yet she was willing to fight him to get home. He'd been that desperate to escape once, taking on the druid, searching for cures that didn't exist. Over the years resignation had taken hold. The only reason he fought on was because of his brother, but the death of each man made it harder to hold the gray at bay.

Roan tapped the Colt on his side. "Too bad."

He drew the scabbard off the sword. The twin blades, separated by a finger width, were liquid in the candlelight. He couldn't remember whose it had been. A summoner chancing his luck only to have it fail? Payment for murder and mayhem? Or treasure taken from a tomb?

Eliza gripped the sword. Her knuckles whitened as if grasping could control the blade. She lifted the point and aimed at his belly.

"Now what? You going to try to decorate my blade with my guts?" A slow death even for a goblin.

"You're going to take me home." Her voice didn't waver. Her gaze didn't lower.

Roan's jaw tightened. The child who had once thanked him now wanted to command him like a slave. Like every other summoner. But she was different. Eliza tested his humanity. While the goblin in him wanted to possess her, the man desired her. The child she'd once been was still there, full of fight she didn't know how to direct effectively. But in the woman it lit her eyes with a fire that gold couldn't match. She might have stopped dreaming of him, but he hadn't stopped thinking of her and wondering what had happened to her—the girl who'd treated him like a person and not a monster.

Now he knew. And he wanted her to look at him like that again. To see him as the man he once was and not the Goblin King. Wanting Eliza was all that kept him from fading and becoming a Hoard goblin, one of the many tribes of true goblins that roamed the Shadowlands. He couldn't fail. He would win Eliza. She would be his.

"No, I'm not."

She pointed the sword at his heart.

He tapped the point down. "My heart was replaced with gold long ago." Driving the sword into his chest would have no effect. It had been tried. Gold didn't bleed.

The twin blades wavered. "How do you live without a heart?"

The golden flecks in her hazel eyes gleamed, drawing him closer. Roan ran his finger along one lethal edge.

"Shadowlands magic," he whispered as he stepped behind her.

Eliza straightened her back, stiffening at his nearness. She grew by all of a hairbreadth. He pried her fingers from the hilt and adjusted her grip, his hands over hers. Her perfume had worn away, but her skin remained sweet and uncontaminated by the Shadowlands. He couldn't help but breathe in her scent as he swung the sword, carving the infinity symbol into the air.

"Be one with the sword."

His hips moved against hers, until gradually her muscles loosened and her arms became fluid. They moved as one. Her hair rubbed against his cheek and her body melded to his. If all he had to do was this for eternity, he would be happy. There were worse fates than the subtle torture of a woman's body. Without the sword they could almost be lovers.

The ice-burn of the metal in his chest spread its fingers. Cold tendrils crawled through his blood. She was already his, she was here, and he could take her. Even this he couldn't enjoy without destroying the moment and seeking to own it forever.

Roan spun away to face her. "Never take your eyes off an opponent." He growled. He should walk away, but he had to have her. His need for Eliza was like his lust for gold. Undeniable.

She raised the points to his neck. "Take me home."

"This is your home."

Her face creased and she shook her head.

"I want a queen." The goblin in him spoke; the words coming out before he could think them through. Only goblins stole queens. But the man he still pretended to be was intrigued by the woman who dared challenge a king with his own sword.

Roan looked at the woman wearing the black evening dress and waving the weapon. He'd taken her—the deal was halfway done. No goblin bride went willingly. Kidnap was the first date, the engagement, the foreplay. Eliza was bringing out the worst in him yet at the same time raising the human. Before her summon he'd been ready to surrender and die just to be free of the curse.

Now, his fingers caressed the hilt of the sword hanging at his side. He wanted to fight until the curse turned his eyes yellow with greed.

Both her eyebrows lifted. "You're holding me hostage. You don't want a queen…you want a ransom. Gold."

He laughed, deep under his breath. "A good idea, but then I'd have to give you back."

At this moment, gold wasn't close to what he wanted. He had more gold than he could spend if he lived forever. Goblins didn't live forever and they never spent their gold.

Still the unavoidable lust for more made him ask. "Besides, who'd pay?"

Hope softened her gaze. "Steve. My fiancé."

"Ah, yes. That charming man who banged on the door while *I* granted your wish." Roan stepped closer so the tip of the blades were a whisper from his skin. "Tell me, what has *he* done for you?"

"You're deranged. Take me home." The blades shook as her arms began to tire.

Her elbows bent, granting him more breathing space. "What's in it for me? Here, you are mine." He closed the gap.

She had the weapon, but he was gaining ground. The end of the sword skimmed the front of his black T-shirt as Eliza dropped the point to his groin. She'd noticed his interest.

"If you were going to take me, you would've done it by now."

"Would I?" He pinched the tip of the sword, side-stepped, and pulled her closer. "Don't you find the anticipation exciting?"

The moment right before the battle cry sounded, the air was always the clearest. Mind sharp. Nerves tight. Release only heartbeats away. Life could only be that raw when death was asking for a kiss.

They turned together in a dance as old as time and more lethal than the sword. Their gazes locked, neither willing to back down. Her tongue slid over her lip, but she remained silent. She hadn't said no. That was almost a yes.

"Here you can have everything you ever dreamed of. Riches beyond your wildest dream. Rule beside me." If she came willingly, it would ease his soul and he could enjoy being human for longer. If he forced her, he would become goblin. It would be a better fate to throw himself on the sword and end the magic that had bound his men and the druid for two millennia.

"Rule what? A desert built of nightmares. Population three?" Her head tilted as she mocked him.

He gritted his teeth. "You forget who you talk with, Eliza. There are others, Hoard goblins. True goblins who would flay your flesh for fun then dance to your screams while they all took turns."

Her skin paled, but her voice still taunted. "What are you then?"

"We were human once. Once there were more. A curse placed us here."

Her eyebrows raised in a move so small he almost missed it. Doubt? Confusion? What did she trust? If she were smart, not him.

"If I were queen, there is one thing you could never give me."

Roan pulled her closer. The blade between them became sharper. The danger of walking the edge of attraction swept over his skin in a rush he hadn't felt in too long. The slide of metal and scabbard. The battle had started. Eliza was considering his offer. The first kiss of conquest was within reach. He could give her anything she named.

He lowered his voice. "What else could you possibly want?"

"Love." She smiled as she trapped him.

Roan snorted. He tugged on the sword, so she was forced to lift her chin to look at him. "Love? Do you love Steve?"

Her mouth opened, but no words followed. First blood claimed. He'd found the weakness in her armor, and he pressed the advantage home.

"Would you die for him? If you swear on your life that you love him, I will take you back to his arms now."

The hilt of the sword clanged on the rock floor as Eliza dropped it. Her eyes were wide as her own words closed around her. She couldn't lie to escape when the Goblin King saw the truth.

"You would marry a man you don't love? You would be a wife but not a queen?" He flicked the sword up, tossing it into his palm.

Armed, the Goblin King went from dangerous to deadly. The sword was held lose in his hand, the point ready to strike, like the metal was an extension of his body or a missing limb now found. He'd probably been born with a blade in his hand and cut his way out of his mother's womb.

"It's not that simple." Her words were nothing more than a dry whisper. How could she explain the ties that bound her Steve? An engagement could be broken...but blackmail and lies bound her more securely than love.

"It's always that simple." He snagged the scabbard off the floor with one of the twin points. "One warning. If you kill me, you kill my men." He sheathed the sword and replaced it between the mattress and the headboard. He smiled and faced her. "Then you really will be stuck here forever."

Eliza stepped back to let him pass. How long would she last before she gave in and became his queen to make for an easy life?

"Wait," she called.

He stopped in the entrance but didn't turn.

She softened the order. Ordering him had achieved nothing. "Please."

The king turned. All that wild, barely contained fire was directed at her again. She stepped closer to the warmth, basking in the heat, while she searched for something to say that wouldn't antagonize or open the unhealed wounds he thought he hid. She needed to know more about the man who'd helped her years ago, the Goblin King.

"How long have you been here?"

"One thousand nine hundred and fifty-one years."

The response was so fast she thought he knew to the day. "Alone?"

This time he seemed to weigh his answer before speaking. "My men were cursed with me. But that's not what you wanted to know, is it?"

Eliza bit her lip. She wasn't sure what she was asking, or why she couldn't let him walk away, only that around him she felt different, like she was awake for the first time in years. Like she could breathe. Like all her wishes had been answered, but she didn't understand what do to.

"For the most part, yes, alone."

No friends or family or lovers. He just existed. It made her life look full, complete, and it was unless you stood in the middle and heard the echo. For a time her memory of him had filled that gap and she hadn't felt lonely, because she'd known he was only a wish away. Even though his warning had kept her from ever calling him, the knowledge had been a comfort.

She placed her hand over his chest where his heart should've been. She hoped something still hid there and that he would want more than the empty promise she had settled for with Steve. "You would take a queen who doesn't love you. A queen you do not love?"

His fingers clasped hers and he slid her hand beneath his shirt. Her palm rested against his skin. No heartbeat under her touch. No murmur of life teased her fingers.

"You see? Nothing." He crushed her hand against him. "I am incapable of loving anything but gold, my eternally unsatisfied mistress."

Eliza tugged on her hand, but he held her there trapped against him. Warm hands, no heart.

How could this be the same man who'd helped her all those years ago? "Why me? Any woman could be your queen." But she already knew the answer. She'd known him since she was a teenager. She'd seen the good he could do. She knew that despite his heart of gold he was capable of kindness...or had been. Now he was cold and selfish like a goblin should be.

"You make me remember what it was to be human. I would rather die than become Hoard."

The king touched her face. His thumb brushed her cheek. Toe to toe, eye to eye, she held a hurricane by the hand. For a man with no heart, life ebbed around him in a constant swirl of energy that drew her in. She wanted to test the depth and strength of the current, but she knew once in she would never be able to step out.

She was more alive here than she had ever been at home. At home, Steve sucked the joy out of living. Here, each second she still breathed was precious.

"You will get used to life here. After a couple of hundred years maybe you will come to like me." One finger traced her lip. "I need a queen. My mistress is a cold companion in bed." He moved closer as if to kiss her.

Eliza turned her head breaking the spell. "So am I."

"We'll see." He lifted her hand to his lips and kissed her fingertips.

Her breath caught at the grace of the simple movement. A smile fluttered over her lips. She was getting charmed by the snake.

Warning bells sounded in her ears, ringing off the walls.

The king dropped her hand and reached for his sword and then his gun. The noise wasn't bells. It was the clash of metal on metal ricocheting off the rock walls. He turned from her and went towards the fight. She started to follow him down the tunnel, but he waved her back.

She hesitated, unsure if she should obey or ignore him. Was he an enemy or just a desperate man, hoping she was his last chance at breaking the curse? Either way, if anything happened to him, she was in serious trouble. Right now he was her best shot at getting home. And at least he didn't seem like he was going to hurt her. The Hoard goblins, on the other hand, would. She went after him. As she drew nearer she heard each scrape of metal, the grunts of the men fighting, and the high-pitched, inhumane hiss of something else. The sound slithered through her body and coiled around her heart.

As if she were in a bad horror movie, she went on, knowing it would be wiser to run back to the bedroom and hide under the bed. The tunnel began to glow with a brilliant yellow sheen and she glimpsed the king disappearing into a cavern. Eliza cautiously peeked around the corner.

Gold.

A cavern big enough to fit a hotel in was piled with gold from pale to red to yellow. The room shone like a sun had crashed in the center of a mountain to give light to the creatures that hid in the shadows. Eliza squinted. The floor appeared to be tiled with coins. One wall was covered in carved amber panels. They were the only break in the endless gleam of gold. The king was bathed in the glow, and for a moment he stopped, as if transfixed by the sight of so much wealth in one location.

Eliza stepped into the cavern. A gray-skinned man wielded a sword, guarding the treasure from Long Hair. The gray man's ears lengthened as she watched, curling over at the top. His nose hooked, and his eyes yellowed like he was absorbing the gold into his very soul. In his beard were strands of gold.

Empty Eyes.

A gasp escaped from her. Eliza clapped her hand over her mouth, too late. The king turned. Before his eyes cleared she saw the lust for gold that blinded him to everything else.

"It's mine. I claim it." The goblin's voice broke as he spoke. The man had been swallowed by goblin greed.

The king flinched, but he kept his eyes on her.

The ring of swords jarred every breath.

"Enough, brother. Step back." The king turned just enough to see if Long Hair, his brother, obeyed.

His brother still circled the goblin that used to be Empty Eyes. His skin was duller and his eyes brighter. "It's our gold."

"Step back!" the king roared. "He is Hoard. It is too late," he added so quietly that Eliza only just heard the words. The king's eyes glistened, but not with the need for gold. He lifted the gun.

Long Hair looked from the king to the gold. He grimaced as if unsure what to do. They couldn't fight for the gold without becoming goblin, yet they couldn't walk away from it either.

Her stomach became a dead weight. "You're going to kill him."

The king spoke, his lips barely moving, "We took a vow. A warrior would rather die than live like that." The king turned from her. He aimed even though his brother still blocked the shot.

Eliza pulled her earring out, a simple gold and diamond creation. A gift from Steve. "I have gold." She held out the tiny jewel, knowing it could never compete with the golden Taj Mahal in the room. "Would you like to see?"

The king's long-haired brother blinked and stepped towards her. His skin brightened as his eyes lost their yellow glow. The crack of gunfire resonated around the room. Eliza ducked, her hands covering her ears. A cold, metallic smell clogged her mouth and sucked the moisture from her tongue.

She looked up to see the king catch the goblin before he fell to the ground. He cradled the goblin that had once been a man in his arms. Their heads were tucked together, but the king shook with each breath. His fingers smoothed the gray mottled skin. She didn't need to understand the words to know that the Goblin King was begging for forgiveness.

Steven placed the suit on his bed. He'd sworn never to buy off the rack again when he'd started working for Gunn and Coulter. He was not Joe Average. His lips thinned into a smile. He was smarter than that. And he had the bank account to prove it. The police would never find anything to pin on him. All the evidence pointed to Eliza—and she was his weak link.

Eliza had reduced him to this cheap suit.

He placed a tie worth more than the suit on the bed. Tailoring would take weeks. Every suit he owned was now only fit for rags. Rage simmered in his blood, but he pressed it down. There would be time for that later. He had to get her back before he could exact his revenge.

And he would make her pay for the inconvenience of calling the police and having them traipse through the house, trawling for evidence. He changed his clothes and checked his appearance in the mirror. The suit hung off his shoulders with no more grace than it had on the coat hanger. Steven took off the jacket.

It was better to be cold than to be photographed in an ill-fitting suit.

Eliza's little game had gone on long enough. A kidnapper would have sent a ransom note by now. Every schmuck knew what Eliza Coulter was worth. Her trust fund was enough to make most men look twice. What he wanted was more basic. Her name. Slade forever linked with the biggest political, and legal, family in the state.

The PI he'd hired had found nothing, but that didn't mean she wasn't hiding, trying to force his hand or make him trip. A breath hissed out between Steven's teeth. If he stumbled, she was going down with him. He was beginning to regret ever telling her. Eliza was becoming more of a liability than an asset.

He picked up the phone ready to act the worried, loving partner. Thirty minutes later the police were taping off the house. The Mobile Police Facility was parked out front. If the neighbors weren't already talking, they would be now. The newspaper reporter snapped photos. Steven did his best distraught fiancé shuffle as the police escorted him to the station to be interviewed.

They asked the same questions. New questions. Only one question.

Where was Eliza?

He honestly had no idea. And that scared him. Eliza was beyond his control.

Chapter 5

DAI, THE KING'S BROTHER, SAT AT THE TABLE WITH ELIZA. He'd introduced himself as he'd claimed her earring and then withdrawn into silence. She'd leaned an important lesson. *Never offer a goblin gold unless you were prepared to part with it.*

"Has this happened before?" Her skin was cold. Trying to coax Dai into conversation was better than watching him toy with a small knife and her earring.

He pointed at the three swords on the wall.

"There were six. He's killed three of you?" After the shooting they'd been banished from the gold room. Eliza had been glad to leave. She wasn't sure if it was a murder or a mercy killing, only that she'd seen a part of the Goblin King she was sure he'd rather keep hidden. Losing a man had wounded him. His golden heart wasn't as cold as she'd thought. What else did he hide?

Dai drove the tip of the knife into the table where it quivered but stayed upright. "No, the druid killed us when he laid the curse." Pain rolled beneath the dark seas of his eyes. She would rather face the endless heat in Roan's eyes than drown in Dai's.

"He shot—"

"Anfri was already gone. His soul was freed. What Roan did was a blessing. Meryn still runs with the Hoard." Dai snorted and shook his head, his loose hair falling over his shoulders. "Back then we didn't know. He gave up so quick. One day he was human, the next…now I doubt he thinks of anything but bloody metal." Dai stood, grabbed his knife, and slid it into his vest with its five identical siblings. "Don't judge Roan by one bullet."

Every time she closed her eyes she saw him fire. The flash of the muzzle, the smell of the shot. Her heart lurched, diving into her stomach. If Dai remained loyal after murder, he wouldn't defy the king and take her home.

She sighed and asked the question that had so far remained unanswered. Her mother's tale of a greedy man wishing for gold seemed too simple. The Goblin King had hoarded gold the way goblins do, but he wanted to be human. He wanted the curse to be broken. Maybe if she understood she could help him. Then they would be even. No more debts between them and she could go home. "Why were you cursed?"

"I wasn't. Roan was. We just came for the ride." He placed his hands on the back of her chair. His hair fell around her like a curtain.

"What do you mean?" She spoke without turning.

Dai was too close. Anger and hurt rolled off him and burst like raindrops on her skin.

"You want to see what happened, want to know why we deserved this punishment?" He pulled her chair back and spun her around to face him.

Eliza nodded since saying no would've been pointless.

"Follow me." He led her towards the cave entrance.

Eliza stopped. "No. I'm not going out there again."

What other nightmares would surge forth to attack her? Would every stray thought come to life?

Dai took her wrist and tugged her over the threshold.

"No, please." She clawed at his fingers.

"Relax. I'm not going to torment you with your nightmares. My creations are much more fun and educational." He sucked in a breath and lifted his hand. Dust swirled, drawn up by an unfelt wind.

"You control it like him."

"No. Not like Roan. He has the power to make anyone's dreams into nightmares and nightmares into reality. I can only call my memories, my fears, my nightmares."

The starless twilight sky glowered over them as out of the dust a clearing in a forest was born. Twenty men filled the space.

She took a step back, expecting one of the sword bearers to turn and attack.

"It's not real. It's kind of like 3-D TV but without the glasses." Dai walked around the scene.

"You get TV here?"

"No. We go to the cinema." He glanced at her. "Plenty of shadows to hide in, no one knows we're there."

Right. She was never sitting at the back of a theater again, just in case. Eliza followed Dai around his living memory. The men all wore swords and cloaks, fighting men—warriors. It was like watching a foreign film with a soundtrack she could only guess and no subtitles. Watching the men speak, listening, she realized it was the same language the three men had used. A language too beautiful to be Goblinese. The lilt and fall of the words wrapped around the furtive whispers in the night. She looked again at their clothing.

"You were Celtic?"

Dai smiled and nodded. "Decangli."

This wasn't a casual meeting. The need for secrecy spread like mist. She was eavesdropping on something she shouldn't hear. No living human should get to re-examine history, but it was a hard offer to refuse.

"What are they saying?" Eliza found herself whispering as if the recreated dead could hear.

"We'd planned a rebellion against the Romans that had taken up residence on our land. It was all set." Dai closed his eyes and listened as if he were hearing a symphony.

Eliza moved closer to the image, towards a man wrapped in a blue and red plaid cloak. His golden torque winked in the firelight. "Is that—"

Dai opened his eyes. "Roan?"

She nodded. "That's the king's name?"

"Is that the name he gave you?"

The king hadn't given her anything except more nightmares. There weren't enough lights in her house to chase away the darkness he brought.

"No. He's not given me a name."

"Then stick with king. It is his rightful title, even then." Dai sighed. "He was a good king. He lived to remove the Roman stain and to continue our father's fight."

A man in a white robe stood. He pointed his finger and spoke. An argument flew between Roan and the druid. The words became jagged and rough. Four men stood up, siding with their king, followed by Dai with his hair cut short, Roman style. The six.

A lump formed in her stomach, sticky and heavy like uncooked dough, and grew with each passing second. "What happened?"

Dai held up his hand. "Shh. Wait."

Roan's hand brushed the hilt of his sword, but he didn't draw. The druid grabbed the pouch from Roan and held it up for all to see, then drew out some coins. His words cut through the night, even though Eliza couldn't understand the language. Eliza's skin prickled as she felt the power in the words without understanding their meaning.

Roan fell to his knees, clutching his torque. His men fell with him all gasping for breath. They were suffocating. The image went black and disintegrated.

Eliza ran forward. "What happened?" She looked around hoping something or someone would appear out of the dust and give her the answer.

"We lost consciousness and woke up here." Dai swept his hand around like he was offering a sumptuous view, not the gray, twisted landscape of the Shadowlands. "Along with the druid. Because of his hatred, the magic trapped him here as well… and he's been trying to finish us off ever since."

The man who'd cursed them was also here and trying to kill them. She glanced across the empty landscape and suppressed a shiver. "Why did the druid curse Roan? What had he done?"

"Roan, myself, and the others lived in the Roman city. The Romans liked pet kings. We were the eyes and ears of the rebellion. I found out that the general had heard of our planned attack. They were ready, waiting, laughing. Attacking would have been suicide. Instead of meeting to finalize preparations, Roan tried to stop them."

That made sense, if it was meant to be a surprise attack. "The druid didn't like that?"

"He accused Roan of selling out to the Romans, of taking their gold instead of leading his people."

Eliza frowned. He didn't seem like the kind of king who'd trade lives for gold. Anfri's death had cut him, and he'd refused her offer of ransom. "Did he?"

"No. By the time the rebellion realized the truth, they lay dying in the mud and gore." Dai spat out the words. "Now you know who we were and what we'll become. Do with it what you will." Dai walked back to the cave.

Not wanting to be left alone outside, Eliza trailed after him, the strange story still swirling in her mind. A cursed Celtic king, trying to find his way home. That idea fit better with the memory of the warrior who'd helped her. It melded with the man who'd brought her here. He would do anything to free his men of the curse, even if it meant shooting them and abducting her. He had a heart, even if it didn't beat.

Inside the cave she paused. One detail was missing from the story. "Dai, who betrayed the rebellion?"

He paused and turned to look at her, a half-smile on his lips. "Our cousin, Drem."

"Is he a..." She couldn't bring herself to call Dai a goblin to his face.

"Goblin? No. Our cousin died on the general's blade that night. A quick death."

———————

The body lay still. Hands folded over the sword. The bullet hole in the forehead couldn't be hidden. Anfri had shaved his head, grown his beard, and for a time ridden with a biker gang. The helmet and leather had hidden his features. He was also the only medic they had. If Dai were to be injured...Roan hissed. He would have to use magic to save his brother.

Centuries had slid past without progress on breaking the curse. Finding a cure had become the sole reason Dai lived. Every moment spent working on a puzzle that would never be complete. Now the bell was ringing. The clock about to strike midnight, yet Dai refused to admit it was over. But if Dai was fighting, so was he. Roan smoothed the red cloak over Anfri's distorted, gray body. He kissed his forehead. The dry, cold skin was already more like dust than life.

Roan closed his eyes. It should be getting easier the closer he came to becoming goblin. Instead, the golden heart in his chest ached. He placed his hand on the wooden boat that was fresh from the dockyard. Someone would curse the loss of the *Summer Breeze*. Anfri deserved the best, not a wreck for his funeral.

"Meryn, wherever you are, may you find peace. I'm sorry." One with the Hoard. Trapped forever by the loss of his soul and Roan's failure to notice. Those first few days in the Shadowlands had been a confused jumble of survival and summons. The loss of Meryn had placed their new reality in striking distance. His fading had been a hard lesson for them all to learn.

"Brac." Killed by the druid. The first send-off he'd had to do. Roan swallowed. There'd not been much left to burn.

"Fane." He closed his eyes. Fane had taken his own life. Not because he was turning, but because he couldn't live only in nightmares. Consumed by despair, he'd left a heavier burden on the living.

"Anfri." Roan's ribs became brittle, crushed by the weight of the metal that made up his heart. His voice fractured.

"Celebrate in the hall of the gods and pray we meet between lives," Dai finished for him.

Unable to speak, Roan lifted his goblet to his lips. He sipped the bloodred wine, then poured the rest into the dirt. The ground blackened then dried, desperate for the acid rain that rarely fell.

In the gold chamber Dai's skin had grayed. If not for Eliza, they would have turned on each other, then faded to goblin and fought to the death. Now she watched the funeral. Not as one of them but as an interloper, because she refused to be queen.

High above a crow circled. How the druid knew when one died, Roan didn't want to know. He ignored the harsh, taunting cries and pushed the boat into the river. It spun around seeking the nonexistent current. The river didn't flow, instead it swelled and sucked like a leech on the landscape. Roan raised his hand in farewell and created the funeral fire for Anfri. The cost to his soul was worth it. Anfri had served him for far longer than any man should have to serve a king.

The river burned by his will, swallowing the boat, the body, the warrior. Roan sucked in a breath tainted by the scent of burning flesh. The flames offered an end. An end to the curse and the endless wait for peace. He stepped forward, knowing that even though there was no heat in the fire, the flames would destroy him. Who would light the fire for him and Dai?

Dai rested his hand on his forearm. "Not yet, brother."

"Am I that transparent?"

"I still have hope of a cure." A smile graced Dai's lips, but no light lit his eyes. For the first time Dai had responded to gold like a goblin should. No amount of hope would save them from fading.

Roan watched the crow draw closer. Dai's activities hadn't escaped his notice.

"Your mystery treasure hunt?" He turned to face his brother. "You spend all your time reading or in burial chambers. When did you last go to the Fixed Realm for something other than your quest?"

Dai's grip on his goblet tightened. "I'm close."

"Then I hope you find it before I am out of time." Roan turned his back to the flames. Their siren song would have to wait. The crow circled to land. "Go to Eliza."

Dai obeyed, crossing the distance to where she watched wide-eyed as the river burned.

The large crow touched the dust then shook its feathers. Out of the ruffle the druid rose. His brown hair and beard were unchanged by time because, as a human, he was unable to leave the Shadowlands via people's nightmares. Like all druids he carried no weapons, but then he had no need when the magic he commanded could make even the ground obey.

The druid Elryion watched the burning river. "Another one succumbed." He didn't bother to hide the glee in his voice. He turned to Eliza and studied her for longer than needed.

Roan loosed the sword at his side. He could end it now and face Elryion for the final time. Roan clenched his fingers over the hilt. Elryion wouldn't fight with weapons, only magic, and while magic couldn't kill Roan, using it would lay waste to his soul. Only weapons could kill a goblin, and the druid was unarmed. If Roan drew first, Elryion would retaliate with magic. He forced his hand to relax. Now wasn't the time, or place. His fading would trap Eliza in the Shadowlands. She would have to be home first. And he wasn't ready to take her back. To be seen as a man one more time was all he wanted.

"Kidnapping, Roan. You get ever closer to the Hoard."

"Anfri's death is on your soul. You wrought this."

"I stand by my judgment. Give up your soul. End your suffering." The druid shook, and the crow took to the smoke-darkened sky.

The curse was so powerful that it had trapped the druid with them. Elryion had refused to retract the curse even though Roan had nothing to do with the rebellion's failure. It was centuries before Roan had understood why the druid wouldn't release them. In the end Dai had unraveled that mystery. If Elryion lifted the curse, he would become a goblin. The only way out for any of them was death.

"We've got company." Dai drew his sword with one hand and a knife with the other.

Three goblins appeared dressed in clothing that blended with their skin and surroundings. Camouflage. They carried an odd assortment of weapons, but they were no less deadly. Above, the crow shrieked and the attack began. An arrow brushed past Roan's arm and skidded into the dust behind him.

Dai threw the knife. It caught the goblin archer in the throat. His battle cry became a gurgle as he choked on his thick black blood. Roan drew his gun—he didn't need another goblin to study—and fired twice. The two other goblins dropped into the dust like hideous, wilted flowers.

He raised the gun and scanned the sky. But the druid was gone. The coward would never face him as a warrior.

He holstered the gun. "Scouts."

Where they were more would follow. The druid had led the Hoard to his home. He glanced at Eliza, but her eyes were locked on the goblins' bodies. He'd shared her horror once. Wondered if every scout he killed was Meryn. He'd learned the hard way not to let a scout live. They'd had to fight until they could barely raise a weapon just to survive after Hoard goblins found their camp. Since then they killed every goblin on sight.

Dai retrieved his knife and wiped it clean on the goblin's clothing. "Do you have to use the gun?"

"It works."

"It lacks class."

"So does dying." Drawing weapons at a funeral would displease any watching god. No doubt that was what Elryion intended. Did the druid still believe the gods would find him innocent and worthy to enter their hall? What would they think of him and all he had done? Would he be damned in every life he lived? An eternity of paying off sins committed while cursed. He glanced back at the goblins. Sometimes being a soulless goblin looked easy.

"You killed them," Eliza said. Her voice filled with disbelief.

"It was us or them." Roan took her arm to lead her back to the cave.

She tried to shrug him off. "How do you know that?"

"Because they are goblins."

Her lips trembled. It was another breath before she responded. "And so are you."

Roan touched her cheek with the back of his hand. She didn't move, frozen by his heartless touch.

"Not yet, Eliza." He cupped her chin.

Her lips were sealed tight, but her eyes were fierce, challenging him to act and prove her right. Magic whipped through his body, raising the hair on the back of his neck. He should remind her who he was and what he could do. Replace her fight with fear. He was the Goblin King.

The man he still wanted to be let her go.

She stared up at him surprised. He turned and stalked away before she could see a similar expression etched on his face.

Eliza was his. Yet he was waiting for permission.

The battle swept across grass that shivered and fell as it was trampled beneath the hooves of the horses and feet of the soldiers. Roan watched the dirt become mud weeping with the blood of the Decangli. He knew every move, every thrust, every man who fell. Yet he still summoned the final battle of the Decangli out of the dust time and time again. This was the result of his failure to win enough support to stall the rebellion. On days like today he liked to wallow in the past, wishing he could go back and change it. Kill the traitor before the general found out. Kill the druid…anything to save his people and change their fate.

He'd been forced to watch the rebellion fail the first time, and had watched it fail a thousand more times played out in the dust as he relived the battle that should never have happened. Watched, unable to do anything as his tribe was slaughtered. Summoned by the Roman general, imprisoned in goblin flesh, he couldn't move until ordered. The orders had made him a slave to Rome.

Bitterness filled his mouth like rancid meat. Seeing the Roman Empire crumble under the feet of invaders had been poor compensation for the theft of their land and lives of his people. He watched on, unable to look away. His sword pierced the ground in front of him. His legs ached from squatting. But the pain meant he was still alive and he would enjoy it a little longer while he could. Did goblins feel pain? Was death the relief he wanted to believe in? Horses shrieked as they fell. Men looked surprised as metal appendages bloomed in their guts. The fortunate ones didn't have time to realize they were dead.

Roan sensed Eliza's approach. She stood behind him. He didn't turn and acknowledge her. The battle was almost over. The remaining few would surrender. Their heads would hang outside the walls until their skulls shone white in the moonlight. Rome would take his home. The military would command where kings had once led.

She sucked in a breath. He supposed the violence was shocking to one who hadn't lived it, and who didn't understand the reasons.

"What will happen to the dead goblins?" she whispered as if she were afraid of interrupting the battle.

"The Shadowlands will reclaim them." Their bodies lay by the river, without life there was no decay. The corpses would remain as fresh as the second they died until the magic stopped working and they turned to dust. No warrior's flame would take their absent soul.

"You said they were scouts. What were they looking for?"

"Gold," he glanced over his shoulder, "women."

Eliza flinched.

Her reaction was almost enough to raise a smile. The Shadowlands wasn't the realm of nightmares without reason. Existing here was dangerous. Roan turned back to the muck of battle.

"Is it safe to be out?"

"No." *Go away and leave me to dwell on my past.* "Go back to the caves."

Her hand settled on his shoulder with no more weight than a butterfly. "Dai said this is the rebellion you tried to stop."

He shrugged and scowled. He didn't need her pity. "I tried to stop the battle. The rebellion would have gone on."

A body rolled to his feet. The eyes were wide open, seeing nothing. Eliza's fingers dug into his shoulder.

With a thought Roan returned the body to dust. "Then Dai told you about Elryion and the other men."

"Yes." Her feet shuffled in the dust. "I'm sorry for your loss."

The once proud warriors of the Decangli laid down their swords before the Roman army. The injured ones were killed. The leaders were tied and taken away. What happened next he didn't need to see again. He had been ordered to kill his tribesmen by the Roman general as punishment for refusing to yield to Roman rule, and he had been helpless to disobey. The compulsion had torn at his skin and cracked his bones. His body was driven forward while his mind protested, screaming silently as his sword was bloodied with his men's blood. He'd learned later that the traitor had also died that night, betrayed by the general after revealing the details of the curse. Using the druid's magic against Roan had been the general's final act of cruelty. But the legend had spread, and other people had called on the king cursed to be goblin.

Learning to refuse an order given by his summoner had taken time. Each order disobeyed had returned his sanity and hope, and each time he ignored an order he had rewarded himself with a bead, which he'd crafted and added to his hair. Years of disobedience now rattled with every step so he could never forget he was no one's slave to command.

"Don't feel sorry for me." He had more than enough to go around. The battle fell back into the ground, no more than a memory dusted off for a special occasion.

"You had to kill one of your own."

Roan stood and spun in one move. "I've turned so goblin that I'm not sad about Anfri. I'm running out of time." He snatched up his sword, sheathed it with a snap. Anfri's death was a reminder of how close he was to the end. He'd lost a friend to a curse none of them should have worn.

"That's not true. I saw—"

"You don't know what you saw. If I'd have looked at the gold and not you, I would have lost my soul. Do you understand? Without a soul I become Hoard." He stepped forward intending to scare her off, send her fleeing back to the dubious safety of the cave, but she stood her ground. "I become like the ones I just killed."

"You kept your vow to Anfri. That took courage."

She took his hand in hers offering support. "You don't have to fight alone."

Roan looked down at their hands. She'd touched him, willingly. Her thumb rubbed against his palm. The contact sparked the tightly packed lust. It caught like tinder and spread, filling his chest, warming the gold of his heart. For the first time in centuries he was warm.

The gold in her eyes softened as if she could see past the curse and understand his pain. He let himself respond. His mouth touched hers in thanks. Chaste. He intended no harm and would take no more than she offered. He would take her back before he faded. She was only on loan from the Fixed Realm.

Then she kissed him as a woman kisses a man. Her tongue glided over his lip as her body moved against his. The warmth became heat that surged, tearing through his body. His hand lifted to cup her face. He pulled Eliza to him, and her body melded to his. Her lips parted, allowing him the taste of humanity he'd been denied for too long and he couldn't resist.

Rain fell from the smoke-filled sky. Fat acid drops burned his skin. The shadows rose at his command, wrapping around them to move them to safety. He had barely thought the location and then they were there. His chamber.

His fingers raked through her hair, tangling the pale, silken strands. Her dress was fisted in his hand. He needed to feel every inch of her. To remember every curve of her body and the way she rolled her hips as he cupped her butt.

Her arms wrapped around his neck as he lifted her and took her to his bed. He laid her down and rested over her. His hips cradled by hers. The ache in his chest was dwarfed by the heat surging in his blood. She brushed her lips against his, seeking him out. Where her fingers traced up his arms and over his shoulders, lines of fire followed. He shivered, anticipating the next touch. Her fingers crept under his shirt. Flesh seeking flesh.

She paused, her hands stilled on his skin, her gaze locked with his. "I shouldn't be doing this. I'm engaged."

"You're with me. My queen." He moved to kiss her again, hungry for something he hadn't felt in too long surging inside him. He wanted Eliza more than he'd ever wanted any piece of gold.

Her hands didn't move, preventing him from closing the gap. She shook her head. "No."

"No?" Eliza wasn't agreeing to be his. He could kiss her, embrace her, but never truly have her. She would always be yearning to be somewhere else.

Roan realized what he was doing. He'd taken a woman from the Fixed Realm, already claimed her as his to his men—and was willing to fight them for her—the only thing he hadn't done was have her. Her fingers remained on his skin, but all he felt was the claws of the curse digging deeper as he became more goblin. And he was more than tempted to surrender his soul for a moment in her arms.

Lying with her would only hasten his fading and he didn't want to steal a queen who would take his soul when he claimed her. He needed a queen who would ground him and help him fight. Eliza wasn't that woman. Lust had blinded him to the reality he didn't want to see. She was temptation—not salvation.

And always had been. He'd wanted to possess her from the moment she gazed at him with awe in the Summerland. A pretty trap, different but no less damaging than the need for gold that filled his heart. But the knowledge did nothing to dampen the raw lust that threatened to incinerate everything but the metal lodged in his chest.

She gazed up at him, her eyes darkened with desire. "You haven't even told me your name. I won't call you king."

He eased away, his teeth clenched, fighting for control. He wanted her and like a greedy goblin he'd do anything, give up everything, to have her. He'd made a mistake in bringing her here. The same mistake he'd made years ago by taking her to the Summerland. He couldn't help himself around Eliza.

"Roan," he said as he called the shadows to take her home. At least she would know his name this time. "If you were mine, you would call me Roan."

The world lurched as he landed on his feet. He released Eliza and melted into the night before she could realize what he'd done. The imprint of her body against his still warmed his skin.

The need to grasp her and take her back to the Shadowlands gouged his metal heart.

She couldn't see him like this. Gray and twisted. Goblin.

Eliza turned. "Roan?" She spun the other way, and then placed her hand on the tree for support. "Roan!"

He bit his tongue so it wouldn't betray him and answer. When it came to Eliza, he couldn't be trusted. He would convince himself she was willing, that she wanted to be there, until it was too late for both of them.

He looked up at the stars. So few now shone, dimmed by the city lights. He was doing the right thing. She belonged here in the Fixed Realm with the living.

He should never have taken her. The urge to possess her rattled in every unsatisfied fiber of his being. Eliza had replaced the lust for gold. Both were fatal to his soul.

Her breath caught like she was about to cry. One hand covered her heart as if it were breaking.

Roan hung his head unable to feel her pain, but wishing he could share it. He could remove the ache in her heart if he took her back and replaced it with something worse. The lack of hope. He fisted his gray hand. He wouldn't do that to the woman who'd once seen him as he'd been. A warrior, not a goblin. A man worth dreaming about. He doubted she'd dream of him now.

"Are you all right, ma'am?" A man in uniform, police, swung his flashlight over her.

She sniffed, then nodded and blinked as if noticing her surroundings. He'd brought her home, to where she would be safe. Back to the fiancé. Roan shook his head. Stealing another man's promised. Eliza brought out the worst in him and raised the goblin to new, dangerous lows.

"That's my house." She pointed to the house surrounded by yellow crime scene tape. A police van was parked out front.

Time had passed in her absence. Roan wasn't sure how long, minutes, weeks, years. To him it was all the same. He waited, not feeling the cold of the night settle on his gray flesh. Eliza would forget him, and once again he would become little more than a nightmare brushed aside like a cobweb in the daylight.

"And you would be?" the policeman asked.

"Eliza Coulter."

Eliza Coulter. Roan let her name form on his lips. He had never forgotten the child who had reminded him to be human. He wouldn't forget the woman who had reminded him what it was to be a man, if only for a moment. Maybe he would've been a better man if he hadn't been king.

Chapter 6

ELIZA EASED BACK ON THE FLAT PILLOW. THE BED WAS too firm, designed to throw the hospital's patients out sooner, rather than later. Her body refused to rest. Her eyes darted to every shadow, searching for a movement that didn't belong or a darkness that couldn't be explained. She could bring him here, but the words wouldn't form on her tongue to breathe the nightmare into life.

She'd lied to police. Claimed she had no recollection of where she'd been for three days. They'd scraped under her nails, taken her clothes, taken blood, taken photos. There was no glass in her feet. The cuts on the soles were too well healed for only three days' absence. But she hadn't spent even one day with Roan.

Already her memories of him were fraying around the edges. Each time she tried to find a detail it became harder to grab the thread. She closed her eyes. Her skin remembered his touch, cool skin, palms roughened from the sword. The way his lips crushed hers and the way his body pressed hard against hers.

She bit her lip. In those few minutes she'd been more alive than she'd been in years. Since Steve had put the ring on her finger. She gritted her teeth and tried to force sleep, staring up at the ceiling, knowing that the real nightmare would begin soon. Her stomach became heavy and her first meal in three days sat like a sunken ship, listing with the currents but going nowhere. Steve would visit and make sure she paid for every inconvenience her absence had caused. No one could save her from the trap he had made. After all, she'd filed the paperwork and she'd signed off on his embezzlement, not that she'd known it at the time. If she didn't go through with the wedding, Steve would make sure she went to jail.

With Roan she had tasted freedom, and the edge of excitement, sharper than a sword, had pierced her heart. She wanted to feel it again—kiss Roan again.

Her eyes flicked open, her body rigid with fear. What if he'd become goblin? Would kissing turn him goblin? Wasn't a kiss supposed to break the curse? Or was that a lie created by fairy tales because they'd kissed and nothing had changed? Her mouth opened to call for him so she could make sure he was okay. She stopped, the words caught in her throat. She hadn't abandoned him. He had thrown her out of his world, out of the Shadowlands.

A lucky escape that felt more like a farewell to a friend and an ache that wouldn't dull as time passed. She shouldn't care. Roan was a heartless goblin, a monster who wore the skin of a man when it suited him. So how did he burn with such intensity that she couldn't touch him without catching alight?

It had been so easy to get swept up and believe he was more than goblin. To her he'd always been more than goblin. He'd been the warrior who'd saved her. And for a moment she'd thought she could return the favor and set him free. She touched her lips. She was a fool. He didn't want her. He wanted a queen.

He'd returned her, and she should be grateful she

had escaped unscathed. But the fate of the Goblin King consumed her thoughts. A breeze lifted her hair, when none should stir in the sterile room. Eliza sat up. Were the shadows a little darker in one corner? She squinted, sure something or someone moved.

"Roan?"

The sound of tinkling beads echoed through the room. Then the darkness lifted, leaving her alone with her heart, longing for the shadows.

Light and color blurred with more hues than Roan remembered the world ever having. He put his boots up on the seat in front of him. The theater in Mumbai was almost empty. The few patrons he shared with stayed clear of the back row of seats without knowing why. To them the dark was best avoided.

The actors broke into song. Love and duty. Should the girl marry the man her father approved of, or take the chance and run away with her true love? That question was older than Roan and would never be answered in a ninety-minute film. The characters danced around. The women's brilliant saris bled across the screen. Their gold jewelry was usually an untouchable torture that didn't bother him today.

Today, Bollywood didn't fill the gap left by his departing humanity. It rubbed salt on the wound and then washed it clear with bitter wine. He couldn't find enjoyment in others' happiness. In laughter, or song, or light. He wanted to be happy. He'd never just lived. He'd been raised to be king from his first breath. With his father's untimely death, he had stepped up as expected. He was killing before kids these days could drive. King before they could vote. Cursed before they could drink. His twenty-first celebrated in goblin blood.

Roan chewed on the heavily buttered popcorn. It didn't matter, none of it did. His life was ancient history that no one knew or cared about. The world had all but forgotten his tribe. Mercifully, most of them had forgotten about goblins too. The summons and commands died out as the centuries slid past in a blood-edged, golden blur.

He sunk farther into the seat. He should've stayed in Texas and watched the shoot'em-up-cop-chase film. But in life, good never won. Evil was rewarded. Honor vanquished. Movies lied. Joyous chatter erupted as the young woman picked her suitor and made wedding plans. Popcorn stuck to his tongue like tasteless balls of polystyrene. The blackness that clung to him wasn't just the normal dusting of shadows that eased his transition between realms as he slid through people's nightmares.

Eliza was getting married. To Steve. He shouldn't have given a damn. She should've been his. His queen. If he closed his eyes, he could feel her presence like a hint of summer. A warmth he could almost touch. Her light followed him across the world not lessened by distance, as if she called to him with a constant beckon he couldn't be free of. And one he wanted to answer. It was still night where she lived. He could watch her sleep. Watch her dream. Watch her wake to the face of a monster leaning over her bed.

Soul be damned.

Roan crushed the popcorn container. Exploded kernels rained onto the floor. It was easier to crave gold than a woman. Both would ruin him. But gold he could have. Gold would never leave. Gold didn't care whether he looked goblin or man. Eliza did. He could never be the man she wanted, and she would never be the queen he needed.

Today was a day for violence and the loss of life and hope. The only problem was what type? Beautiful-impossible-anime? Or brutal-bloody-slasher? He weighed the decision knowing the answer would be both. With his mind made up, Roan stood. First, he'd check out his favorite German art-house theatre, the one where Goths mingled with thugs looking for ideas.

With only a thought he was leaving Mumbai for Berlin.

"Welcome back, honey."

Steve's voice cut into her sleep. Eliza kept her eyes closed, knowing he wouldn't be put off that easily. He was too used to getting results to back down.

The bed shifted as he sat down. "Wake up, Eliza."

His breath on her ear was hot like a dog sniffing out dinner. She blinked a couple of times, turned, and tried to look surprised to see her fiancé visiting. He smiled and kissed her forehead, but his eyes were cold, like rain-slicked steel. She could never find her footing with him. Never be in the right place, never be safe.

Steve remained, leaning over her. "I'm so glad you decided to come back."

"I didn't decide—"

"Shh, I'm talking. We both know I had nothing to do with your disappearance. Regardless of what the police think."

"I don't know what happened." The words tumbled out as she apologized for living once again.

He did this to her every time. And she bent to his will, but their relationship hadn't always been like this. He'd rescued her when her world had collapsed. When her father, the last of her family, had died of a heart attack in parliament. He was dead before he'd hit the floor. Her degree had followed. A one-year deferral to deal with her grief had become five. In her family's law firm she was a legal secretary, filing Steve's paperwork.

Steve had been her father's protégé, a self-made man, the poor kid made good. And he played on it, manipulating everyone around him. He'd had her fooled for three years before she'd seen the truth. By then it had been too late. She was caught.

He lowered his weight, crushing her chest. "You can't lie to me."

She couldn't breathe. The tiny half-breaths he allowed her were not enough. Eliza tried to push him off. But he held firm. To a nurse passing by he was merely attentive. There would be no help coming.

"Keep still." He pinched her earlobe where her earring should have hung. "Where have you been?"

Eliza shook her head. Her lungs burned for more than a gasp of air.

"Is this payback? Do you think anyone but you cares who I screw?" He kept the embrace tight but let her breathe.

She gasped, sucking in the air tainted with expensive aftershave. There was nothing honest or natural about Steve.

"We're not married yet," she choked out. When they

married, everyone assumed he'd get the partnership she'd refused him two years ago. Two years ago this nightmare engagement had begun.

"Is that a threat?" His nose touched hers.

If he kissed her, she would be sick.

He drew back and laughed, patting her hand. "It's your name on the documents."

Nausea clawed the back of her throat. Those documents were the one thing between her and freedom. She'd seen them once. Perfect documents that looked the part and siphoned money into an account Steve had set up. The poor boy had become a rich, corrupt lawyer, and she would take the fall. The documents had her signature and her handwriting on them. She filled out paperwork like that all the time. She'd done the paperwork for Steve's fraud without knowing. Her signature had locked the chain around her throat.

"Choose carefully, Eliza. You wouldn't last a week in jail." He stood and smoothed his charcoal suit. A replacement for the ones she'd ruined. "I've ordered new suits. You'll settle the bill, won't you, dear?" He turned and left without waiting for her answer. His visit left no more than a depression on the sheets. Eliza smoothed them away, wishing it would be as easy to remove him from her life.

In the afternoon, the detective assigned to investigate her disappearance stopped in to see if she could remember something she hadn't told the uniformed police. Eliza gazed out the window. She wanted to be outside, to feel the sun and taste the fresh air. She wanted to be free of Steve and his fraud for a few moments. She'd tasted freedom for a few short seconds with Roan as their lips had met and she'd forgotten she was Eliza Coulter and should know better.

"Just a few more questions, Ms. Coulter." Detective Griffin brought her back to the hospital room.

She nodded, sure that she'd answered the same ones last night, but she couldn't be certain. Had she fainted before or after the questions? She couldn't remember getting to the hospital. But she couldn't forget where she'd been. She couldn't forget Roan.

"What time did you leave the party?"

"I don't know. Elevenish?" She should know that. She should remember what time she'd caught Steve with his pants down.

"Your fiancé is a lawyer, yet there were no suits in the house. Do you know where they might be?"

Eliza frowned. "No…" He'd cleaned up. The cheating bastard had removed the evidence of their fight, evidence that might have been important had she been actually missing. The bastard had only thought of his own ass. The weight of Steve's lies became too heavy for her to carry. "They should've been in the bathtub."

"The bathtub?" Detective Griffin smiled, his face an invitation to spill all. He could keep a secret. Who would he tell?

"I took them down and soaked them in hot water and wine." She swallowed the laugh that bubbled in her throat.

"After the argument."

"Yes." There was no argument. Just her yelling and locking herself in the bedroom with a bottle of wine. Tearing down his suits, jumping on them as the water flowed, staining them with the red wine and cursing him. Cursing everyone. Cursing herself for being so stupid.

"That's an expensive way to fight." Griffin nodded as if he understood her life perfectly.

"We don't usually fight." *I usually give in.*

There were several breaths of silence. She could take off the burden if she told the truth. She could tell Griffin everything. Her eyes flicked to his partially concealed gun. Cuffs would lurk not far behind. How would the metal feel around her wrists? Gooseflesh rose on her arms. Steve was right that she wouldn't survive in jail, and she wouldn't ruin her family's good name for Steve.

"When can I go home?" She'd inherited the Coulter family residence after her father's death. While it was home, it had never felt like it was hers.

"The doctor said you can leave today. Your house is still being processed. Have you got somewhere else to stay?"

Eliza's eyebrows pulled together. She wanted to get out, get some real clothes, and sleep in her bed. "I'm no longer missing."

"You have no recollection of where you were for seventy-two hours." Disbelief flashed in Griffin's eyes before being hidden behind the warm mask of concern.

She knew that look. She may never have finished her law degree, but he was keeping something from her. Something that made him doubt her amnesia. Had Roan left something behind?

"Is there a problem, Detective?"

"Why did you argue?"

Steve wanted payback. Well here it was with interest. Let the police make up their own minds about him. "I caught him cheating."

"He said you overreacted, that you had been drinking heavily. Do you normally drink?"

Eliza forced a breath out between her teeth. Her fingers twisted the bedsheets. "I was drinking because I caught him screwing some skank in *my* house."

Griffin nodded, his face showing nothing. "Where do you keep your handbag?"

"Was it stolen?" Spending a day canceling cards and replacing her keys, phone, and purse was not what she wanted to do.

"No. Where did you leave your handbag?"

"In the bedroom."

"You didn't leave it in the cloakroom by accident on Saturday night?"

No personal belongings ever went in the cloakroom. Raincoats, umbrellas, sun hats, never her handbag. "No, that's generally for guests."

"Your bag was in the cloakroom. The suits haven't been found. Do you know why Mr. Slade would move things before the police arrived?"

Because he didn't want them looking into his affairs. The police might find the documents she'd signed, and maybe more. Something that she'd missed in her hunt for the paperwork and a way out.

The words that would reveal the fraud rested on the tip of her tongue, but before she spoke they twisted and reformed. "I don't know."

The detective leaned back in his seat. Without saying a word Eliza knew that he didn't believe the lie. She held her breath waiting for him to ask again and force the truth out of her.

"I'll make sure you get your handbag back before

you leave hospital. Have you got somewhere else to stay until your house is released?"

She knew where she was going to stay—in a hotel far away from Steve. "Yes. Thank you."

Detective Griffin reached into his pocket and withdrew a business card. "You've had a rough couple of days. Have a think about things. Give me a call if you remember anything."

—⁓—

Roan appeared in Dai's library and sat opposite his brother. A twenty-four-hour movie marathon chasing the night around the world had coated his tongue in salt and made his fingers greasy but accomplished little else. It was a poor substitute for an all-night bender, drinking until he couldn't walk. These days even that small release was out of his reach. If he let control slide for just a moment, the curse would gobble him up without a burp.

He set the almost empty bucket of popcorn down on the ivory map inlaid in the desk, where Australia should have been, where Eliza was. The ancient map, while beautiful, was incorrect and obsolete. Like every other map in the library, it belonged to a different time.

Dai looked up from the shiny black tablet he was reading. Or translating? The two were almost one and the same when time wasn't a factor. Between the two of them there wasn't a language that had existed over the past two thousand years that they didn't know. Most were dead, remembered only by cursed men. So much knowledge would be lost when they died. Such a waste of time, life, and learning.

Dai didn't take his eyes off the tablet. "That stuff will give a heart attack. All that butter and salt."

"How many buckets would that take?" Roan held up his hand as he reconsidered. "No, don't tempt me." It probably wouldn't work anyway. He didn't have a heart to stop.

Dai set down his pencil and held out his hand. Roan reached into his pocket and pulled out a bag. He tossed Dai the multi-colored jelly snakes. There was no escaping where he'd been and he never hid it. There was no point. The candy was a small bribe for peace.

"That your latest find?"

His brother had never gathered gold the way a goblin should. Dai collected books and scrolls and tablets, anything that might refer to goblins, curses, or magic. The shelves were littered with relics. When they got full, Dai simply acquired another set of shelves. When the room got full, he had Roan enlarge the cavern. He wouldn't be doing that again. He didn't have enough soul to waste on renovations. If he'd known what damage the magic did, he would've been more restrained with its use.

"Mmm. Where's yours?" Dai said as the tail of a red snake disappeared into his mouth.

"I took her back." Roan licked his fingers and started worrying a dread, rolling it between his fingers. His fingers skipped over the beads; some of the gold and amber had been there for centuries. The first one he'd placed in his hair now adorned Eliza's wrist. Sacrificed because he'd responded to a summons and granted her wish. His lips thinned. Now he owed her a second bead.

"So you've been skulking around Delhi, or was it Mumbai?" Dai flicked the bag of snakes with his pencil.

"*Tumse matleb.*" Roan squashed the popcorn bucket into dust. The dark magic of the Shadowlands was always calling to be used. It was easier to give in than to ignore it these days. Would it hurt when it took him?

"I care because I'm your brother."

"Because your fate is tied to mine." Today he resented Dai. If not for his brother, he would've given in already. Holding on to his humanity hurt like a rusted knife lodged in his back. Eliza had eased the wound before twisting the blade. Now he couldn't get the itch out of his skin.

They glared at each other. How many times could they have the same argument? Did it matter how he whiled away eternity? He preferred movies to books. Living people to dead trees. Life instead of legends.

"I thought Eliza was keeping you human."

Roan shook his head. He wished that were true, that he could make it true. Make her agree to be his, but no woman wanted to be a goblin's queen, banished to the land of nightmares—it's why the Hoard resorted to kidnapping on the night of solstice. He wasn't quite that close.

His brother frowned and bit through a snake. He waved the green head at Roan. "You've lost ground?"

Somewhere over the centuries his younger brother had become the guardian of his soul. Self-preservation or brotherly love, the result was the same. Dai would never let him fade. He might be king, but he answered to his advisor.

"I'm running out of time. I can feel it with each breath." It was the admission he knew would come eventually, but he wasn't ready. Not yet.

"You're drawing too much from the Shadowlands."

Dai picked up his pencil and tapped it on the paper covered in unintelligible markings. "Stop using magic."

What he could speak, Dai could write and read. Roan's writing was limited to Greek, Latin, and English, and that was only at Dai's insistence that he would need it when the curse broke. His brother had always been more scholar than warrior.

"The druid is still stronger." Roan sighed. He both yearned for and dreaded their confrontation. For centuries, he had honed his use of the dark magic so he would be able to meet the druid on equal ground. But the price had been heavy, stealing more of his soul with each use of the magic. Was he even worth saving anymore? "I have to face him before I lose what is left of my soul."

"Don't rush. While you live we have a chance."

"If I kill him, we could be free." He said it as though it were fact, but in truth, killing the druid could just as easily bind them in the Shadowlands forever. But when there was no other option, it was worth trying. He'd be damned if he'd fade without putting up a fight.

"And we may not." Dai placed his hand over the tablet. His eyes were an unreadable tangle of thoughts. "If Eliza anchored your soul, why did you return her?"

"She tested me." Roan fisted his hand. "An itch worse than any gold lust. If I'd taken her to bed, I would've succumbed. Then where would you be, brother?"

Dai closed his eyes. His fingers traced over the grooves in the tablet as if he were reading an ancient Braille. "She seemed willing."

Roan snorted. His hands still remembered the warmth of her skin gliding under him. The sweet taste of her mouth was like water to a man dying of thirst. "Yeah, like every woman, she dreams of waking next to a goblin."

"Did she ask to leave again?" The calm in Dai's voice stemmed the bitter flow of thoughts.

She hadn't. But she wasn't willing to stay as queen either. "She wanted a man. Not the Goblin King. Get out, Dai. Enjoy the Fixed Realm while you can. There is no cure to the poison in our blood."

"I'm not looking for a cure, just a way to stop you from fading to gray." Dai made some more lines on the paper.

Roan leaned forward. Dai was always looking for a cure. Something had changed. "What have you found?"

"A really nice tomb under the Sahara." Dai pointed to Africa on the map in his desk. "Tablets and trinkets. You'd like it."

"Goblins are supposed to take gold, not texts." The curse had never settled on Dai the same way it had the rest of them. Those years of compulsory Roman education had changed him. They had given him more than just a thirst for knowledge and a hatred of Rome that ran deeper than Dai ever mentioned. But Roan didn't pry. A man's secrets were his own.

Dai lifted his head, his dark blue eyes momentarily empty. "I did." He pulled an ornate gold and lapis lazuli clasp out of his hair. "That's how I know *I'm* sliding."

Roan's golden heart grew colder and the ice spread to his ribs. His little brother was starting to fade and he had no way of stopping it. No way of preventing Dai from becoming goblin except death. Unable to say anything, Roan drew the shadows to him and left Dai to his study. He went where he always went when he needed reminding of why he was fighting and why he couldn't give in and fade—why the only choice was death. He went to see Gob.

Yellow eyes wide and unblinking, Gob sat as he always did, like the lights were on, but no one was home. Roan sat on the floor unsure if Gob saw him or if he was lost in a mindless haze of unsatisfied gold-lust.

The cell next to Gob was empty. The first time they'd caught two goblin scouts to study, both goblins had been dead within hours. Killing each other through the bars. Even jailed there had to be a pecking order. They'd been so crazy for status they'd been willing to die.

The next time Roan was more careful. He'd caught only one scout and killed the other ones. It was too dangerous to let them live and report back, but it was no easier killing the goblins now than it had been at first. He only did it in defense. He told himself that keeping Gob here was better than killing him. Some days he wasn't so sure.

Gob spent his days alone unless Roan or Dai felt like facing their future.

Roan pulled the rabbit he'd snatched from the Fixed Realm on his way down out of the bag. The animal was still warm in his hands. Scenting the meat, Gob threw himself at the bars. He lashed out and tried to grasp the out-of-reach flesh. It had been a while since Gob had eaten, yet starvation seemed to have no effect on goblins. It was as if the Shadowlands kept him alive and food was a luxury. A luxury Roan lacked the hunger for. He forced himself to eat and to act human because the alternative salivated in front of him like a mad dog.

"Him wants meat." Gob writhed and hissed with his face mashed against the bars.

Roan sat back and waited. Sometimes the fit would last minutes, other times hours.

"Who are you?"

"Meat. Meat. Meat," Gob whined. His voice changed from rage to wheedle. His fingers curled as he beckoned, pleading for pity.

Disgust rose rancid and thick in the back of Roan's throat, choking out hope that he would find something in Gob that would make fading palatable. He knew all goblins had been human once. A priest of a religion that had died unnoted by history had explained that greedy souls found a place where their dreams could be fulfilled. Gold and power. Roan forced himself to gaze into the goblin's yellow eyes. No humanity remained in Gob.

No humanity would remain in him. Everything he was would be stripped away like flesh off a carcass until only the bleached bones of need remained. His soul would truly be swapped for gold. Roan touched his torque. The sign of his kingship was locked around his neck until he died. The druid's error in casting the curse had caused this aberration.

Soul of a man. Heart of a goblin. What man desires let the gods make true.

With those words Roan had suffocated. The dreamless dark had been replaced by endless gray and the horror of realizing they weren't dead, or human, or goblin. He should be thankful the curse was incomplete and he'd had a chance—and a choice.

Roan threw the rabbit through the bars, revulsion souring his blood. That would never be him. He would die first. Gob snatched the rabbit up, his eyes bright with lust. Roan walked away to the noise of breaking bones and the slurping of blood. That wasn't living. That was a living death.

And he wasn't ready to die without seeing Eliza again. From the Fixed Realm her call pulled on him, drawing him to her the same way it had when she'd been younger and she'd dreamed of him. Back then he'd been able to resist. Now he couldn't. But he also knew he couldn't let her look upon the body he wore in her world. That of a goblin.

Chapter 7

ELIZA'S BREATHING WAS THE ONLY NOISE IN HER ROOM. No, not her room. A hotel—why wasn't she at home? Roan skimmed her thoughts as she slept. Eliza's house was still a crime scene. At the edges of her mind, swathed in fear, lurked her fiancé. She didn't want to marry him. Roan frowned. She didn't want to be near him.

What bound her to Steve?

He reached out his hand and touched the ends of her pale blond hair. He preferred the dark honey gold she'd had when she was younger. She flinched in her sleep as if feeling his cool touch. He stepped back, making sure the shadows hid him in case she woke. Her thoughts still pulled at him, strong like summons, ripping at his muscles as if her call remained unanswered. He was here with her, yet it wasn't enough. She was dreaming of him, calling him to the Summerland.

He gave in and let the sound of her voice lure him from the Fixed Realm to where she wanted him. At first he'd used nightmares to travel between worlds, then he'd learned to travel by will alone. Unlike true goblins, he could travel between realms. Dai thought it was because they still had a soul and were connected to the Fixed Realm. Once his soul was gone he would be like every other goblin, trapped in the Shadowlands until winter solstice. But Eliza's pull was different from a summons. Lighter, clearer.

The compulsion to go to Eliza left his body in peace as he arrived in a grassy field. Trees swept around three sides, a river on the other. The landscape was so familiar, yet so alien, like the Shadowlands had been colored in using the bright palette of a child. He inhaled the summer air, sweet with fresh grass. Then he closed his eyes for a moment and tried to remember when the world had been so pure. He couldn't. This wasn't the Fixed Realm. It was too perfect, as if all the best bits had been brought together in one place.

On his back the sun was warm, and his skin didn't burn the way it would in the Fixed Realm. But the heat didn't reach his cold metal core. He opened his eyes and lifted his hand, examining his flesh by daylight for the first time in too long. He was human in appearance. Roan lifted his face to the sun. A simple pleasure he'd almost forgotten. Beads chimed as the breeze caressed his hair. It was too good to be real.

And it wasn't.

This was the Summerland. Eliza had called him into her dream. She'd tried many times when she was younger and he'd been able to ignore the requests. Now he couldn't. Now she fully believed in his existence and her visit to the Shadowlands had strengthened their connection.

This was the place he had brought her so she wouldn't have to look on his goblin body. It was where he'd given her the bead, and where she'd looked at him with something other than fear. It was where he could pretend to be human.

The calf-high grass rippled and shied away from him as he walked toward Eliza, who was clad in a filmy nightgown. The sky was perfect summer blue and the sun shone brilliantly. Butterflies cavorted among the wildflowers of the field, only he noticed the gray clouds gathering on the horizon. He swallowed, not wanting her dream to end, but knowing he was already destroying it by being here.

"Eliza." Her name sounded like a prayer on his lips. He wasn't hiding in the shadows and skulking through nightmares. He was safe and he was human. And he was with Eliza. She had called him and for the moment his soul was intact. The few delicate threads that tied it to his body held.

She turned and her pink lips parted like a blossoming flower inviting a taste. "I was thinking of you." She cocked her head and frowned, eclipsing the joy his presence had caused. "Are you real or a dream?"

Roan took her hand, drawing her to him. "Real."

He should know better, but he couldn't resist holding her again. "You called to me in your dream, and I couldn't refuse." That sounded better than saying he was too weak to resist her. He stepped close and brushed her hair behind her ear.

Eliza grinned, brilliant and untainted. She threw her arms around his neck. The lightweight nightgown offered no protection to either of them. Her heart beat against his chest and echoed against his ribs. He slipped his arm around her. Her skin was warm from the endless sun and blue sky of her dream. Unable to stop himself, he leaned into her so his lips brushed hers. Her mouth opened offering more, a taste sweeter than the wild summer strawberries of his youth. And he couldn't refuse. His body responded to her lightest touch and the hint of a suggestion that couldn't be. He shouldn't be here.

"You never came before."

Roan took a breath and released her. "I wanted to."

This was a dream, an escape, but for who? He ran his fingers through her hair, spun strands of sunlight that could bind him more firmly than any rope.

Her fingers skimmed his cheek and his skin burned from within. "Why didn't you? I wanted to see you again."

"Because this isn't reality. And it isn't right." He caught her hand and tried to catch his breath.

"What do you mean?" she asked.

Roan watched the sunlight shimmer in her eyes, not sure what to say. Not wanting to break the spell, but not believing in the illusion. He told her the truth.

"This is the Summerland." The eternal perfection of a summer day. The high of life that would never die. Everything the Shadowlands wasn't. "The land of dreams."

Around him a current flowed, pulsing with life and magic fed by the creation of imagination. Roan wanted to cover the field with pink flowers the same shade as her mouth. She was the perfection he was denied. He reached out to the magic to use it as he would in the Shadowlands, but it slipped from his hand as if he was trying to catch moonlight.

At his feet the grass died. Then the blight spread. The color faded from the sky. The trees shed their leaves and twisted in grief.

Eliza gasped and looked up at him. "It's happening again."

The Shadowlands was once again taking over Eliza's

dream. There were no dreams for him. No escape. There was only one thing he could do to avoid dragging her into his nightmare.

"It will always happen. I am not who you want me to be." She was not who he needed her to be. Roan kissed her cheek and whispered in her ear, "Wake up, Eliza."

She shimmered and vanished, then returned to the Fixed Realm where she belonged. But her scent remained, clinging to his skin as if she were trying to hold onto him, pure like flowers just budding and untouched by his darkness. Roan opened his eyes. In the distance the last sliver of blue sky put up a brave fight against the gray before succumbing.

Alone, he stood and watched as the Summerland died, death spreading from the dead heart. Him. Everything he touched was corrupted by his dark magic. It was becoming impossible to separate himself from the Shadowlands.

He crossed his arms, surveying his kingdom. Almost-black clouds tumbled on the horizon, a smear on the perfect monotone twilight. They shouldn't be there. There was no weather, no night, no day in the Shadowlands. They were left over from Eliza's dream. A dream he'd wanted to believe he had a part in, if only for a moment. Roan pressed his lips together, his body tight with unspent desire. No matter how sweet the temptation, he couldn't exist for Eliza only in dreams.

Sunlight slipped past the cracks in the curtains. Eliza blinked and tried to orient herself in the strange bedroom. She wasn't with Roan. But she had been. She'd felt his hands on her back and his arms around her.

It was more than just a dream. She touched her mouth. Her lips were cool from his touch. Eliza pulled the cover over her head and closed her eyes. She tried to reclaim sleep and find her dream-lover.

"Roan, I need to see you."

Smothered in the dark she waited, knowing he wouldn't appear. He'd sent her away as her dream had been leached away by the Shadowlands.

The curtains rattled on their tracks. Eliza sat up throwing off the cover. The hotel room was awash in pale morning light. The fabric swung from the ghostly hand that had tugged them open. No shadows clung to the edges. Only her breathing disturbed the silence. Roan was already gone.

"Damn you. Why won't you come?" How could she live knowing that Roan was fighting for survival?

She groaned and lay down, not willing to formally summon him as if he were her slave. She just wanted to be with him…and he kept sending her away. Did she have to agree to be his queen, to spend the rest of her life in the realm of nightmares just to spend time with him?

A chilling thought swept over her. Maybe he was really goblin. No, she couldn't believe that. She'd seen him as he'd been before the curse. Even back then he'd tried to do the right thing by his people. He was an honest man. And that was all she wanted.

Her cell phone vibrated, rustling against the contents of her handbag the police had returned. The phone went to voice mail before she could retrieve it.

Twenty-three missed calls.

Eliza started listening to the messages. Steve reminded her about the final wedding dress fitting. Like she could forget. She'd lost three days of freedom but gained a day with Roan. Eliza chewed her lip. She'd meet him again in the Summerland. She could live through the days with Steve if she could find Roan at night.

Eight calls in, Steve became more demanding, wanting to know where she was and why she wasn't with him. When the police released her house, she would go back home to Steve. Until then she would do what she wanted. Eliza hung up on the message back. She didn't have the stomach to listen to the rest of the messages. She knew how the game ended, so why bother playing?

As she thought, she flicked the cell phone open and closed. The flick, snap marked the time. Ten o'clock. The dress fitting was in an hour. She could make it if she hurried. Her niece would be at school and her sister-in-law was scheduled to meet her at the fitting.

Her thumb moved without thought.

With each ring her nerve faltered. This was the equivalent of poking a beehive. She was going to get stung for this. Maybe it wasn't worth it? If Amanda didn't pick up in one more ring, she'd go to the dress fitting.

"Eliza. Are you feeling better?" Amanda still sounded guilty about not visiting in the hospital.

"Yeah, I've slept the worst off. Can we get coffee?" She needed to get out and tell someone what had happened. But, like before, she knew she wouldn't tell a soul about the goblins. Couldn't.

"Ah, sure, before the fitting or after?"

Eliza licked her lip, then took a breath. "Let's skip the fitting."

"Skip?" Amanda asked like Eliza wanted her to jump off the Bell Tower and fly.

"I need clothes, not a wedding dress, and all my clothes are locked in the house." Except for the few items Steve had deemed appropriate and left for her at the hospital. "Let's go shopping." Shopping for clothes Steve would hate and that he'd never let her wear in public. A grin formed. She was going to live every hour that she had until she had to go back home.

"Are you sure about this? Maybe the bump on your head was more serious than the docs thought."

"I'm good. Pick me up?"

"Okay. If you're sure."

Eliza's heart thumped a nervous rhythm. It would betray her. She nodded and spoke with more confidence than she felt. "Never been surer."

Two hours and several shops later Eliza had found the perfect dress for wearing in the Summerland and meeting Roan. She spun and the white sundress floated around her. The gathered peasant bodice flowed into a full skirt that skimmed her knees. For the first time she was grateful summer fashion was invading the stores in the middle of winter.

Amanda leaned next to the changing room mirror with her sunglasses perched on the top of her head. She had the casual jeans and T-shirt look done perfectly. The streaks in her brown hair were natural from the time spent at the beach. That was where Amanda and Matt had spent all their free time, where she'd lost him and where his ashes were scattered. Amanda had been six months pregnant with Brigit.

"Steve wouldn't let *that rag* enter the house." Amanda took a sip of soft drink.

Eliza checked the price tag. It was an expensive rag.

With the white dress, pale skin, and bleached blond hair she looked like an empty shell of a woman. The life sucked out until she was little more than a weathered bone. What had happened to the girl whose future had seemed so bright? She could have been anyone, done anything. Instead she'd buckled and become what everyone else expected.

"Buy it. Hide it at my house and wear it when you visit."

"I shouldn't have to hide it." Eliza lifted her hair. Imagining it shorter, darker, different. Like she could be a different person by changing the way she looked.

"Where were you, Eliza?" Amanda put her hand on Eliza's arm. Her fingers brushed the gold bangle as if she sensed the connection. "What happened?"

Their eyes met. How could she explain? Where did she start? Nine years ago when she'd first met Roan? Five days ago when she'd vanished?

"Is there someone else?" Amanda gave her a look, as if she knew Eliza was keeping a secret.

Yes. But he's cursed and lives in the Shadowlands where he hoards gold because he's a goblin. He's scary at first, but once you get to know him he's gentle and caring. We've kissed twice. He wants me to stay with him and be his queen.

Eliza shook her head and her hair tumbled down her back. Anything she imagined with Roan was pure fantasy. He didn't exist in the real world, and she couldn't give up her life to live in the twisted world he inhabited as a queen in name only.

"You don't have to marry Steve." Amanda had never liked Steve. Not because she was jealous, but because he was too uptight.

But Steve had been there for Eliza. They had been in love, they were going to run Gunn and Coulter when the old men retired to play golf. They'd had plans. He'd helped her through her father's death when she'd had no one to lean on—Amanda had been too fractured from Matt's death and struggling with a two-year-old and studies. Then something had changed. Something so small she hadn't noticed at first. By the time Eliza had realized what was happening and where their relationship was going, it was too late. She'd declined his partnership request, dumped him, and found herself blackmailed and engaged in the same breath.

"It's a bit late now." It had gone on too long, her compliance adding to her assumed guilt. Without all the documents, not just the ones she'd signed, Steve held all the aces.

Amanda shrugged. "So you'll lose the deposit."

And my freedom.

The details of her relationship with Steve she'd never shared. Telling Amanda now would place her, and Brigit, in danger. She didn't trust Steve even when she was looking straight at him. His hands were always moving. Some things were best kept secret.

Eliza smoothed the dress. "I'm getting it."

—✺—

Eliza emptied the contents of the shopping bags onto the bed. With the scissors she cut the tags off the clothes. The sharp blades sung with each snip. Jeans, T-shirts, panties, bras, there was nothing exciting in the pile. But it was hers, selected by her because she liked it and not because it would make the right impression. She was tired of looking the part of expensive fiancée. She wanted to look like Eliza.

The hair dye lay on top of an electric-blue bra. *Maya gold*. A warm, honey-brown according to the box. As close to her natural color as she'd been able to find. Eliza held the scissors in one hand, the dye in the other. This was more serious than buying clothes. Amanda had bet fifty dollars she wouldn't do it. And another fifty that by the time of the wedding her hair would be blond again.

Eliza dropped the dye on the bed. She bent over and gathered her hair into a ponytail that sat ridiculously on her forehead. Then she cut. Six inches of hair fell on the floor. One more inch than Steve ever had. She stood up and looked in the mirror. The layers fell around her cheekbones, and the ends of her hair skimmed her shoulders.

Her stomach clenched, but a smile teased the corners of her lips. Steve was going to kill her. A giggle sneaked out. She was dead. She dropped the scissors and covered her mouth.

Shit.

Steve was going to lose it. After he'd planned the wedding down to the napkin rings, she'd ruined the day by chopping off her hair. He'd talk to her like she was a puppy who didn't know better, and then suffocate her with what he called love until she stopped fighting. For a moment she didn't care. He would've found something to complain about, so why not her hair?

But the haircut looked good, and while it wasn't her usual three-hundred-dollar cut, it was even and layered. Who needed to know she'd done it herself?

She tossed her hair and let it flick and settle. What the new style needed was a change in color. If she was going to be shot, she might as well face the bullet. She opened the dye and covered her hair in purple paste, popped a hotel shower cap over the top, and set the alarm clock for thirty minutes.

Eliza sat down and opened the first gossip magazine she'd read in two years. Minutes crawled past. Hollywood's latest breakups and hookups didn't offer enough distraction. With each passing second her mouth dried as if she'd been eating Shadowlands dust. She forced out a breath and rolled her shoulders. This wasn't right. She shouldn't be tormenting Steve. It would only come back and bite her on the ass. She tapped her foot and checked her watch. It had been working perfectly since she'd been back. But it was too late to change her mind—the dye would've already taken.

Her phone buzzed and she glanced at the screen. The number was too familiar. Steve. Her skin heated as if he could see what she was doing. She knew she couldn't continue to ignore his calls, yet it was another two heartbeats before she could pick up.

"Hello."

"So, you do remember how to use a phone."

"It was on silent. I was sleeping." The lie came too easily and was less troublesome than the truth.

"You missed the dress fitting. Donna called me. She made excuses for you."

Of course the wedding planner had rung him. She'd wanted nothing to do with the wedding preparations. She hadn't wanted the engagement. "I'm sorry, I was tired."

"Re-book. Pull yourself together, Eliza. No more

stunts. One phone call and I'll make sure you spend the rest of your life in orange."

The line went dead.

Her hand shook. She ripped off the shower cap. A tendril of purple-goo-coated hair slapped her face. She brushed it aside, her eyes burning. Just because she was marrying Steve didn't mean she had to obey him. She could disrupt his perfect, pretentious plans.

She searched her contacts for WPD. Wedding Planner Donna, or as Amanda had named her Wedding Prima Donna. It was time to show some interest in her wedding.

"Hi, Donna. Eliza Coulter."

"Oh, your dress fitting. I can get you back in on Friday at two. Okay?"

She knew without checking her diary she was free, and Amanda didn't work Fridays. Too perfect, she could almost see Steve's hand in it. She gritted her teeth. The fitting couldn't be avoided. WPD already thought a bride not having input was weird.

"Thank you." Eliza paused and softened her voice. Being brittle and tense wasn't going to help. "I'm sorry about today. I got my days mixed up."

"I heard from Steven. How horrible not knowing where you were. Is there anything else?" WPD, sympathy was part of the job.

She should've said no. She'd shaken the boat enough today, but her tongue had a life of its own. "Um. Yes, actually. Can I make a menu change?"

"Sure, what would you like to change?"

Eliza didn't know what was on the menu. Knowing Steve it would be beef or chicken.

"Some of my friends are vegetarian but eat seafood,

so I'd like the entrées to be either vegetarian or prawns."
She was going to hell for this.

Stunned silence followed as if she'd asked for a blood
sacrifice.

"Steven is allergic to seafood." Donna spoke slowly
as if Eliza didn't know her own fiancé.

"I know, but he can eat the vegetarian option." The
boat started to sink. He would never eat the vegetarian
option. Steve was a *real* man.

"He was very specific in his instructions, Ms. Coulter."

Eliza stood up. "Well I'm being specific in mine.
Who do you think is paying your fee?"

"Vegetarian and prawns. Anything else, Ms. Coulter?"

"That's all. Thank you, Donna." Eliza ended the call.
Adrenaline tightened her skin. She shivered. Temporary
insanity. Maybe she'd banged her head harder than the
doctors thought.

The alarm went off and a rock song punched through
the room. She let it play as she went into the bathroom
to see the damage done by the dye.

———

Steven watched the cab pull up. A woman with shoulder-
length, light auburn hair got out, her arms laden with
shopping bags. He clenched his teeth not wanting her to
turn and prove him right. She closed the cab door and he
saw her face. Eliza.

His fingers curled. How could she do this to him?
How would the wedding photos look? He'd have a
brassy bawd on his arm at the biggest wedding in town.

Steven unlocked the front door and let Eliza in. She
smiled with her lips pressed tight. He leaned in to kiss

her, but she turned her head so he caught her cheek. Anger buzzed inside him. Her defiance had gone on long enough.

He snatched her hand, so she was forced to face him. He saw the burst of fear in her eyes, quickly blanketed in calm. Her lips moved in a silent prayer.

"Been shopping, dear?"

"Got some clothes for the honeymoon." She lifted her chin daring a challenge.

"You know you can't shop alone." The clothes Eliza liked lacked the styling and branding that reflected their place in society. At first he hadn't cared, he'd thought she'd grow up and become smart and sophisticated like her mother. But that hadn't happened.

"I managed."

This new Eliza was rebelling, and he didn't like it. Rebellion was dangerous, and he had too much riding on her compliance.

"What happened to your hair? You look like a cheap whore."

A door slammed upstairs. The both glanced upwards.

Eliza tried to pull her hand away. "What did you want, an expensive one?"

He gripped tighter. "You can't play me and win, Eliza."

"I want more than being your blow-up wife."

He laughed. "Is that where you went for three days? Got a lover? Found someone who says he loves you? Says he can help you?"

She gasped. The private detective may have found nothing, but that simple breath told him everything.

"When I find him, I'll make sure he won't want anything to do with you."

The classical music that had filled the house fell silent. Around him the walls cracked and seemed to laugh. The noise from the neighbor's wind chimes filtered into the house, even though all the windows were closed. The hair on his arms dug into Steven's skin, needling his bones. He released Eliza.

She backed away, heading for the stairs, her eyes on him. "I'm sleeping in the guest room." She retreated upstairs with her head held high.

Steven let her go. He knew when to choose his battles. And soon enough he would have the perfect family.

Mozart came back on, but a brittle chill had settled over the house. Eliza was slipping through his fingers and the tighter he grasped the less he held. His threats were no longer working. He straightened his tie. The PI was going to have to dig harder. Whoever this person was, giving Eliza hope, he could be paid off. Everyone had a price.

Eliza closed the bedroom door with a thump that rattled the windows. She turned the privacy lock and leaned against the door, waiting for Steve to follow. To argue. She held her breath as she listened. The lock could easily be opened from the other side. It offered only the illusion of security. Her pulse pounded in her ears and the burn in her lungs increased. Nothing. No footsteps followed her and the handle didn't turn. Eliza let out the breath and glanced around the room. The shadows swelled and sighed. She wasn't alone.

"Roan? Are you here?" She hadn't called him. Was he watching over her?

His presence was the faintest brush against her skin. He was in the aching darkness she couldn't touch.

"Why won't you speak to me? Why can't I see you?" Her breathing rubbed over the silence, scratching away the surface until it was raw.

She swallowed and sniffed. "You keep sending me away. Now you follow me. What do you want from me?"

The shadows growled and grew, expanding to consume the room. Eliza put her hand on the light switch to fight the darkness that had terrified her as a child. The bulbs blew before she could turn them on. She flattened her back to the door. Her hair lifted as the jangle of beads swept past her. She turned her head to follow the noise, then the darkness was gone.

Pale sunset splashed on the floral quilt. In the middle of the bed was a piece of paper. Eliza walked over and picked up the thick, cream paper edged in gold, never-ending Celtic knots. The invitation looked like wedding stationary. On the paper were three words in elegant gold scrawl.

Be my queen.

She dropped the paper but never saw it hit the floor. It vanished, taken by the shadow cast by the bed.

"I can't." The words were almost silent. She couldn't live in the perpetual nightmare of the Shadowlands as queen. Yet she couldn't live without seeing Roan. To see Roan she had to sleep.

She dressed with care, one ear listening for Steve, but her mind was already on Roan and the way he'd smiled at her in the sunlight. The beads in his hair shining. It was hard to believe he was a goblin with a heart of gold when he looked so human. Her lips curved as she settled into the guest bed. When she blinked, she opened her eyes in the Summerland.

The grass was an ocean of green, banked by trees. Exactly the same as last time, as every time she'd waited for him as a teenager. Try as she might Eliza couldn't change the setting. Above her clouds hovered in the distance, like a bruise on the blue dream sky.

Roan appeared in front of her. Arms crossed. The grass cringed away from his touch.

"I didn't think you'd come." She smiled but didn't get one back.

"I have to answer *all* summons. Even dream ones now."

The bitterness in his voice held her in place. "I'm not summoning you. I'm just thinking of you." Dreaming of him…except he was really here. "If this is just a dream, why can't I change where we are?"

"This is the Summerland. Dreams start here—they don't stay here." Roan caught the end of a dreadlock and worked it through his fingers with his arms still folded. "Most people don't know of this place. They pass through and move on to the dream."

"But you know of it." The white sundress swished around her knees. She tucked a strand of hair behind her ear, but the shorter hairstyle refused to be tamed and it flicked free again.

"Dreams and nightmares can't exist without each other but can't exist together. I shouldn't be here." He tossed the beads to his back in a melody that was all Roan's. "You shouldn't be here, waiting for me."

Eliza stepped toward him, unable to resist. "But I want you here in my dream."

"You have to stop calling me." He watched with eyes

bluer than the sky but less forgiving. The dry aching heat sucked at her soul.

Her tongue moistened her lip. "I call because you watch."

His mouth quirked up on one side. "I watch because you call."

"I needed to see you. To talk to you." She felt like was seventeen again with her first boyfriend. No boyfriend had ever been able to match up to the man she'd imagined the Goblin King to be. "How about a picnic? Stay awhile with me." A red and white checked rug and wicker basket appeared on the grass at their feet as soon as she'd thought it.

Roan looked at the spread of food, and then at Eliza. He shook his head yet sat. She sat next to him. Her pale legs stretched out next to his black-clad and booted ones as if they were enjoying a summer picnic. Next to him she felt safer than she had in a long time.

"I'm here as you desired. What did you want to talk about?" He leaned back in a pose that on another man would have passed for relaxation.

Her smile faltered. He was playing along for her, not because he wanted to. "I don't mean to command you."

"No?" He lifted an eyebrow. "Then what is it you want from me?"

She glanced at him under her lashes. What did she want? A friend? A protector? Her cheeks warmed under the sun. A lover? "I...I don't know."

Roan kissed her. His lips moved gently over her mouth. She yielded to his questing tongue and let herself be lowered to the picnic rug.

"You cut your hair." He nuzzled against her neck.

"I wanted a change," she said too fast, defending herself from the coming attack.

"And changed the color." His hand traced around the neckline of her dress. "It suits you."

He soothed her surprise with a kiss. Her nipple peaked as his fingers circled her breast. The dress gave her no protection, but with Roan she didn't need any. Her back arched, pressing her body closer.

"You're not wearing underwear." His hand stilled and the cool of his palm seeped through the thin fabric. The sun haloed his head with dazzling pure light.

And Eliza knew why she'd called him, why she had to see him. The need for Roan burned in every cell of her body, cold and bright. "I want you."

She'd wanted him for years.

He closed his eyes and groaned as if she'd stabbed him. "Then be my queen."

Eliza cupped his face. "I don't want to be queen in the Shadowlands. I just want you."

Roan gazed at her for an eternity before moving. He shifted to lie over her, his weight stealing her breath. The kiss that followed was rough and hard like a warrior taking no prisoners. Eliza surrendered to his touch. Then the world turned black, became airless, and spun.

She gasped and found herself on the spare bed in her house. The room glowed yellow with an unnatural light that left no shadows to hide the goblin that knelt over her, trapping her hands. Her eyes widened but her voice was lost, left in the dream. She couldn't scream as the nightmare became real and seized control.

Round, yellow cat's eyes glowed from gray skin

stretched tight over his skull. In contrast, his lips were wide and fleshy. Long, pointed ears that curled over at the top were almost hidden by his hair—the only part of him she recognized. The beaded dreadlocks could only be Roan's.

The goblin didn't move. "Is this what you want?" His voice rasped like a file over rust-riddled iron. "Is this what you want to see every time you summon me?" He released her hand. His knotted fingers traced her cheek. As a man the gesture had been kind, now his hand only promised cruelty.

A tremor started deep in her body, rattling the breath in her lungs. The scent of leaves left to wither on the forest floor filled the room.

He placed his lips on her cheek and whispered in her ear. "Is this what you want to lie with? Do you want these hands on your skin?"

She didn't fight and didn't push him away. Her limbs wouldn't move. This wasn't the man she knew. "This isn't you."

"This *is* what I am. I am the Goblin King." Despair and anger swept the room. "Not a forgotten warrior, not a dream-lover, not a man." He stared down at her, stripping her emotions bare, laying open every fear for him to see. "Without you as my queen this is what I become. Forever. I want to keep my soul, Eliza."

She gasped, understanding why he'd brought her back. Not because he didn't want her, but because he wanted her so much it would cost him his soul. The realization made her dizzy.

"You're a man. I've seen you." The words tore her throat.

"Not in the Fixed Realm." His voice lowered. "Not in your world."

He was truly a goblin. The man she'd seen was nothing but a mask worn in the Shadowlands to lure her into being his queen. An eternity as the goblin's bride, warming his bed.

"No." Tears burned her eyes. She shook her head as if she could remove the sight of the goblin. Like denial could make the horror go away.

He released her and stood at the foot of the bed. "Think hard before calling me again. Next time there will be no choice. I will take the summons as your acceptance. You will be mine." The shadows coalesced around the Goblin King. "Marry your fiancé, Eliza. At least he is human."

Chapter 8

THE DUST BENEATH HIS FEET SURGED AND WRITHED AS IF a million ants sought their way to the surface. Shadowlands magic flowed through him dark, slick, tempting. An ice-cold oblivion from the constant fight to remain human.

Was it worth the fight?

Was being human really so grand?

He had the power of every fear ever thought at his fingertips. He could control nightmares. He could make them reality, so every moment became a delicate hell that would never end. But it had only taken one look at his face to reduce Eliza to tears and to ensure that he would never again be included in her dreams.

Roan stared into the endless, lusterless twilight. No dark, dreamless night lit only by stars. No hope of a fat, fertile moon. No promise of a bright, bleeding dawn. Just the endless quest for more gold, as if goblins could create their own sun if they only had enough. It was never enough. There wasn't enough gold in the universe to fill the need that bored through his chest. Only Eliza could've stopped the rot.

And he'd made sure she regretted ever summoning the Goblin King.

He clenched his fists. This ended now. No more games. The druid would die, or the curse would take Roan completely into its embrace. The ground quaked as if he was tearing out the center of the world.

"Elryion!"

The huge crow appeared in the sky. Magic burned Roan's fingers as he attacked. Lightning arced out of the ground, and the bird dodged. It rolled like a fighter pilot, then dived. The ground at Roan's feet tore, trying to swallow him whole. He sealed the gaping maw without losing his footing. His soul loosened and flapped like a flag in a tornado, waiting for the right moment to tear free and be lost in the storm.

Hail the size of fists fell from a cloudless sky, forcing the crow to land. One hundred paces away the druid became a man. Too far away for Roan to fight him as a warrior should, hand to hand. The druid was too smart to ever let that happen. He may have been wrong in placing the curse, but admitting it would mean forfeiting his own soul. A price he was too proud to pay.

So it was always a magical fight, both left spent but alive, and Roan just a little closer to the abyss that nibbled at his toes. Today he didn't care how much power he drew. The cold magic scoured his veins. The gold in his chest expanded, fed by the rage at himself. He'd pushed Eliza away. He hadn't given her a chance to understand. He'd just expected her obedience as if she were a slave to command.

He melted the ground beneath the druid. Lava bubbled. Red blisters popped and oozed. The druid reformed ground, so he stood in a sea of weeping magma. Roan stalked toward the druid, but the ground sucked at his feet. It clung to his legs as unseen hands dragged him down into the gray muck.

Roan laughed as he sunk up to his knees. If he didn't fight, he would be entombed in the dust. Not dead. Not alive. One with the Shadowlands forever. It was the fate he deserved.

The mud clawed at his thighs. Roan snarled and yelled, "Is that the best you have?"

The druid smiled, and beside him on the island appeared Eliza.

Roan stopped. The blinding rage cleared and left him hollow. No. Not possible. Elryion lacked the power to pull people through from the Fixed Realm. He couldn't leave the Shadowlands. Roan drew the gun and fired at the druid. The bullets fell to the ground well short of their target, stopped by magic. He would never get close enough to kill.

Elryion pushed her to the edge of his island. Eliza screamed. Roan fought against the thick gray mud, sinking with every step. Wading through it without magic he would never get there in time.

All he had to do was cool the lava and close the ground. Let Elryion win. His fingers throbbed with unspent power. He could save himself and Eliza. He curled his hands. That would be all it took. That little morsel of magic would gobble up his soul without a second thought. He would be Hoard, Eliza would be his, and the druid would be free.

Eliza begged, pleading for her life. Her long, pale blond hair whipped around her face. As Roan stood still, sanity took residence. She was exactly as the druid had seen her at Anfri's burning. Eliza had dark golden hair now. The color made her skin glow—lit with an inner fire he had done his best to taint. Roan let his breath ease out. This Eliza wasn't real. The druid was using fear, his fear and his nightmare of a world without Eliza.

He raised his hands. "Do it, Elryion. Prove how far you have fallen."

The druid shoved the Eliza-illusion into the lava-lake. Roan's stomach lurched, punching his ribs. He reached out a hand, barely stopping the magic from leaping to do his bidding. The instinct to save her was so powerful he almost obeyed even though he knew the truth. Her death was over in a second. It may not have been real, but the loss was. He had lost Eliza. A man would have cried. He was just numb.

Unable to tempt Roan into surrender, the druid took flight. The crow lived to fight another day. Another day when Roan would lose to a man who was as lost as he was.

Roan climbed out of the dust and lay down. Two thousand years and he was just as fucked now as he had been that first day. If it had only been him cursed, he would have ended it long ago. He couldn't die without taking his brother with him. He lay motionless. The cold from the ground seeped into bones that should have turned to dust centuries ago and left no trace of his passing. He was old. He was tired. He was alone.

—⁓—

Roan found Dai sitting at the desk where he spent most of his days. A pile of scrolls and maps sat to one side. Occasionally Dai would find a report of some misdeed they were commanded to commit and they would toast the bad old days before they'd had control. He'd seen evil men rewarded. Good men assassinated. They'd changed history without anyone knowing who they were. He wanted Eliza to remember who he was—not the goblin he was becoming. He'd screwed that up.

"Finished your pissing contest with Elryion?" Dai looked over the gold rim of his glasses.

Roan slumped into a seat. He ran his hand over his face. Gray dust clung to his skin like he was already halfway goblin. He'd made himself walk back to the caves. Distance in the Shadowlands, like everything else, shifted to make the individual suffer. In his case, he was sure he'd walked a solid day with his sword in his hand, looking out for goblin scouts who wouldn't hesitate to challenge him for a crown he was ready to surrender.

"This might cool your heels." A faint smile crossed Dai's lips as he tossed Roan a pouch.

Roan caught the dull black leather bag one-handed. He tipped the contents into his palm. The black gems were beautiful but lacked the lure of gold. They seemed to absorb the light then reflect it, like it was their own fire and they burned from within. His hand warmed, the magic that tied him to the Shadowlands gone. In shock he threw them down and the gems scattered over the table.

"What are they?" Roan flexed his fingers to assess any damage that had been done.

"Black diamonds." Dai took of his glasses, his fingers going through the empty gold frames. He had no need for lenses. "They are said to protect the wearer from the Shadowlands. I take it they work."

"I'm not an experiment. Without our magic, we are at the mercy of Elryion." Roan summoned a glass goblet of water. His throat was dry after his walk. He relaxed a little when the goblet appeared. The diamonds hadn't stolen the magic permanently.

"With every battle you get closer." Dai placed three

small silvery bars on the table. "If the diamonds stop the fade, I say wear them."

"Is this what you've been searching for?" Roan toyed with a diamond, feeling the retreat and advance of magic but no movement from his heart.

Dai looked away, distracted by a scroll on his desk. "Not exactly." He traced a line of text. "Black fire fell from the sky, blessed by the gods. No evil survived." He opened another scroll.

Roan pinched the diamond between his fingers and stared at his brother. He wanted the simple answer, not the thesis including references. "What exactly were you looking for?"

"These diamonds were ripped out of the earth. I chased every reference, searched every tomb. The diamonds that fell to earth remain missing."

Or never existed. It wouldn't be the first time the writers of old had been less than honest in their scribblings.

"Would the sky diamonds have broken the curse?"

Dai shook his head.

Roan clamped his teeth together. They had fake mythical diamonds that appeared to protect the wearer. That did them no good when he faded. He put the diamond down.

"How does this help to break the curse?"

"A stay of execution, brother."

"What good is a stay of execution when the axe will still fall?" Roan pulled out his gun and placed it on the table. Could Dai not feel the drag of the Shadowlands? He didn't want a reprieve, he needed a cure. Death would suffice.

"We will find a way to break the curse. I need more time." Dai's gaze flicked between Roan and the gun.

"How much? A decade? A century? Another thousand years?" Roan traced the smooth contours of the metal. He flicked the safety off. It would be over in an instant. No more fighting. No more weight in his chest. No more tugging on his soul. Peace and an eternity of dining in the Hall of the Gods. They wouldn't deny him. They denied no warrior who fell. He hoped they wouldn't force him to be reborn. He wasn't sure he could manage another lifetime after this one.

Dai pulled the gun over the table. He thumbed the safety back on. "Is the gray that close?"

The muscle in Roan's cheek twitched. Dai wasn't ready. He couldn't take his brother's life just because he was tired of living.

"Until today I had hope." Roan closed his eyes and made himself breathe. "I believed that one day I could have everything I'd been denied by the gods. A wife, a family. Things men take for granted."

Roan used magic to pull the gun back into his grip. He knew he shouldn't be drawing on the Shadowlands, but it had become habit. And it would be a hard habit to break. He holstered the metal, saving its promise for another time. "That day will never come."

"What of your queen?"

"There will be no queen." Roan traced the edge of the goblet. The glass returned to sand. Water splashed over his fingers, and he let it spill onto the desk, washing the diamonds that would stop him from using the magic that was claiming his soul. "She knows me for what I am."

—⁓—

Sleep wouldn't come. Eliza sat on the bed with her knees drawn up to her chin. The bedside light's glow left half the room in shadows. She checked the clock again. One o'clock in the morning. Hours remained of the night. It wasn't fear of Steve that prevented sleep. Every time her head lolled and her eyes closed, luminous yellow eyes appeared in her mind. She could almost convince herself they weren't human. But the lust and pain that raged behind the surface were too familiar. She'd seen them in the clear blue eyes of a Celtic king.

She had to stop thinking of him. She didn't want to summon him by accident. In frustration she threw back the covers and gave up on sleep. Eliza opened the guest room door and peered out. The house was silent. She padded down the hallway, placed her hand on a door handle, then hesitated. Would going back to where it had started answer any of her questions or breed more ugly, unwanted questions?

There was only one way to find out. She pushed open the door and turned on the light. Forgotten treasures of her childhood lined the shelves. Certificates hung on the walls. The bed was made. The white and rose quilt was pulled tight with disuse. A doll and a stuffed lion were propped on the pillow, waiting for the child to return. She touched the lion's ear. He had been her nighttime protector. Her cheeks tightened in a sad semblance of a smile. No monsters would dare come near her while she slept with Ruff at her side. Now her faith was too damaged to believe. She pulled her hand away and her fingers came away dusty. The room needed airing.

Across the hall was Matt's room. Untouched since the day of his death. Her father had just closed the door, unable to pack up the room. Her father may not have agreed with Matt's choice to shun the four-generation-old family business and study medicine, but he wasn't cruel enough to cut him or his unscheduled wife and child out of the trust.

When Steve had moved in three months after her father's death, their first fight had been over where to sleep. In the end he'd bought a new bedroom suite for the master bedroom and she'd given in. The first of many fights barely fought and too easily lost. Now he wanted to turn her old room into a home gym. It was a constant sore. A reminder that this was her house and would always be hers, not his. The pale pink roses should've been updated years ago, but her mother had picked the colors, and Eliza had never had the strength to erase what little remained of her mother.

She glanced at the photo on the bedside table. Her mother's perfect smile and easy elegance captured as she placed a kiss on a twelve-year-old Eliza's head. Too gangly to have grace, and the braces a hindrance to beauty, her mother had decided that Eliza should concentrate on her studies. The stage was not for her. Her mother had been right. Eliza was more than happy to drop the drama club and step away from the limelight.

With her mother's death, her father had shrunk. Work had become his sole passion. Eliza closed her eyes. The day she'd been accepted into law school was the first time he hadn't looked through her in search of his wife. The acceptance letter was still pinned to the corkboard. She opened her eyes and ripped down the letter. Once it had filled her with pride, now it was worthless. She scrunched the paper and let it fall to the floor.

It had been five years since she'd studied law. Her shoulders sagged.

She'd be lying if she'd said she missed it. But working as a legal secretary at the family firm, the half-hidden looks of pity from the other lawyers, rankled.

Had law ever been her dream? Or just a cry for attention?

If she'd never summoned the Goblin King the first time, where would she be now?

The same place.

Alone. Roan had given her a chance to change, to take charge of her life, and she'd thrown it away. She'd worn his bead as a reminder but hadn't learned from the lesson. She'd remained the girl everyone expected her to be. She'd never grown up and become who she was supposed to be. Who was that?

Her life was her fault, every decision she'd avoided making had led her here—to the point where she was facing jail or being married to a man she didn't love while longing for a man she couldn't have. With no one to blame, the reality was harder to swallow. Nausea rose, thickening at the back of her throat. She sucked in a few deep breaths and swiped at the tears forming in her eyes.

Law had taught her one thing. The power of research. In among the books of fairy tales was a slim, plain brown volume on goblins. She'd bought it on a whim shortly after her mother's funeral, hoping to keep tales of her childhood alive. After her first meeting with the Goblin King, she'd read it again cover to cover, desperate to find evidence that would prove her encounter and reveal something about the warrior who ruled the Shadowlands.

She traced down the spine. The book's details she'd forgotten with time, only the skin-tingling rush of fear remained. Some people feared vampires or ghosts, but the monsters in her dreams were goblins.

Eliza pulled *Goblins: Myth or Truth?* from the shelf. She moved the doll and lion and sat on the bed. This time she knew goblins were real. So what other pieces of lore could be true? Now that she was looking at the stories in a whole new light, she might be able to get some answers.

Roan couldn't stay away. His body ached and he wanted to sleep even though he didn't need to. But closing his eyes provided no rest. Eliza filled his thoughts even if he didn't disturb hers. In the last few hours before dawn he gave in and went to her. To the woman who now feared him more than death.

She'd moved rooms, unable to sleep with the memory of the Goblin King on her bed. She leaned against the headboard of a single bed. Her head rested against a pillow and a book lay limp in her hands. Barely asleep, the light on. He'd made her afraid of the dark. He couldn't touch her, not with these hands, not now. His nails curled into his palms. Watching Eliza sleep was more painful than parting with gold.

He tore himself away and went back to the bedroom where he'd pressed his gray body to hers. Her scent

permeated every corner of the room and haunted his
life. Roan hung his head. She would never be his—he
should have never granted her ill-thought-through wish.
From the corner of his eyes he saw a slip of paper poking
out from under the bed. His gilded invitation lay on the
floor forgotten.

Better he was forgotten.

Better Eliza never looked on his face again.

He drew the shadows to him ready to leave, but
another presence lived in the house. Roan paused. The
fiancé. It would be easier to leave Eliza if he knew she
would be safe and loved. He glided through the darkness to the room where Eliza had summoned him before
passing out. The same room she'd summoned him to
years ago. This time there was no youth hunting her,
only her sleeping fiancé. The temptation to stalk him
was too great. He could climb through his dreams and
convince himself that this man was worthy of Eliza despite what he'd seen in her mind.

Roan dipped into his thoughts. Dreams of celebrity
and pomp and splendor. Self-obsession. Steve stirred as
Roan dug deeper, peeling back layers of thoughts. He
wanted to find substance, a man who could be trusted
to care for Eliza. Anything that would free him of the
delusion that she would come to him willingly.

He failed.

Beneath the surface lurked a goblin in a man's skin.
Obsessive and driven. Hungry for only one thing—power.

White-hot bitterness flooded Roan's veins. He
wanted to wake the bastard and hear him scream as the
goblin squeezed his throat until his eyes burst and his
voice was a broken croak. But that was too fast. No.

This man needed something that would make him rest-less every night for the rest of his life.

With a whisper in his ear Roan took away everything. He conjured every fear and balled them into a night-mare. Then he watched as the man tossed, clenching the sheets in white-knuckled hands. His cries were muffled by sleep. Roan would have traded his soul to be this Steve. To take his place by Eliza's side. To have a wife and not a queen.

The man reached out, seeking help. Roan didn't have the heart to ease the man's suffering, nor the stomach to watch anymore. He'd done enough damage for one night. Tomorrow he would do more. The call of the Wild Ride already sung in his blood.

Winter solstice was almost here.

Eliza stared at the golden-haired stranger in the wedding dress. White lace and beads frothed around her, smoth-ering her will to live.

"Get it off me." She tore at the tiny buttons at the back.

They bounced to the floor in a hollow mockery of the music of Roan's beads. Her skin quivered at the reminder of his cold, gray hands. She'd sat up all night until exhaustion had claimed her. She was too scared to sleep in case the Goblin King returned and she agreed to his demands. The goblin she saw wasn't the man she knew, yet she couldn't have one without the other. She knew that now and still she wanted him.

"Get it off me, now."

The shop assistant rushed to help before she ripped the dress that cost as much as a family car.

"Eliza, stop." Amanda grabbed her hands. "What is wrong?"

Eliza pressed her lips together to stop herself from screaming and revealing the madness that was taking over. That would never do, the new wife of prominent lawyer Steven Slade paying a visit to Graylands Mental Hospital. She could see the tabloid headlines already. She swallowed, fighting the urge to be sick. She didn't need the Shadowlands. She was living the nightmare. She was marrying Steve. Steve was human. He wouldn't crawl out of the darkness with kisses, threats, and magic, demanding her soul. He did all of that in daylight.

The assistant peeled the dress away and she could breathe again.

"It's the dress," she said through her teeth. In her heart she knew it was the man.

Amanda's eyebrows pinched together, but she said nothing.

"I want a different dress." The idea rolled over her tongue and tasted good. "This one isn't me."

"But the wedding is next week." The assistant, who could pass through a sieve without touching the sides, hovered, confused by the sudden change.

Amanda rounded on the woman. "Plenty of time. Show us some new dresses."

"But the groom, the bridesmaids, nothing will match." The woman stepped back.

"It doesn't matter. Bring us what you have." Amanda closed the door to the changing room, then turned and faced Eliza. "It's not the dress. You've been different since you came back."

Eliza sat in her white bridal underwear. The thought of Steve undressing her spun her stomach. She ran her hands through her hair. "How did you know Matt was the one?"

"He was going to be a doctor. I got knocked up. We eloped. Case closed." Amanda shrugged like losing Matt hadn't nearly cost her the baby as well.

"Seriously."

Amanda sat on the floor of the changing room. For a moment her eyes were seeing something else. A memory kept close. "I just knew there would never be anyone else."

"Not even now?" Eliza lifted her head.

Amanda removed her sunglasses from their perch on top of her head, folded the arms, and placed them in her handbag. "I've never met anyone who comes close. It's hard to live in a dead man's shadow." She looked up at Eliza. "Steve's not the one, is he?"

Eliza bit her lip and shook her head.

"You can't marry Steve if he's not the one."

"Why not? Maybe not everyone gets that feeling when they just know. When nothing else matters as long as they are there." Roan would never be there because he didn't really exist. Only the Goblin King existed. That was how she had to think of him, unless she wanted to become a goblin queen…would that even save him?

There had been no hints in the book—only a confusing array of stories that contradicted each other as many times as they agreed. There was no one legend of the Goblin King. It was like Roan's story had fractured and each part had taken on a life of its own. In some he was a hero, in others a villain, in her mother's he'd granted wishes, in another he scared greedy children into behaving. All failed to recognize his struggle to hold on to his humanity.

"You met someone."

Eliza ran a finger along her lower eyelid before her mascara could run and smudge.

"I thought…" There'd been something, something in the way Roan had looked at her, touched her, but it had died when the goblin had held her hands. She shook off the ache that lurked beneath her skin. "Prewedding jitters."

Eliza stood. The Goblin King made Steve look like an angel.

There was a tentative tap on the door. "What kind of dress, Ms. Coulter?"

"Something simple," Eliza said. She held out her hand to Amanda and helped her up.

They went through the shop, guided by the assistant to racks of dresses from arctic-white to rich-buttery-cream and every shade in between. Some had splashes of color, a peacock ribbon, a crimson train, a hot pink bodice.

She pulled out a simple A-line dress. No frills or trains that went for yards, just a small amount of beading. What she'd wanted all along. Even the color was perfect, a silken shade of pale cream.

The dress looked better on her than it had on the hanger.

"That's a beautiful dress. It suits you." Amanda nodded as she spoke.

"The wedding is black and white. We can make this one in time, in white to match." The wafer-thin assistant smiled encouragingly.

Eliza sighed. Steve and his lack of imagination, that and Wedding Prima Donna telling him black and white was super chic. She should've been involved instead of running away. She'd made her choice years ago, and instead of going to the police when she found out about the fraud she wore his ring. She looked at herself in the mirror. How had it come to this?

"Ms. Coulter?"

The dress had to match the rest of the bridal party. It would have to be white. White like the sundress she wore to see Roan in the Summerland.

Eliza shook her head. She couldn't do it. There was one other option. "Black. I want it in black."

Everyone gasped as if she'd blasphemed in church.

"You can't wear black." The assistant's eyebrows hit her hairline and kept crawling.

Eliza shrugged. "Everyone else is." She'd worn black when Roan had granted her wish and saved her from Steve. Maybe it would bring her luck if not joy.

"Are you sure, Eliza?" Amanda touched her arm.

"It's not done. It can't be done." The assistant reached for a fabric sample book. The page fell open to a lustrous black satin.

Eliza touched the square of cloth, and calm wrapped its arms around her, soothing away her worries. Her lips twitched. The answer was staring at her as it had been all along. She may have to marry Steve, but it would be done her way. She would take control of her life, one piece at a time.

"It is now."

Five hours later Eliza had put thoughts into action. She finished stuffing the last designer label shirt into an oversized orange trash bag and tied it up. Then she placed it next to one full of shoes and paused to admire her afternoon's efforts for a second before she dragged the bags downstairs, the bundles making a satisfying schlump as they bounced down each step.

She placed them outside on the veranda by the front door next to the box of classical CDs. In the front yard darkness bloomed under every tree and shrub. She peered into the night, fearful and hopeful of what she would see. She closed her eyes to listen better for the chime of beads.

Nothing stirred the leaves except for the wind that bubbled off the gathering storm clouds. She ran her teeth over her lip. She hadn't called Roan, and he hadn't visited to watch her from the shadows. She straightened her back and tried to convince herself she didn't need him or his curse. Wishing to be taken away didn't fix anything. She had her own problems in her real life that only she could deal with. Throwing out Steve's things was just the start of reclaiming her space and removing her curse.

She pulled the two dollar coin from her pocket and threw it on to the lawn. It had been many years since she'd left gold out for the goblins that were allowed to roam the world during the winter solstice. She'd grown up and forgotten about them, but her fear of the dark had remained. She didn't feel like tempting fate tonight. She'd already done enough.

Steve's red BMW swung into the driveway. The headlights on high beam burned away the darkness. The car slid into her garage. He would have seen her standing by the open door. Her stomach rolled over, but it was too late to back down. She touched the back pocket of her jeans. The papers that would secure her newfound independence were tucked inside.

Eliza closed the front door and waited, listening for Steve as he made his entrance. The car door slammed. The internal door between the house and garage opened. His keys landed on the sideboard. She waited, knowing he would march into the foyer to confront her. He didn't disappoint. His face was tight, ready for a fight.

This time, so was she. She'd learned to play the game his way. Eliza smiled, part nerves, part excitement, and crossed her arms. She leaned against the door as if she threw out his belongings every day of the week.

Steve's eyes narrowed. His lips didn't move, but she knew he was thinking about what to say. Start the argument right and win at all costs. She fired the first shot.

"I took the liberty of packing your clothes. You won't be staying here anymore." Eliza's voice was a thousand times more steady than she felt. Her hands sweated against her arms, and her stomach was clenched so tight it would be days before she would be able to force it to take food.

He swallowed, digesting the turn of events. "We will be married next week. It's hardly worth me moving out."

"Married. We don't have to live together."

"I'm not moving out." He loosened his tie.

Eliza pulled the folded piece of paper from her pocket. She smoothed it out slowly, making him wait for a change. He watched her hands but kept himself in check.

"If you don't leave, I will ring Alistair and have every cent, every property, every share owned by the trust turned over to Amanda and Brigit." She handed him the piece of paper—a copy of the instructions she had lodged with her lawyer after the dress fitting.

His gaze flicked over the page. His face paled, but his features were carefully schooled. Would he allow this piece of new evidence to be admitted into the argument?

Steve folded the paper back up and placed it into his jacket pocket. "What is the meaning of this?"

"You want marriage. You want the partnership. It's yours. But it is a marriage in name only. We will not live together. You don't get access to any of the trust. No more suits, cars, holidays unless you pay for them."

"It's too late to negotiate."

Eliza stood straight. "No, it's not. You see, I got to thinking. I am of more value to you as a wife than I am in jail."

Spots of pink flushed his cheeks. His lips pulled back in a grimace that was like a smile wrapped around the mouth of a dried out corpse. "Has that bitch been in your ear? Ever since you've been back—"

"I woke up."

"You can't throw me out. People will talk."

"Let them." For the first time she didn't care what people thought. She'd spent so long living up to the Coulter name. Now she wanted to be just Eliza.

Steve raised his hand. "In one week you're my wife. You're mine."

"In one week I own you," Eliza corrected. She stood just out of reach. She didn't drop her gaze or back down. She'd found the crack in his armor and was prepared to deliver the lethal blow. She would rather go to jail and hand over the trust fund than live life as man and wife with Steve. And he knew it.

"You can't do this. I'll call the police, I'll tell them everything."

Eliza pulled her cell phone out of her pocket. "Good idea." She dialed emergency services. Not Detective Griffin's number. She wasn't desperate enough to tell all. She would only do that when she had the documents that proved it was Steve doing the stealing.

He watched, daring her to stop. She put the phone to her ear. The line connected.

"What are you doing?" He reached out to snatch the phone away.

Eliza spun away and the vase of silk flowers hit the floor. "Hello, police."

"Give me the phone." Steve caught her hand.

"Coulter, Bay View Terrace, Peppermint—"

He wrenched the phone out of her hand and hung up. He glared at her. She returned the stare, refusing to cave or bend to his will. Not this time. It may only be a small part of her life to regain, but it was a start.

"You can explain to the police, if they arrive, that you were making a scene."

"What I tell them depends on where you are." She opened the cloakroom door and pulled out the raincoat he kept there. He might need it tonight; the weather was getting wild.

Steve took hold of the fabric and pulled her close. "You can't win."

"I lose either way. The difference is I don't care." She tugged on the coat, pulling him toward the door.

She used her elbow to turn the handle and her foot to kick open the door. She pulled Steve out the door with the raincoat.

"You're crazy." He jerked, trying to snatch it back.

"I should've done it years ago." She tightened her hold, her muscles burning from the effort. "You get what you want, but I get the house. I get my life."

He pulled again and she let go. Steve went sprawling onto the veranda. Too late, he realized what she'd planned. He scrambled to get up while she slipped inside and closed the door. The lock snapped into place.

Steve pounded on the door. The wood sung beneath his fist and reverberated through her body. She sobbed without tears. She'd wounded the beast but not killed him. Steve was more dangerous than ever.

The night went silent.

Eliza peeked out the glass pane at the side. A white car had pulled into the driveway. Her heart constricted, preventing her from swallowing. Two uniformed police walked up the driveway, then up the path, their serious blueness a sign she'd gone too far. They stepped around the orange bags. "Good evening, sir. Got a call about a disturbance. Is there a problem?"

"I seem to have locked my keys inside."

One of the officers looked at Eliza. She held her breath not wanting to miss a word of the conversation.

"Your partner won't let you in?"

"She's PMSing."

The female office nodded. "Mind if I chat with her?"

Steve glanced over his shoulder. "Not at all."

Eliza wanted to be sick. It was never supposed to come to this. Steve was supposed to leave knowing the wedding would go ahead. He wasn't supposed to challenge her to a game of chicken with the cops. Her fingers wouldn't work properly. She fumbled the lock twice before getting it open.

"Good evening, miss." The cop walked in, and her gaze left Eliza as she took in the broken vase and scattered flowers.

"Coulter," Eliza filled in.

The woman's eyes flashed in recognition. "Was it you who called?"

Eliza nodded. Steve was talking, but they had moved away from the door so all she heard was the rhythm of speech with no definite words. The handcuffs at the woman's side beckoned. Eliza rubbed her wrists.

"I asked him to move out." More like demanded, but she wasn't ready to divulge their under-the-table deals.

"He didn't like that." The woman glanced at her partner.

"No."

"What started the argument?"

"Wedding plans, my missing days." If she'd known it would get this far, she wouldn't have started. It was easier to toe the line than make a new one.

The other officer signaled his partner. The policewoman went outside. They both spoke to Steve. Eliza kept her back straight, but inside she was wilting. He'd spilled. She was sure of it, and she was going to jail. Steve turned and gave a look so bitter it should've been accompanied with a slicing gesture across the neck.

The man pulled out some paperwork. He filled it in and then approached her. Her eyes widened.

"Evening, Ms. Coulter. Can you please get Mr. Slade's car keys?"

"His keys?" The simple request gave her hope…Steve hadn't told them. Maybe his fraud wasn't as well hidden as he claimed.

The policeman nodded.

Eliza bit back a nervous smile as she walked through the house and retrieved the keys. She placed them in the cop's hand not sure what to expect. In exchange he gave her a piece of paper.

"This is a twenty-four-hour police order. Mr. Slade must stay away from the house. If he breaches the order, ring and he will be arrested."

It was a magical lifeline. Her fingers crushed the paper, making sure it was real. Steve was leaving. "Thank you."

The officer remained standing on her veranda. "Is there anything else I can help you with?"

She shook her head, not trusting herself to speak.

"Good night, ma'am. Make sure you lock up." The cop walked away.

Eliza locked the door. The house breathed a sigh of relief that echoed around her. She was truly alone for the first time in years. She wanted to cry, but if she started she'd never stop. She blinked and drew in lungfuls of air. She'd done it. Only one thing remained.

She picked up the phone and dialed, then spoke to the computer operator.

"Locksmith."

She was going to lock up so Steve never got back in to her house. Removing him from her life was going to be harder.

It was midnight by the time the locksmith left. Every door lock had been changed. The house didn't move around her. The silence waited to be filled by music or voices or footsteps. Instead, every light burned to push back the emptiness.

Outside a storm was in the making. The clouds had erased the stars from the sky. Wind coiled around the trees and shook them. Inside the house remained untouched. The stains of Steve's life here remained, but they could be wiped clear. The house would be hers. She double-checked all the locks again. The reality of spending the night alone had her jumping at her own heartbeat.

Eliza set the alarm and ran up to the guest room. The room was lit only by the bedside light because she hadn't replaced the main bulb. She dropped her new keys into her handbag and surveyed the room.

The bed still held the imprints of the goblin's knees. She shuddered. With a tug she wrenched the sheets off the bed. They resettled smooth and unmarked. The memory of the goblin's face wasn't as easy to remove. She couldn't sleep in this room. How could she not call him in her sleep when he was all she thought about?

From the corner of her eye she caught a glimpse of cream paper poking out from beneath the bed. She dropped to her knees to retrieve it. She picked it up, knowing what it was but holding it like a treasure. The gold words bored into her heart. She wiped her face and her hand came away wet. Why had he proved what a monster he was? Why couldn't he let her believe he was a man?

Her cell phone rang. Private number. Thinking it was the police she answered.

"Hello, Eliza." Steve's voice was razor sharp.

She stood, dropping the paper, and rushed to the window expecting to see Steve out in the front yard. The driveway was empty except for the shivering shadows of trees.

"Very clever. I saw what you did. Tut tut. I'm going to need new keys in twenty-four hours."

"Never. The house will be Amanda's before I let you back inside." Her heart hammered in her chest. Thunder churned the clouds, clotting the sky. Were there goblins out there already? Eliza drew the curtain. She couldn't see Steve, but he might be able to see her.

"You've won this battle, but it's not over, Eliza."

"It'll never be over. Would you have let me go in five years? Ten years? How many until you destroyed the evidence and let me go?"

"Never. You're mine, Eliza. Just like your father wanted."

"If he'd known what you were like—"

"He was a politician. I worked for him and his mates. You think his hands were clean?"

Eliza covered her eyes and shook her head. "Stop. He's dead." Her father had faults, but she couldn't believe he was corrupt.

"They all are. I'm all you have left."

Eliza stared at her feet. "Then I still have nothing." She hung up. No matter what she did or how much space she carved around herself, she would always be known as Steve's wife. A title no woman deserved.

Roan's invitation lay on the floor. Would he become human again if she accepted? Is that what he was hoping for? So far the book had mentioned nothing about curses or queens. Accepting was a risk. If nothing changed, she would be stuck in the Shadowlands. A goblin queen. She licked her lip. If she accepted she could be with him, maybe save him. She closed her eyes and imagined Roan in her house, by her side. Human.

Her phone beeped twice. She opened her eyes and read the text message.

Lights out.

She heard the electricity die milliseconds before the lights went out. Alone in the dark. Eliza screamed. She dropped the phone. It bounced on the carpet. She lunged for it before its blue light faded.

The house was silent, but outside trees creaked and groaned. She waited for the cackle of goblins and the patter of feet as they ran through the house. Nothing. They would see the gold in the yard and ignore the house.

The light on the phone died. She pressed a button to get the light back. Her hands began to shake. She'd always feared the dark. Steve knew that. He was just trying to scare her. And it was working. Her heart beat hard, trying to break out of her chest. Roan's name lingered on the tip of her tongue. All she had to do was call and he'd come.

She could find candles. She would be fine. She could call the police.

No she couldn't. Steve wouldn't hang around, waiting to get caught. The fuse box was outside. All she had to do was flick the switch and the lights would come back on. Her legs refused to move. What if he'd taken the fuse out? What if he was waiting for her to go out?

A knock on the front door echoed through the silent house. Her breath caught. He was downstairs waiting to be let in.

In her hand her phone rang. She answered knowing it would be Steve.

"Go away or I'll call the police."

"You haven't yet."

No, she hadn't because she didn't really want them

involved. Steve's threats about her going to jail while he lived the high life still had power.

"Turn the lights back on."

"Let me in."

"Steve." She wanted to sound strong but her voice came out as if she was pleading.

"It doesn't matter what you do, or where you go. You can't get away, we are bound together."

He was right…but she didn't have to stay here. In the Shadowlands Roan was waiting for her. She hung up on Steve and picked up the invitation. Then she closed her eyes and whispered the word that would make her queen.

"Yes."

Chapter 9

ROAN GLANCED AT THE SHADOWLANDS' SKY ALIVE WITH the golden lights of a thousand human cities. Tonight was the night of cold and darkness, the magical border between the worlds was thin, and the two could bleed together. Tonight all goblins were free to wander the Fixed Realm. To run the streets and wilds of earth as they had done through all time.

From the dust Roan called his horse. She was as black as his mood with more bones than muscle and eyes that burned with the devil's own fire. A mount worthy of a Goblin King. Roan dropped the appearance of a man. In the Shadowlands he could be either. It was more habit than anything else that made him keep the form he had worn as a man. Now it was little more than an illusion—a memory of what he had been.

He ran his hand over the horse's molting side. Breath didn't trouble her flanks. A black and gold saddle formed. The leatherwork was as immaculate as it was unnatural. The mare stamped and her razor-edged hooves cut the ground, but the dust didn't stir. Through the Shadowlands a horn sounded, calling to the goblins. His flesh prickled already anticipating the storm and the race across the sky with the Hoard. He wasn't the only king, just one of many. Tonight there would be no fighting between the different troops of Hoard goblin. All hostilities would be on hold until after the ride.

Dai appeared at the cave entrance, still a man and horseless. He leaned on the rock, his lips tight.

Roan swung himself onto the twisted mare's back. "You will not heed the call to ride?"

"I hear no call." Dai touched the pendant that lay against his skin. Black diamond and platinum made by Roan's hand.

"As your king I command you to ride with me." This year the call was strong and as unavoidable as a direct summons.

The mare tossed her head. Her ears flattened in anger at the disturbance to her rightful slumber. Roan gripped her with his knees.

"As your brother I ask that you stay." From his pocket Dai drew out a ring.

A plain platinum band marred by a chip of black. It would slide onto Roan's finger and fit perfectly. He'd made it at Dai's insistence but refused to wear the ring. Not until the last thread of his soul was about to snap would he wear a black diamond. He'd rather die than admit defeat. The magic of the Shadowlands was part of him. Without it he was nothing but a man trapped in a world without dreams or hope.

He would shatter out of grief if he were a man and not with Eliza.

The horse pawed the ground. Steam rose from her nostrils as if she breathed and lived. Her agitation boiled through his blood, pounded at the metal of his heart. Roan tightened his fist around the reins. The sky was opening. Heaven was theirs if only for a night. The horn sounded again. The sour note promised sweet reward.

Roan gritted his teeth and growled. "Allow me one last look upon the world at solstice. We both know I won't get another."

"Very well." Dai nodded, his face grim. "Greet Meryn for me. I pray you don't join him tonight. I don't want to test the strength of a gem."

"Have no fear. I will return."

Dai drew his sword and raised it in salute. "Ride for the living. But remember the dead."

Roan returned the salute. He was one of the dead. He pulled on the reins and the horse galloped over the Shadowlands to join the amassing army of goblins. At least Dai would be in no danger from the Hoard tonight. And it had been a long time since the druid had tried to tempt Dai into doing something stupid. Roan allowed himself a tight smile…maybe because Dai's knives were a little too threatening.

He approached the Hoard army and was greeted with hisses and nods from the other kings. Weapons and gold and lopsided stolen crowns. More metal than meat on the horses. Compared to them Roan was barely identifiable as a king. But they all knew of him. All feared him. All would kill him on any other night. He could cross between worlds at will, a power true goblins lacked, because he had the remains of a soul.

Roan glanced behind him. An army pounded, rolling in the storm clouds, waiting to descend on the sleeping, night-cloaked earth. Were they all true goblins? He'd never bothered to ask during the solstice truce. The rest of the time he stayed clear of the goblins in the Shadowlands. A battle over gold wasn't worth the risk if they could break the curse and be free.

If Meryn was alive, he would be there. Did he remember anything of his life? His wife and daughters? Or was he as empty as Gob? He hoped he'd found freedom in death along with the others who'd been cursed with him. His final ride as king was for them.

The kings raised their weapons to start the ride. Roan raised his sword.

"For the dead," he said under his breath.

The Hoard descended into the Fixed Realm. The howling of goblins echoed off streets and entered buildings. People would remember nothing but a storm and a fear of the dark as the magic of the Shadowlands followed the army.

The Hoard spread out, dispersing the mayhem. Any woman unfortunate enough to be caught out was likely to wake up in the Shadowlands as a queen to any goblin willing to fight and kill to keep her and become king. A job Roan would hand over without a second thought. He'd done it for too long.

He broke away from the group, riding the solstice alone with the storm at his back and the world at his feet. It was strangely empty and held no allure. He was taking his last ride alone. Was a king without men really a king? His lips twisted in a goblin's grimace. He didn't care.

Roan let his mount lead, grateful he was still able to enjoy the easy pleasure of riding. The surly beast chased down streets, past cars that swerved and found nothing to hit, yet left the driver blinking and swearing.

His dead horse chewed up miles of road, hooves sparking on the asphalt. She cleared rivers and raced over rooftops. The earth turned under the blanket of the storm. So much had changed in the Fixed Realm that even if he found his way back he would have no place. Cities sprawled, roads snaked the surface of the earth. The world he had fought for was gone, replaced by the one he watched from the Shadowlands but would never get the chance to experience.

What would it be like to sit in a movie theatre and not skulk in the shadows? To go out with Eliza on his arm? To sit in a restaurant instead of stealing plates of food?

He kicked the horse on, knowing she wouldn't tire. He wanted to catch the edge of the sunset half a world away. Roan's skin tightened and cracked. His head snapped up. He jerked the reins. The horse reared, but he held her with a firm hand. His knuckles whitened around the leather. She pranced in a tight circle in the middle of a freeway. Cars raced past. Roan's hand dropped to the hilt of his sword.

She wouldn't dare. Dare to test his vow.

Tonight of all nights. The solstice most treasured by goblins. He listened again, but the voice was in his head. She called. She summoned not Roan, but the Goblin King to her side.

He threw down the reins and released the horse of her duty. The glow of her red eyes lingered as she dissolved like mist and then was gone, returned to the dead.

His skin peeled at the edges, dragging his body to answer the summons. It was a fight he couldn't win and a promise he couldn't break. With a cry of anguish Roan threw himself into the night to claim his queen.

The air tasted like ozone and rippled with power. Eliza's hair crackled with static. It was too late to take back the summons. She pressed another button on her mobile, the faint blue light all she had to keep the darkness away. Her heart pulsed in her throat. Shadows chased each other over the walls and under the bed. She refused to watch their macabre dance.

The jangling of beads broke the silence. Eliza looked up from her phone, her hands clenched around the plastic. Her heart slid down her spine and slowed to one beat that seemed to last for hours.

Before her stood the Goblin King in black camo, armed with an ancient sword and a modern military handgun. The gold torque gleamed in the pale light, but his face was hidden in the shadows. His dreadlocks looked alive in the unnatural battle between light and dark.

"Why do you call the Goblin King?" His voice rasped out and slithered over her skin cold and rough. "You know my nature." He placed a finger under her chin and tilted, so she was forced to meet his gaze. "Or do you test me?"

The light from her phone died. She swallowed. He was more fearsome than she remembered. Had he already lost? No. She had to believe that beneath the power that crawled around this goblin was Roan. The alternative was...unthinkable. That she had called the Goblin King and surrendered herself to a monster. She licked her lip but words wouldn't come.

"My patience grows thin, Eliza." The air in the room snapped and sparked, lighting the bulbs. They burned bright and hopeful.

"Prove you are Roan."

He laughed. The sound cooled her blood so it thickened, coagulating in her gut.

"If I had faded, I would have the peace of not being summoned by a woman not sure if she can stomach what she has agreed to." He released her chin and leaned close—so close their noses almost touched. "You haven't forgotten the arrangement?"

Eliza inhaled the stale air. No, not forgotten—she'd been counting on it. It was better to be queen to a cursed man than wife to a man who made living a nightmare. This was her chance to be free of Steve forever and to rescue Roan from the druid's curse. She glanced at the yellow eyes that seemed so alien yet held the hurt of the man they hid. This had to work—for both of them.

"I'll be your queen. But first I need your help." She could push Steve away, but he would always be part of her life while he held the papers. Where she had failed to find them, she was sure Roan would succeed.

The goblin spun away dragging a cape of shadows with him. He faced her again. "You make demands?"

She wouldn't fold now. Eliza straightened her back, acting brave to convince herself she was.

"If I am to truly be with you, I need to free myself from Steve first." Eliza dipped her head a fraction but kept her gaze on the goblin. Roan didn't respond to orders well. And he was in there, behind the yellow eyes and gray skin.

He took her hand and slid her engagement ring off. It fell silently on the floor. "Is it so hard for you to be free?"

"It's not just the ring." How could she make him understand when even she was hard-pressed to explain how her life had become so tangled—how much power Steve held over her? Power she intended to sever, permanently.

He tilted his head and froze. His bulging eyes watched her, weighing her. "You want me to kill him?"

"No!" she gasped. "But there are documents that bind my life to his. I need to find them so he can't use them against me. So I can be free."

Before Roan, she'd forgotten what it felt like to breathe without fear.

He spread his arms. "You think this is freedom. You accepted my offer. You can't walk away from me the way you can Steve. We play this to the end." He placed both hands around hers.

The cold of his flesh hurt her hands. "When does this end?"

"When I say so." The air hummed, alive with the pounding of her heart and the magic of the goblin. Eliza's eyebrows pinched together, her voice was a whisper. "What if the curse doesn't break?"

A look of pain twisted the goblin's face as if the thought caused such agony that hearing it spoken wounded not only flesh but also his soul.

"There's only one way to find out."

The air was pressed out of her lungs. Her vision went black as the shadows invaded her body and ripped her out of her world and into the Shadowlands. She gagged and gasped, drowning in the blackness. Pins and needles in every limb. This is what it felt like to die.

Her feet hit the floor of the cave chamber in the Shadowlands. She stumbled but was caught by the man who lived in her dreams. Roan held her to his chest. Raw desperation burned in his desert blue eyes. Aching for something the way the sand cries for rain, and she was the first to try to quench his thirst.

She touched his skin, fair but tanned like he'd spent all his time under the sun. Her fingers traced the lines of his face. Strong like a king should be, but not arrogant. With his dark, almost black, hair and clear blue eyes, he was the perfect Celt. A scar ran under his jaw, almost hidden by stubble. She raised an eyebrow in question.

"Wooden training sword...thrown by my sister." Where a smile should have lit his eyes and turned his lips there was only emptiness. Ancient history had preserved the pain of loss.

Eliza kissed the long healed scar. Her tongue flicked over its length. Then she reached for his lips, her mouth touching his. Roan's hands ran up her back and tangled in her hair. His fingers dug deeper until he cradled the back of her head. Her lips parted and she tasted the man who craved her more than water. Her body tingled as if drawing current out of the air.

This was wrong to be in his arms, to be here, yet it felt so right. The sharp edge of temptation had never sung so sweetly. She'd always been the good daughter, the good girlfriend. Being with Roan was pure magic. Magic that pulled on her soul, warm and thick and rich.

Eliza leaned into him, seeking to melt against his skin. She ran her hands over his shirt, searching for the fastenings. Roan ripped off the belt that held his weapons. The curtain that had swung over the entrance to his chamber became an iron-bound door that shut with a bang, and a reminder that she wasn't with a normal man.

Her tongue wet her lip. The show of power was sexy—in a dangerous way. The way people loved to watch tigers, as long as they were behind bars. And she was alone with the hungry, hungry king of the Shadowlands. He pulled off his shirt. The green candlelight softened the hard planes of muscle but did nothing to hide the wealth of scars. Some were a small nick of a blade and nothing more. One must have been life threatening. The knotted mass was strung from collarbone to mid-chest.

She placed her hand over the puckered line that crossed his heart.

"Rome tried to take my heart before the druid succeeded." He lifted her hand, kissing her palm then her wrist, working his way back to her throat.

Breath slipped from her body the way a soul might depart its flesh, slowly but with longing. Her hands tried to absorb the texture of his supple skin made firm by the muscle beneath. So different, so much more life trapped inside. Roan was nothing like Steve. He lifted the edge of her T-shirt. Her nipples tightened, waiting for him to skim his hands over her breasts as he lifted the shirt. Instead he undressed her without touching her. Her top was removed by the magic that curled around them. The zipper on her jeans tracked down without a hand to help as if he was peeling a forbidden fruit with all the grace and decorum he could manage.

Roan's hand caressed her waist and eased her jeans over her hips. She stepped out, her hands on his shoulder. He kissed her inner knee over the thin white scar that had required stitches.

"My brother let go and I fell out of the tree house." The one scar she'd gained at seven wasn't in the same league as Roan's.

He nodded, beads creating background music. His hands ran up her legs until his fingers danced over her panties. He paused to kiss the top of her left breast. Her heart raced beneath his mouth. With a single flick he unclasped her bra. She instinctively tried to cover herself.

"Too late for second thoughts." Roan gently moved her hand away.

"Dim the lights." The candles burned too bright. There was nowhere to hide.

"No. I want to see you." His gaze rested on her. Heat flushed her skin pink like sunburn. "And I want to be seen." He slid the bra-straps down her arms.

She waited for a comment. *False advertising*. Her bra enhanced her assets by an extra cup size. She'd refused plastic surgery. If Roan noticed, he said nothing. His calloused palm closed over her breast. Her back arched as he brushed his thumb over her nipple. Braver, she snaked her hand around his neck, her fingers brushing against the gold torque, and drew him into a kiss. His beads were like rain on her skin, bouncing cold against her flesh before taking on her warmth.

He nipped at her lip, and she responded in kind. Her stomach tightened, caught between excitement and fear. There was something in the way he handled her, with care, with desire, but also a firm intent. He knew what he was doing. Roan pulled her to him and lifted her, his forearm under her bottom. Hip to hip. The length of his shaft pressed against her belly. Her breath hiccupped, but her body responded to the unspoken demand, shifting against him. He groaned and broke the kiss.

Without the all-consuming attention, her doubts bubbled to the surface.

"Will I become…" She let the word hang unspoken. She didn't want to be goblin.

Roan pulled her to the bed. The crimson sheets turned down by thought alone. "None of the other women did."

Eliza pulled her hand back. Roan didn't let go.

"What other women? Other queens?"

She resisted the tug on her hand, her toes curling on the rock. Roan held her gaze.

"Centuries ago, when we could still part with our gold, women would come and…" He paused as if searching for a suitable word. "Entertain."

"Whores." She wrapped one arm over her breasts. Being cursed, being goblin, was one thing, but using hookers was another. She wanted a free hand to wipe her mouth.

"Yes. Whores. Did you think I'd been celibate since the curse choked out my life?" He pulled with enough force to send her stumbling into his arms and onto his lap. He twisted, laying her on the bed.

Eliza gasped at the ceiling. "Why didn't you take one of them as your queen?"

"They came for the gold. Back then I didn't want or need a queen." Roan loomed over her, confusion raising his eyebrows together. "I want you. You called me. Different from every other summoner." His lips touched her throat. He trailed kisses to her heart. "You keep me human."

"There are no vows to become queen?"

"No. I brought you here. You are mine. That is enough."

Her resistance melted under the heat of his mouth. His tongue flicked over her nipple, then drew the peak into his mouth. She flinched trying not to respond, but the fire was already lit in her belly. Her nerves pulled tight, waiting for the touch that would release them. She put her hands on his chest.

"How do I know you didn't catch a disease from one of them?"

His laugh vibrated through her chest. He lifted his head. "I tried to catch the bubonic plague—twice—hoping to die. But then I'm not technically alive. My heart doesn't beat. I exist outside of time."

Yet four swords hung on the wall, one had faded, one had died by bullet. "How did the others die?"

"A goblin can only be killed in battle." Roan traced an elaborate pattern over her skin. "You've asked about everything but children." He pressed one nipple.

"I can't. I have an implant. I never wanted kids with…" She was cheating. Or had they broken up, and she hadn't gotten around to telling Steve? Her finger was naked, and she wanted to be with Roan.

"But you can have children?" His hand slid along her side and flicked the edge of her panties, making light of the weighty question.

There was no slap against her skin. They were simply gone. His knee dropped between her thighs.

She nodded. Two thousand years and Roan still wanted to be a father. No goblin would be so unselfish. She'd seen the sacrifices made by Amanda for Brigit. "The implant can be removed."

Eliza squirmed into the bed as his fingers found her clit and circled. She bit her lip, not used to anyone else touching her so intimately. Sex had always been about Steve and what he was getting. Her eyes closed as her insides became liquid under Roan's sure hand.

"Open your eyes." Roan rolled onto his back, dragging her onto him. His black camo appeared on the floor with the rest of the clothing.

Eliza sat up, her knees dropping to the side as she straddled him. One hand held her hip and rocked, so she slid over the length of hardened flesh. His shaft caressed her most delicate folds. The ache built, blocking out all other doubts and questions.

Roan watched every move but waited only for one. She knew this had to be her doing. Her choice or he would keep her here untouched. She wrapped her fingers around his shaft and smoothed over the already slick head. His hips bucked, pressing deeper into her fist. A darkness rose in her blood. The cold taste of power was like ice on her tongue. Roan needed her. Without her he would fade. In the Fixed Realm she was nothing.

Here she was queen.

But she hesitated and in that moment the power dissipated. She wanted Roan, but not like this. Not like she was claiming him. Their eyes locked and she knew he was giving her the choice, even though it wasn't what he wanted. He wanted her surrender.

She lay back on the bed. Roan followed, his body flowing with hers in one smooth motion, perfectly in synch. A glimmer of a smile curved his lips. The ends of his dreads tickled her skin. His beads whispered a hundred promises, a hundred secrets in a hundred languages. They only needed one.

His tongue skimmed her lip, teasing until she opened her mouth. The head of his shaft pressed against her sex. She lifted her hips and moaned as he entered. Each thrust a little deeper until he was fully seated within her core. With just the slightest move, he began with a slow irresistible rhythm. Her skin was fevered as if she'd sat too long in the sun, basking under the endless blue heat of his eyes.

The air around them thickened. She lifted her legs to wrap them around his hips. The edge was so close, she wanted to fall and take Roan with her. With that wish, every tight nerve snapped and sent her spiraling through the dream until she landed back in the bed. The crimson sheets scrunched around them. Roan lay over her. No beat echoed the racing of her heart. His fingers tapped the rhythm of her slowing pulse. His eyes were closed. He was locked in his own world of broken hopes and bitter dreams. She tasted the edges but didn't know what to say.

The curse held. She'd failed to save him.

Roan looked at her. Pain and regret were chained together in his eyes. They stole the desire that had razed her senses. He vanished without a sound.

Warmth seeped from her skin, but she lay still half expecting him to return. He should be here with her, lying close with her hand on his chest, feeling his heart beat for the first time in nearly two millennia. After several small breaths Eliza realized he wasn't coming back. He couldn't bear to look at her. She drew the sheet around her body and curled up. Numbness crawled through her muscles until even breathing was a burden.

The walls groaned in sympathy.

Steve would be waiting for her to return. How many days had she been gone already? Even as she asked the question she didn't care what the answer was. Let him be accused of her murder. Her other life was over. She was here now, with Roan. They would find a way to break the curse.

The caves screamed as they tore themselves apart. Anger reverberated through the rock demanding an end. Eliza sat up. Only one man could be tearing up his world. But if he kept on drawing on the dark magic, he would become one with the Shadowlands.

Roan would become Hoard.

Chapter 10

IT SHOULD HAVE WORKED.

Tonight, while the solstice closed the gap between dreams and waking, out of all nights it should have worked. Roan held out his hands and rock splintered off the walls leaving furrows as if they'd been attacked by a giant cat or a demon. No wall was safe as magic ripped through him. Nothing was safe from the absolute desolation that cradled the gold where his heart should've now been beating.

Eliza had been willing. She knew the truth of his being. She had seen his face in the Fixed Realm and still wanted him. Him, not gold or jewels like the concubines who'd performed with too much enthusiasm, too much finesse, and too little emotion.

He fisted his hand and the tunnel collapsed behind him. He stalked on, no longer caring where he walked. It didn't matter. He would die here, trapped beneath a mountain of rock of his own making. He ground out a breath and cursed. First in Decangli, then in every language he knew. The words fell effortlessly off his tongue. He cursed the Romans, the druid, and finally himself for thinking that such a simple act would free him. That he could have used Eliza and brought her here with the sole intent of freeing himself. When all she had ever done was have the misfortune of having him answer her summons.

With a twist of his wrist Roan tore a slab of rock out of the wall. Gold coins spilled at his feet. He'd walked the maze of tunnels and ended up here. Like any goblin he'd sought comfort from the one thing he knew. Gold. Tons of empty, lifeless, shiny gold. Gold would never judge him or make demands.

In his bed waited a woman and he didn't know what to do with her. He couldn't take her back to the Fixed Realm. She was already too deeply embedded in his skin. She was his queen until the end. Losing her would take too much from him. Keeping his lover would cut too deep. Seeing the broken dream in Eliza's eyes was unfaceable. He picked up a coin and threw it across the room. It ricocheted off the wall and rolled back to his feet offering him another chance.

Roan picked up a handful of gold coins and threw them into the air.

Eliza traced the claw marks in the wall. The tormented swipe of an animal lashing out, searching for freedom. A man with nothing to lose. Each new piece of demolition was another wound that wouldn't heal. She climbed over piles of rock that almost blocked the tunnels with only one thought in her mind—she had to reach him before he faded. Finding Roan was as easy as following the debris left by his destruction. But would she like what she saw when she found him? The warning rose in her thoughts.

If Roan was lost, they were all lost.

A two-foot-high slab of stone lay across the tunnel, gold weeping from the gash. Through the hole was the gleaming golden cavern. The brilliance brought tears to her eyes. She'd watched one man fade and die in there already. What if it was too late? Could she do anything if it wasn't?

She leaned against the wall with her fists clenched at her sides. The rock pulsed against her back. Magic. Eliza stood up and placed her palm on the cave wall. It shuddered as if buffeted by a strong wind. Her mouth dried. Whatever waited on the other side, she had to face it. Waiting longer only guaranteed she would find a goblin.

With her shoulders back and her courage screwed up as tight as it would go, Eliza peered around the corner into the gold cavern. Her mouth opened and her breath was taken by the impossible, terrifying beauty. Coins rushed past, little more than a golden blur, part of the hurricane whipping around the room. Lethal and brilliant and mesmerizing. The metal would shred anyone who dared to enter. A lone figure stood in the eye of the storm.

❦

Roan flung more coins into the air. They joined the fray at his bidding without him touching their surface. The magic coursed through his veins thicker than blood. Hotter than a wildfire it burned through his body. But it was never enough. He could never channel enough to break the curse and free himself. Another pile of coins got caught up in the deadly dance. The gold in his chest became soft and molten, but it wouldn't release his heart from its grip. Nothing lived within his flesh.

In the cage of his ribs something tore as if trying to

break away. The coins dropped to the floor in a heavy, metal shower. He sucked in a breath, but the feeling didn't leave. Like a severed muscle, it ached and throbbed. He closed his eyes with his hand over his chest as if he could stop the hemorrhage of his soul.

He saw the edge of the abyss. There was no light at the end, just soft, deep black waiting to embrace him. The darkness had always been safely out of reach. Now it reached out with needy, grasping hands. He stepped back as if he could step away from the edge. The voices in the dark called to him with a seductive promise of rest and no more fighting.

Such a small cost for eternal peace. You can keep your gold. We just want your soul.

Why was he fighting when he would fail anyway? He bent, his hand on his knee and every breath cutting deeper.

"Roan?"

He snarled, but the whisper of her voice made him look over his shoulder. The arms of the dark sirens became the bleached white hands of skeletons snatching at the edges of his clothing. Eliza's grip was stronger. He was under her spell more than she knew.

She dipped her head, her gaze falling to the floor as she refused to look at him. "I was just…I…I'm sorry it didn't work."

Had he faded and not noticed? Roan glanced at his hand. It was still his, not the gray, gnarled hand of a goblin.

"I'm fine." His voice cracked as he spoke. The rasping grate of the goblin he was trying not to become.

To prove the point he stood. His chest burned, the pain much the same as when a Roman sword had cut through his leather armor and come a finger width from killing him. The only difference was this time blood didn't stream through his fingers and the world didn't turn black. He forced his hand to drop casually to his side.

Eliza's eyes were wide and watchful, her skin pale. Not the warm glow that should have dusted her skin after sex. If he lived for nothing else, he had to return her to the Fixed Realm before he faded. He couldn't leave her here for the Hoard to find. She was *his* queen, not a goblin queen.

Roan reached out a hand. Her teeth worried at her lower lip, but she stepped forward carefully over the gold. Her gaze remained on him. He'd expected her to be scooping up the gold, filling her pockets and then demanding to be taken home, much like the whores that had visited before paying had become more painful than going without human company.

Her fingers closed around his hand. He lifted her knuckles to his lips and kissed her. The gold flecks in her eyes shone brighter than all the metal in the cavern. His lust for power and magic was replaced by a desire that had existed long before gold was valued.

"My king." She smiled, but the edges were forced and her eyes guarded.

Roan's lips thinned. She didn't want him. She wanted to escape her fiancé. Someone always wanted something from him. Eliza was no different.

"My queen." He inclined his head almost chocking on the forced politeness. What would it take to cross the chasm and be with Eliza?

For her to look at him the way she had when she'd writhed beneath him. Her body dancing to his touch, sweat glistening on her skin. Raw need in her eyes. By leaving he'd lost that privilege. Her eyes had grown cold.

A handful of coins spiraled into the air twisting, dancing for her. She had nothing to fear from him. She watched, lips parted. The spiral became a dragon, each coin a scale, chasing the shadows over the walls. Her face lit up, and her eyes glittered as she turned to watch the dragon fly over the ceiling.

She frowned and tore her eyes away from the dragon to Roan. "Is it safe to draw the magic?"

It was a parlor trick. Nothing more. The dragon took no more power than removing clothing. The magic was different, clearer. It lacked the begging-song and the demands to release more. Like all magic, intent determined the cost. Anything wrought in anger or with the desire to do damage demanded a high price. One he could no longer afford. He would never be able to defeat the druid with a handful of pretty tricks. And he would never be able to keep Eliza if he didn't find a way to break the curse. Roan let go of her hand and the dragon collapsed on the floor nothing more than a spread of coins.

"Perfectly."

They regarded each other. The silence stretched like an elastic band pulled tight. He snapped first.

"Don't trouble yourself with my soul. I will return you before I fade."

"That's not what I meant."

"No?" He crossed his arms over his bare chest. He hadn't bothered to dress fully, too intent on destruction.

Her eyebrows drew together. "Please don't give up hope."

He snorted and tossed his head. The beads clattered

around his shoulders and rained on his back. "I can count my remaining time in days." Before his private hurricane it had been weeks. "Days until I slide silently into the Hoard and forget I was ever human."

"Only days?" Her face crumpled.

It took Roan several seconds to realize she was upset. Not because it would be days until she could go home, but because his life would end. His demise was going to have an effect. But it brought him no joy, only discomfort as if sandpaper was being rubbed over his skin. He tried to soften the truth.

"A week tops."

"No." She shook her head not wanting to hear or believe. "There must be another option."

Roan pursed his lips. How much did he tell her? What did she need to know? She waited for an answer.

"I find a way to kill Elryion without magic." He made it sound easy, like he could've done it centuries ago if he'd wanted.

Her mouth opened, preparing to argue. Behind her eyes he saw the machines turning, weighing his words and finding them too heavy to be the truth.

"Will that work?"

Not even his queen was willing to back him and believe he could kill the druid and break the curse. The quick lie sat ready on his tongue, but instead he forced out the truth. She was part of this now. Bound to him by Shadowlands magic.

"I don't know. Despite Dai's research we are guessing blind, and unarmed."

She tucked a strand of hair behind her ear, but the golden wisp didn't stay put. "If it doesn't, what then?"

"Then it's over. Goblin or death." He should be reveling in what time he had left. Should be buried in Eliza with her legs around his waist until he couldn't resist the pull of the Shadowlands any longer.

"There must be another way."

"You think you can defeat Elryion where I have failed?" Roan ran his hand through his dreadlocks and looked away. Once he'd shared her easy hope.

"There's always a way to break a curse."

"And how many curses have you broken, Eliza? How many cursed men have you saved?"

Not one. Bringing her here as queen had changed nothing, and everything. Unlike the concubines, he couldn't walk away from Eliza. Queens never left their king's side. Returning her to the Fixed Realm when his time was up was going to be like cutting the gold out of his chest. Bloody. Painful. Fatal.

She dropped her gaze to the floor. "Is there nothing I can do?"

Roan sighed and lowered his voice. "You are here. You slow my fade. I don't know how." Around Eliza the gold dimmed and rusted. All he wanted was her. He pulled up a handful of coins. They became liquid in his hand. The gold stretched forming a stem, then a bud. The bud of the rose bloomed, glistening, almost alive.

Tentatively she touched the petal. "It looks so real." Her finger traced the veins in the leaf.

His hand tightened around the stem. *She would take his gold.*

"Thank you." Her lips pressed on his cheek. Her hand rested over his, yet she made no attempt to take the rose.

Eliza may lessen his lust for gold, but he still couldn't

give it away. Not even to her. He was more goblin than
he wanted to believe. The rose wilted, faking death until
it fell to the floor, nothing but golden dust.

Her lips pressed together and crept up at the corners.
She took his hand. "I prefer silver."

He laced his fingers with hers. The gold dust trapped
between their palms. Roan nodded, his mouth twisted in
a bitter smile. She was making excuses for him.

"I'll see what I can do."

Eliza assessed the piles of gold coin, bars, and nug-
gets stacked high against the walls. The statues and
thrones and crowns. One wall was covered in amber
panels backed in gold leaf, stolen from the amber room
before it was destroyed in World War II. His desire for
gold had been quenched with priceless artifacts humans
thought lost, destroyed, or simply fables.

"If this were in a bank, you'd be immeasurably rich."

His chest swelled with pride before he could stop
himself. "I am immeasurably rich. I know exactly how
much is here. And how much is in the bank."

The silver and gems they had gathered had been
banked when they'd had hope, before they needed to
constantly touch and see their wealth. The only clause
on the bank contract was they had to be human to acti-
vate the account.

"Really?" Her brows raised in obvious disbelief. "How
does a goblin walk into a bank and open an account?"

"Like everyone else." Human banks were relatively
new. There was a much older bank. "Birch Trustees
caters to people with special needs. I check in periodi-
cally to let them know I'm still around. The compound
interest over fifteen hundred years is," Roan sucked in

a breath, inhaling the cold metallic scent of gold. Just imagining the pile of gold stored in the vault was enough to make him hard. "Staggering."

Eliza stood, mouth open, unblinking. "There's a special bank?"

"Did you want to see a statement?" He had none in the Shadowlands. He only ever saw the totals stack up when he visited a branch. It was enough.

She shook her head, her golden-brown hair falling around her face. "Why didn't you bank all of it?"

"I can't be separated."

The reflected gold colored her skin. The light teased the shadows, tempting them to play. He reached out and ran a finger down her cheek.

"I need to be able to touch what is mine." He'd succumbed to another beautiful object. Another perfect treasure for his never complete collection. But this one made him feel less goblin. Roan tilted her head and touched his lips to hers. She yielded without force. Her lips opened as if she craved his touch. With Eliza he could pretend he was a man and nothing more.

"You fear me, yet offer yourself," he murmured against her cheek.

"I fear what you will become." She nuzzled just below his ear. Her free hand skimmed his back and traced the line of another scar. "You've fought a lot of battles."

"It was the way of the world." He pulled her top over her head. She hadn't bothered with underwear.

This time she didn't rush to cover herself. A trail of gold dust followed his hand. He brushed his palm over her breasts so the tips gleamed gold and pink.

"How old were you when you became king?" She

gasped when his mouth closed over her nipple. It firmed under the caress of his tongue.

His fingers opened her jeans. "Eighteen."

He pushed them down. She wiggled, helping, then stepped out. Naked except for the glow of gold. One finger slid past the dark curls on her mound. Circled her clit. Her hips rocked, and her nails dug into his shoulders. She lifted onto her toes, but he held her firm.

Her eyes half closed. "And when…ah…were… you…ah…mm…cursed?"

He teased her clit until her shaking had subsided and her breathing was rough. Music to a deaf man.

"Twenty-one, almost." He pulled her to the floor.

"You're so young." She knelt in front of him.

He placed her hands on the floor. "I've lived ancient history. Celebrated two new millennia." He ran his hand down her spine, learning each bump of bone. "I'm old, Eliza. I'm weary." He took off his camo and knelt behind her.

She turned and looked over her shoulder with a cheeky glint in her eye. "Is the age gap too much?"

Roan slid two fingers into her wet core. She moved in time with his hand, so he gave her more. His cock ached for similar treatment.

"I wish that were our only problem."

He shifted and pressed his cock into her slick heat. Eliza moaned and dropped onto her elbows. He held her hips in an attempt to slow her down, but eventually he gave in to her need. He thrust deeper and faster. Each time she met and raised the challenge, igniting a fire that would never be smothered. She cried out, and her muscles contracted, milking him. He brought one hand to her swollen bud and circled. She shuddered and groaned, rubbing against his hand. With Eliza held tight against his hips, he came, still thrusting within her. Roan closed his eyes and breathed, trying to hold on to the moment when he almost felt fully human. That second was better than finding the lost city of the Incas and stripping it of gold.

A new sensation climbed into his body. Warm and gentle. The slow swell of satisfaction. Peace. Happiness. All lust and need fulfilled. For the first time he could remember he'd enjoyed something without paying a price.

He ran his hand over her damp skin, and she jumped at his touch. He opened his eyes to drink her in. A gold handprint lay across one buttock. His handprint.

He eased back, reluctant to leave her body. He wanted more of Eliza, but not in the all-consuming way he wanted more gold. She sighed at the loss and sat up on her heels. Taking his offered hand, she stood. He handed Eliza her clothing and they dressed silently.

The silence didn't prickle or try to provoke words. It wrapped around them like a blanket of protection. Roan summoned the rest of his clothes. He couldn't go anywhere without weapons. One day he'd walk out of his front door and find the Hoard waiting to kill him. His sword belt snaked through the loops and buckled as if it lived. But all the armor and weapons in the world wouldn't protect him from Eliza. She placed her arms around his neck and kissed him. He responded, hoping to extend his fragile happiness a little longer. One doubt gnawed at the carcass of his conscience, spoiling the joy he'd found.

"Why did you call me, Eliza?" Roan pulled her away and held her at arm's length.

"You helped me twice. I wanted to return the favor."

"You wanted to escape your fiancé." He couldn't blame her for that when he agreed. The man was worth a fraction of the value he placed on himself. But he needed to hear her say the words, if only to reassure himself that he wasn't just the best out of a couple of bad choices. What woman chose nightmares over dreams? Monsters over men?

She bit her lip and nodded. "That wasn't why I called." She looked away to study the coins on the floor. "I thought I could break the curse. That everything would work out and we could be together."

"That was a gamble you lost." *We both lost.* A bitter smile almost turned his mouth. They were both fools with too much hope.

She lifted her chin, hazel eyes burning. "I'd do it again. I have nothing to lose."

Roan placed his hand over her heart. The rhythm called like an ancient drumbeat he'd never dance to again. "You have everything to lose. Don't trust a goblin with your life."

Eliza covered his hand with hers. "I see a man who I trust with my heart."

He wished that were true, but he would end up breaking her heart.

Chapter 11

STEVEN FLICKED SHARDS OF GLASS OFF HIS JACKET. IT crunched under his shoes as he walked away from the broken window. If Eliza hadn't called the police, he wouldn't have had to break into his home. Since she'd paid to change the locks, she could pay to replace the glass. The alarm screeched at his presence. He punched in the code. She hadn't changed it yet...she hadn't changed it ever. It was the same code her father had used. She insisted the alarm be set every night. The upper floor was left off so the occupants could move around. Then he called the security company to assure them everything was fine.

"Honey, I'm home." His voice fell on a dark and silent house. Her twenty-four hours was up, the police order had expired, and he'd been generous. He'd let her start a second night alone.

He turned on lights as he walked through the house. It had taken him less than a minute to replace the missing light fuse. Eliza wouldn't spend a night without power; she was like a child, terrified of the dark. But he'd watched, and he hadn't seen her leave the house. Steven stomped up the stairs. The guest room door was closed. He knocked.

No answer.

She wasn't here. He clenched his teeth. Anger welled and slipped past. He swore and thumped the door. He'd

been expecting her to grovel, to apologize and beg forgiveness for stepping out of line and risking everything
he'd worked for. With a flick he opened his cell phone
and rung her. Maybe she'd sneaked out to the bitch
sister-in-law's. Her phone responded from the other side
of the door, breaking up the rage.

A trickle of cold sweat tracked down his back. With
a sick sense of déjà vu he hung up. She'd gone AWOL
again. With the calm of a dead man he opened the guest
room door. He tried the light. Nothing happened. He
turned on the en suite light. It was enough to see what
was wrong. That her disappearance was too similar to
last time.

Empty room. Unmade bed. Clothes on the chair. Her
handbag rested on the bedside table. Her cell phone
lay on the floor. Steven bent to pick it up and stopped.
Next to the phone was her engagement ring. A two-carat
white diamond ring left on the floor for the cleaner to
vacuum up. This behavior was becoming a worrying
pattern. An escalating pattern. He slipped the ring into
his pocket.

It was too close to the wedding for her to fall apart.
Eliza obviously had an undiagnosed mental condi-
tion. Why else would she walk the streets, yet have no
memory? If she was lying, she was doing a damn good
job. But then her mother was an actress. If he needed to
medicate Eliza to get through the wedding, so be it. But
there would be a wedding.

This time he couldn't call the police. He was sure
someone had watched him leave the hotel this morning.
Tailing his car until he'd lost them by looping through
the city and going extra slow. It had almost made him

think twice about coming back here even though he was now legally allowed back in his own house. Steven sat down and ran his hand over his hair without ruffling a stand. He would wait for her to come back. She had to come back. There was nowhere else she could go.

He stretched his legs and dozed in the chair in the guest room. When daylight struggled in through the window, he went downstairs for coffee. He pulled the milk out of the fridge. The stench lodged in his nostrils. He checked the date, still good for another week, yet it stunk like it had been left in the car on a summer day. He dropped it in the bin and drank his coffee black. Again.

He sat alone at the dining table, his coffee half drunk, his fingers drumming on the wood. At nine he called the office and told them he was working from home. He called a glazier and while the man replaced the glass, Steven toyed with the diamond ring in his pocket. He wanted her back. Before her father's death he'd asked permission to marry Eliza. Then everything had turned. His career had taken off, along with his personal investments made with other people's money, while Eliza had dropped out of university. She became dependant on him, and he on her. Without her name and backing he would sink back into obscurity. The kid with no lunch and the alcoholic mother. He was going to be someone and Eliza was part of his plan. Plenty of marriages were built on less.

Once the glazier left Steven lay on the sofa, one arm draped over his eyes. He couldn't afford for his plans to unravel now. Telling Eliza about the fraud may have been a mistake. He'd thought she'd be impressed at how clever he was. She hadn't been. He was man enough to admit it, lawyer enough to never say it. Losing the house and money would be an inconvenience but not insurmountable.

His cell phone rang. "Steven Slade."

An overly pert female voice rattled a greeting at one hundred miles an hour. "Anyway, just to let you know that your accountant has finished auditing Chiverney Holdings, and it's all okay."

The muscle below Steven's eye twitched. He sat up. "I gave strict instructions not to call me regarding that job. That I would stop by the office next week."

"How odd, the regular receptionist left no instructions. Oh well. Looks like I saved you a trip. Have a nice day."

"Listen, you little chit—" The line hummed at him. "Bollocks." He threw his phone. It bounced into the opposing sofa.

"Fuck." Steven scrubbed his hands over his face. Had the temp receptionist called the office first?

What had started as game, skim a few dollars here, a few thousand there, had become a source of independent wealth that couldn't be explained. Access to the trust fund covered some of his tracks. People assumed it was trust money he was spending. But he was buying his way into society without Eliza.

"Take a breath. No one gives a damn about Chiverney. No one knows about the company." It was safe. He was safe. Only Eliza knew what he was doing, and she didn't know the company name—he hadn't told her everything. However, she was becoming less pliant. Steven pressed his fingers together.

It was time to change strategies.

Exclusive. A location to die for. The only five-star restaurant in the Shadowlands. The white cloth on the table was set with gold. In a crystal vase were two silver roses so lifelike Eliza wanted to pick them up and see if they also had a scent. She smiled at Roan. He shrugged one shoulder and sat.

In the center of the table there were enough plates to feed six men a three-course meal. Each plate presented the food as if it were a masterpiece. Sauces painted into a pattern, vegetable curls, and delicate piles of succulent seafood.

"Eat before it grows cold. Be a shame for the magic to go to waste." Dai gave his brother a sharp look. He had kept away for most of the day, said nothing about the damage done to the caves or that they were still goblins, not men.

A whisper brushed over her skin. Words she didn't quite catch. She brushed it off. "Did you make the food?"

"No. But someone's order is missing and their meal will be late, probably on the house if they whine enough. These things happen." Roan indicated for her to pick a plate to start.

"You stole the food?"

"Have you seen anything to hunt here?" Dai said as he studied the meal as if he couldn't decide what to choose.

"I guess not." Eliza took a plate of scallops wrapped in prosciutto. They melted in her mouth. "What did you eat at the start?"

"There is plenty to hunt if you know where to look. Wild animals have always lived in people's fears. Some nightmares never change. New ones arrive, old ones persist." Roan stretched his legs.

Their feet collided. He smiled, his lips curving easily instead of being strained. Then his smile became crooked and one brow lifted with suggestion. Heat uncurled from her stomach and spread through her limbs. Roan locked his ankles with hers, trapping her feet.

Dai made a comment as he selected a couple of plates and picked up cutlery so he could eat elsewhere. She didn't need to speak the language to understand the meaning. *Get a room.* Warmth colored her face.

Roan responded and the brothers argued across different languages. She was glad she couldn't understand; she was sure the conversation had slid under the tablecloth.

The stray thought tugged more firmly. The words still unclear. Eliza tilted her head to listen more closely. She put down her fork. If Roan and Dai would just be quiet for a moment, she would be able to hear the words. They were almost audible. She pulled her feet free and tucked them under her chair.

"Shh."

Roan and Dai stopped talking, and watched her as if she'd turned goblin.

"Can you hear that?" She stood and turned, trying to locate the source. A soft voice called to her, no more pain, no more heartache, no more broken promises. "Why can't you hear it?"

Roan pushed his chair back, all humor gone from his face. "What do you hear?"

"I don't know." As she looked at him the voice became quiet but it waited. She closed her eyes. This time the voice returned inside her mind. It was part of her. "Talking."

She held her breath to listen better, to hear what the voice was saying and find out why it was calling her. Magic coiled around her limbs and tugged on her flesh. The voice lulled and soothed. She relaxed, believing the voice wouldn't hurt her.

A hand closed around her wrist. "Eliza, can you hear me?"

Her eyes snapped open. The voice was gone, leaving her with an ache as if she'd lost someone of great importance, but she didn't know whom. Like she'd lost part of herself but wasn't sure who she'd been to begin with.

She blinked. "Yes."

Roan was staring at her, his blue eyes clouded with concern. "Do you still hear Elryion?"

Elryion, the druid. The sweet, seductive call had been a summons. An unfightable whirlpool that spun until it was fed. If Roan hadn't held onto her, she would've been unable to resist. She shivered like a bucket of ice had been thrown over her soul. She'd almost been called to the druid—the one responsible for Roan's curse. She had no doubt he would've used her against Roan.

Roan lifted his hand up. Cupped in her palm was a pile of black rocks, gems that burned with a fire that would never be released.

Dai spoke quietly to Roan and Roan's reply was short. Two words. Dai shook his head and left with his dinner.

"What's going on?"

"Dai thinks I should take you home. That you are my weakness and Elryion will use your hand to gut me."

"You don't agree." Eliza turned her hand so the gems caught the light from the never-melting candles.

They were beautiful and captivating. Their secrets were locked tight inside.

"With you I'm stronger. My grip on humanity is tighter. But I can't claw back what I've lost." He held her hands to prevent her from slipping away while he watched. His hands were cool and rough, grounding her in the moment.

"You won't get rid of me that easily." She tried a smile on, pretending the druid's call wasn't serious.

"I hope not. Choose one." He lifted a gem.

"What are they?"

The one between his fingers sucked in the light so it burned from the inside.

"Black diamonds."

"You want me to choose a diamond?" Regular white diamonds merely sparkled. These had been carved out of fallen stars. A universe caught in each gem. Every diamond in her palm was more than a carat. A couple were the size of a fingernail. Was it some kind of goblin test? If so, what was the right answer?

"Unless you want Elryion to call you to his side."

To use as bait remained unsaid. But they both knew it was the truth.

If the diamond was to keep her safe, there was no wrong answer. A midsized diamond burned with a fire as black as night, as dangerous as it was beautiful. She picked up the gem.

Roan gathered the others and placed them into a bag. He produced a small silvery bar. "Platinum. I'd give you gold, but we both know that wouldn't work."

He held her gaze for a fraction too long, and she glimpsed the ache he kept chained behind his fierce exterior.

"Platinum's a nice change. Steve always gave me gold."

Roan's lips thinned. "Give me your hand."

"What are you doing?" Eliza offered her left hand. Her white diamond and gold ring had been left behind along with her old life. Her heart fluttered in her chest like a butterfly in a net. She swallowed, not wanting to release it too soon.

He touched her fingers. "Replacing the ring you left behind. Other hand."

"Engagement rings go on the left hand." She kept her left hand out and studied Roan's face for any sign that giving her a diamond ring meant something to him. Because she needed it to be more than a replacement of a ring she hated.

His eyes were as desolate as the desert. Nothing stirred. There was no emotion was brave enough to confront the glare of his golden heart.

"I'm not marrying you. I'm protecting my queen. Marking you as mine." He lifted her right hand. The platinum melted, coiled, and slithered in his palm.

The trapped butterfly died. Roan wasn't offering a future together. They had no future together. His future could be counted in days. She would end up back in the real world trying to resurrect a life she didn't want. What she wanted was a hopeless dream.

The metal glided toward her like a snake. Wrapped around her finger, the liquid warmth circled and split into strands no thicker than a hair. The ever-moving metal held the diamond in place, embracing it as part of the ring. Watching the creation was fascinating. Roan was bending the elements to his will. A tremor of power tickled under her skin. No matter what she wanted to believe, Roan was more than a man.

Eliza licked her lip. "How do you do it?"

"A strong thought." He shrugged. "Sometimes not even that. I use the magic but I don't know how it works."

The ring took shape. Details formed on the delicate strands, leaves and flowers no bigger than the head of a pin.

"And your soul?"

"There is enough of the Shadowlands in me that some magic is almost free."

She nodded, feeling slightly safer. He wasn't risking his life every time he used magic…just sometimes. She needed longer with him than the time they had.

"Can you alter time?"

Roan lifted an eyebrow. "No man controls time."

"Last time I was here it seemed less than a day. But I'd been missing for three." She'd fainted as if she hadn't eaten for three days, but she couldn't have slept for two whole days in his bed.

"Time is subjective. Boredom lasts forever. Some moments are over in an instant."

"How long have I been here, Roan?"

He didn't look at her, his gaze focused on the ring. "A minute, a week, a year, does it matter?"

"The police thought I'd been murdered the first time. I need to spend time in my world. This will—"

"End." Roan watched the platinum. It solidified and the unused metal fell like silver tears into his palm. "Are you regretting your choice?"

"No."

"Yet you want to leave already?" He looked her in the eye.

She wished he hadn't. The sadness in his face was too

much. He knew how this would end but wasn't ready to face it. The crushing weight of fate was a burden she couldn't ease no matter how long they had together.

"I don't want to leave you—" Not when every second was more precious than the ring he'd given her for all the wrong reasons.

"You can't, until I release you. You are my queen."

"I will have to return to my world eventually." Eliza blinked back the tears that stung her eyes. She wasn't going to cry until he was gone. Until it was over. Until she had to face her reality alone.

"I'm sure the fiancé you don't love will be waiting."

Eliza shivered. An eternity trapped in the Shadowlands with a man who couldn't love her but wanted to was preferable to an hour in the company of Steve. "I will never go back to him."

"Can you learn to love me?" He lifted her newly made ring to his lips and revealed a glimmer of the man she was looking for—the man he could be if freed from the curse.

Her breath tightened, she glanced down not wanting him to read the truth in her eyes. She didn't have to learn to love him. She had graduated. She was in love with him and, like everyone she loved, he would die too soon. Only Steve was safe because she didn't love him, the young lawyer she had fallen for was long gone. She couldn't tell Roan. She may not be handing out his death sentence, but she didn't want to bring the end closer than it had to be.

"Everyone I love dies."

"Then grant me that blessing." Roan released her hand. A king would never beg, but every line on his face was asking for her permission to die.

"I can't." She shook her head, her hair skimming her shoulders.

—m—

Roan didn't blink as he regarded her. He was damned anyway, but it would have been nice to have been loved by someone, especially the woman who was slowing the fade with one hand while drawing it closer with the other.

"Well, we're well matched. Unable or unwilling. There is little difference." He took a step closer, tempted by her presence.

Eliza smelled like flowers and gold. The metallic taste lay over her skin, attracting the goblin, repelling the man. Beneath that she smelled like sex, like him. The way a woman should, although his memory could be wrong after so many years.

"Tell me, Eliza, when you lie with your fiancé do you think of him? Do you call out his name?"

She glanced away, but he caught her chin and turned her head. Her hazel eyes refused to meet his. Her full lips pressed together so no reply slipped past. It should be enough, she'd chosen him, embraced him, taken his ring. But he was driven to press harder, to force what he wanted to hear from her lips.

"You called my name. But I wonder whose face you see when you close your eyes."

"Yours." The word was forced, like admitting it would wound them both.

His lips brushed her cheek. Her skin was soft like a warm, ripe peach. Her hand slid up his arm, and her body moved closer.

"Is it easier to sleep with a monster than love to one?" His tongue traced the shell-like contour of her ear.

"I don't see a monster. I see a man." Her breathy words cut like white-hot knives.

Roan dropped the embrace. "Then you are blind and careless with your affections."

How could she ignore what he was? See only what she wanted? She summoned the Goblin King to reach the man, forgetting they were one and the same.

Without touching the magic that ran beneath their feet he changed and become the goblin Eliza refused to see. The part of him she wouldn't accept. In the Shadowlands he chose to be a man, but it was easy, maybe easier to be a goblin. At least then he could give up the pretense of being human.

"That isn't you. It's a mask you hide behind." Her face contorted. But she didn't scream or look away. She didn't reach for him either.

Had he really expected her to? The thought of her mating with this monstrous body made him sick. He knew no good would come out of kidnapping her, yet he'd done it anyway and was now reaping his reward. A longing for something he could never feel. A hunger for something he'd never tasted. Even when confronted with the twisted truth she refused to believe. Until she believed in goblins, she wouldn't believe in love. Love he was more than willing to return if he'd a heart made of flesh.

He laughed. The high pitch rang off the walls like an off-key bell, a sound that would sour milk still in the udder.

"If it were a mask, I would have discarded it many

centuries ago." Roan pulled up the shadows and slid into the Fixed Realm, away from his queen who wanted to believe he was nothing but a man.

Away from the woman who made him believe there was still hope, when all he saw was death.

centuries ago, Roan pulled up the shadows and slid into the Greel Woods, away from his queen who wanted to believe he was not a monster.

Away from the woman who made him believe there was still hope when all he saw was doom.

THE ROCKS SANG WITH TWISTED LAUGHTER THAT MADE HER blood ice. Eliza reached her hand out but grasped only air where the Goblin King had stood only a heartbeat before. She sucked in a heavy breath.

"Damn you. Come back!" Like a child cheated of candy, she stamped her foot.

No swirl and tangle of beads answered her call.

"Roan, please." How could she be with him when he kept forcing her to see the goblin that he didn't want to be?

"Fine." Eliza crossed her arms and tilted her hip. She could wait. She had all the time in the world. Roan didn't.

The candles stood unmelting, a surreal silent vigil that marked no time. She could wait a lifetime and there would be no change to anything here. The earth would spin, another day would roll past, and she would be standing here waiting for her lover to return. He would return. Roan wouldn't leave her stranded in the Shadowlands. The Goblin King she wasn't sure about.

Eliza sighed and dropped into a chair. She could wait just as well sitting. The diamond in her ring flashed like a burning sun in the candlelight. It was an inhumanly exquisite piece of work. The flowers were tiny, glistening roses, some in full bloom, others tightly wrapped buds. The tendrils coiled around her finger and clasped the diamond to its center with a whisper of leaves. But almost hidden by the beauty were tiny thorns. She tugged the ring to remove it and have a closer look. It remained put. She twisted and her skin turned with the ring. Her blood cooled and drained away.

The ring was one with her flesh.

Created for her alone. Born of magic, but lacking the one thing she'd wanted from her next diamond ring.

Love.

By protecting her, he was shielding himself from the curse. Roan had told her he craved only gold. There was no room for anything else in his solid, metal heart. She hadn't believed him.

Icy fingers tickled her spine and coaxed the hairs on the back of her neck to attention. Eliza turned in her seat. Dai stood in the doorway. All trace of friendliness was scrubbed away by the curl of his lip and the dullness of his eyes. Would he fade while she watched?

"How long has he been gone?" Dai dropped his empty plates on the table. The rest of the food remained on the plates, cold and uneaten.

"How long have you been there?"

"Long enough." He sat opposite her. Around his neck swung a pendant. Black diamond and platinum.

"Did Roan make that?"

"Yes." Dai filled a golden goblet with wine. "The diamonds protect the wearer from corruption by the Shadowlands."

She rubbed her fingers over her ring. Roan didn't wear one. There was no hidden jewelry on his body. Dai watched her as he drank. Sitting here with him wasn't the best idea, but leaving would be rude, so she leaned back in her seat. If they were going to chat, he could fill in some blanks while they waited for the king to return.

"Why doesn't Roan wear a diamond?"

Dai ran one finger around the rim of his goblet as he considered her request. "He can't use magic while possessing a black diamond. If we don't have magic, Elryion would kill us."

"Goblins can only be killed in battle." Both Roan and her book had mentioned that, so she'd taken it as fact.

Dai hooked his thumbs in his Kevlar vest. "This isn't for decoration. Battle weapons, not necessarily a battle."

Eliza pushed her hair back off her face. She'd cut it a little too short. It wouldn't stay tucked behind her ears. "How does magic stop—"

"Ever stood in a rain of bullets? Fought an army of skeletons wielding battle axes? How do you fight ghosts who look like family that died a thousand years before but now seek your blood on their weapons?" Dai lifted his cup in salute. "Magic."

He took a swig of wine. "And every time Roan uses magic he pays with his soul. Much easier for the druid to chip away like a coward than face a warrior like a man."

Yet, Roan used magic without a thought. Sacrificing himself to protect her with a ring. How much of his soul had he used to make her ring? "Will the diamond stop you from becoming—"

"Goblin." He twirled the goblet in his fingers. The gold tossed sunspots over the walls. "Not if Roan fades. We'd thought…" He shook his head and drank deeply. "We thought that you coming willingly could break the curse." He slammed the goblet down with too much force. It bounced and tipped on its side, then rolled spilling the last trickle of red wine.

Eliza jumped. The wine glistened on the table like fresh, blood-filled blisters. Bursting a blister led to infection, but she took the risk.

"I thought it would too." If breaking the curse was as easy as wishing it, then it would've been broken a hundred times over every day she'd known Roan.

"Why do you care?" Dai flicked the goblet back onto its base and refilled it.

He drank as if he was breathing. The gold framed glasses suited him, but he wore them as goblin treasure. Her gold earring hung from his ear. Dai had given up. He was hoarding treasure ready for when he faded. The pendant only prolonged the inevitable.

The temperature in the caves plummeted and she burned as if ice pressed its bitter lips to her skin. "Because there are too few good men."

"None of us have been *good men* in a very long time. Wake up and smell the rot." He waved his hand toward the food.

The food that had been edible what seemed like moments ago was discolored with mold. In the meat, maggots writhed. Eliza clamped her hand over her mouth in an effort to keep her stomach in place. It tumbled trying to throw out the small amount she'd eaten. She turned her head away and drew in several deep breaths in an attempt to quell the rising nausea. She was sure she could feel the cold bodies of the maggots in her stomach. Eating her from the inside.

Dai smiled and took a drink. "What you've eaten is fine. The Shadowlands claims what is left. Quick and the dead."

"Would you rather I was dead?" She kept her eyes averted from the decomposing food. She didn't want to know what happened to the food next.

He pressed his lips together and thought.

The pause was enough. Short answer, yes. Dai would prefer it if she were dead.

"No. But every action has a price. Your presence denies Roan death. If he were only gambling with his life, I wouldn't care. What a man decides is his own business." Dai pointed with his goblet. He'd judged and found her guilty of offering life. "He will risk fading for one more second with you."

One more second with her. Eliza snorted. "I can tell by the way he vanished and left me here."

"What did you say to him?"

This wasn't her fault. Roan's brother didn't have the right to question her. She wasn't on trial. "Didn't you overhear?"

Dai blinked. The glaze over his eyes loosened for a moment so she could see the intelligence that had once been applied to breaking the curse. Now he wallowed waist deep in wine, waiting for the end. Both brothers were trying to face death while still holding out for a cure. But each shattered hope cut deep, making a wound that wouldn't be given time to heal.

Eliza softened. How would she deal with an unwanted fate? By hiding in the Shadowlands. "I said I can't stay here. I need to live in both worlds."

Except she hadn't said it exactly like that. Maybe if she had, Roan would have understood. He didn't have enough soul to keep lashing out and releasing his hurt.

"As queen you have to remain. You are another possession." Dai ran one finger over the rim of the empty spectacle frame as if he was thinking. "Modern life makes kidnapping so much harder."

Eliza sat up a little straighter.

Dai laughed. "A goblin joke. You were his first kidnap." He raised his drink. "And his first queen. Just another sign how close he is to the edge."

"What do you mean?" Roan had said he had days. Did he have less time? However long he had, he was wasting time by running away. Surely they could talk, make love, and laugh…she remembered the grating laugh as he left…maybe not laugh. They could steal time and make it stop just for them.

"Goblin Kings always steal a queen. A woman captured over the solstice."

He waited for the words to sink in past the barrier of her skin and deep into her body. Her heart slowed until she could feel the squeeze of the muscle as it pushed her unwilling blood onward. She had come to Roan on the longest night of the year. Samhain might be the night of the dead, but winter solstice belonged to the goblins.

Dai placed his cup down and leaned on the table. "Perfect, isn't it?"

"He could have taken any woman." Her voice was quiet and shaky.

He shook his head. Long black hair slipped over his shoulders. "You don't understand what you tamper with. Kidnapping and rape would have completed the curse. No other woman would do. You were willing."

It had nothing to do with her and everything to do with what Roan was. He wanted a queen that wouldn't

cost him his humanity. And she was desperate enough
to fall into his hands. She slumped back into the chair.
It supported her body but not her spirit, which slipped
through the wood and lay on the floor, waiting to be
reconnected with life. Her skin resisted and argued. It
remembered and trembled under the imagined touch of
his hands. The summer heat of his eyes that had burned
through her, searching for something, but not knowing
what it would be if he found it. Did she believe the man,
or the goblin?

"What happens to the human queens?" She wasn't
sure she had the stomach to know, but she had to ask. If
the curse won, she would become one of those women.

"That depends. The lucky ones succumb to the
Shadowlands magic, surrender their souls, and fade."
Dai refilled his goblet.

Eliza's fingers curled as she resisted the urge to
snatch it from him and make him sober up. "And the
unlucky ones?"

"If they are captured by a rival troop, they are eaten."
He pulled one of the knives that decorated his armor out
and stabbed the table. "They don't kill their food first."

Her throat closed. Roan had made a comment about
goblins sending her bones back. She'd thought it a
threat, not the truth.

"And those that aren't captured find out how long the
human body can last in the Shadowlands at the mercy of
their king, before they get the relief of death."

As a goblin, Roan was all anger and raw power. There
would be no gentle touch or kind word. The hands that
touched her would be cold and gray. She squeezed her
eyes shut as she tried not to think about the night he'd

revealed himself to her, his body pressed against her, his yellow eyes glowing in the shadows.

"He promised to take me home before he fades."

"Bit hard when he's not here." Dai pulled the knife out of the table. He ran the tip along the table, lifting a curl of wood.

"Roan will come back." She said it to convince herself as much as Dai.

"Maybe. Or maybe it's easier to face death alone." Dai flung the knife at the wall. It quivered, stuck in the rock between two of the swords hung for the dead.

"You mean to keep the vow."

"I have no wish to be goblin." He thumbed the hilt of another knife.

She couldn't give up on Roan. If she did, she was giving up on a life she'd only dared to dream. "There must be a way—"

"What do you think we have done for close to two thousand years? I have trawled through forgotten tombs for forgotten texts written in forgotten languages." Dai pulled the knife free of the rock and returned it to his vest. "Roan visited magicians, wise women, religious leaders, hermits, gurus. Nothing. The magic the druid used is forgotten."

Eliza understood why Dai had given up. He'd failed. It had been his responsibility to find a cure. Now they were truly at the end of the line. If Roan fought the druid and didn't kill him, Roan would fade, dragging Dai along for the ride.

Sadness bubbled up and drowned the hope she'd been clutching. "There's really no solution."

"No." Dai removed his necklace. He dropped it into

a black bag and tucked it into a pocket. "I will take you home." He held out his hand.

"I thought I had to stay here since I'm queen?" Eliza slid off the chair, placing it between them. Dai had already admitted he would rather she not be here, involved with Roan.

"I doubt he has the heart to take you back."

Roan had no heart, it was gold. "Why should I trust you?"

"You shouldn't. I'm more goblin than man." His eyes blinked yellow then blue so fast she could have imagined the change.

"I'll wait here for Roan."

Dai looked at the ceiling and sighed. "After everything I've said." He gritted his teeth. "You aren't safe here alone. Elryion would use you to kill Roan. The Hoard creeps around in the dust looking for tasty human. And every breath you take is one closer to corruption. The longer you spend here the more you become part of the Shadowlands."

Eliza glanced at her hands. She could fade by just being here? She looked back at Dai, if he wasn't staying here with her…"Where are you going?"

"To find Roan."

She jumped like an overeager puppy being taken for a walk. "I'll come."

Dai shook his head. "He'll find you when he's ready."

Her toes gripped the inside of her shoes. They both knew that may never happen. She wanted to wait for Roan, needed to see him again before he was lost to her forever. But the price required, remaining trapped in the Shadowlands on a chance, was too high.

"Swear you'll take me home."

Dai placed his hand on his sword. "On my life. Besides, I can't take you anywhere you don't want to go while you wear his ring."

Eliza glanced at the ring; as beautiful as it was, the intent was as black as the diamond in its heart. She was Roan's until the end.

"I'll wait for him in the Fixed Realm." She clasped Dai's offered hand and hoped he was telling the truth. The candles blurred, and she blinked clearing the tears. "Tell him I'd like to say good-bye."

"I can't make promises for a king."

———— ∞ ————

Roan stretched out his legs. A black spider danced past, away from the intruder who'd ripped through its silk interior decorating. The tree house had been vacant for years. It sighed around him, longing for the laughter of children to call out from its windows. He was a poor substitute.

Through the window he watched the house. The lights remained on, but the man no longer flickered against the blinds. He slept. If Roan reached out, he would be able to snag the edge of the dream and twist until it broke. Roan forced out a breath. This time he let Steve sleep.

With a yellow nail he flicked a red-backed spider away. His gray fingers were more like spider legs than a man's hand. It was a body he hated, yet he expected Eliza to overlook the disfigurement. She wanted a real man, not a part-time, damned man. He couldn't live up to her expectation. He'd been set up to fail before they first met.

And he would fail her a hundred times over and still not be able to walk away and let her be. And she would call him back. And he would come, caught by the promise that maybe if the stars aligned, or fell from the sky, the curse would break.

He drew his sword. The blade was still and black in the dark. Untarnished by time, or stained by use, it had been at his side for most of the curse. No doubt it would go on without him. Slashing, cutting, biting into flesh. Never his. A bullet was faster, surer. He wanted the end to be clean.

His fingers traced the length of the blade. She would be chatting to Dai. He would be telling tall tales of ancient tombs and hidden treasure, making them come alive in the dust to entertain. But she would sigh and wonder where he was and when she could come home. Eliza was right. Keeping her in the Shadowlands would ruin her real life. This was where Eliza deserved to live. Her home. Her world.

The idea of leaving her with Steve, her fiancé, turned his stomach worse than the stink of death after battle. As men they both had one thing in common.

Eliza.

Steve feared losing Eliza, too vain to realize that he'd lost her a long time ago. She was too scared of him to leave because of a few pieces of paper he kept hidden. Steve's fears had revealed the usual obsessions of a man concerned only with appearance. His fear of being exposed as a fraud, of being laughed at. Losing Eliza was down the list.

The man was a fool.

Roan lifted the sword and rolled his wrist. The motion was fluid, pure muscle memory with no thought.

With a nick, not even a full cut, he could free Eliza from whatever web Steve had built. Her wish was simple.

Be free of Steve.

Roan closed his eyes and kissed the blade. Cold against his lips. Cold in his heart. Colder in the grave. No goblin could resist a fight. He left the spiders to their repairs and went to confront his rival.

Chapter 13

HER STOMACH LURCHED, BUT HER FEET SUNK INTO carpet. She opened her eyes and fell to her knees. She was home. Relief, regret, and loss burst in her chest like an overfilled water balloon. Her throat ached. She didn't want to be here in the silent house. Eliza titled her head. The sensor winked red with every movement, but no alarm was triggered.

She'd set the alarm.

Only she and Steve knew the code.

For three heartbeats she didn't move. Steve was back for round two. Her cell phone was upstairs in the guest room. The nearest landline was in the kitchen. She listened for anything—a door, a footstep, a breath. The silence buzzed, swamping the pulse of her blood in her ears.

She took a tentative step, then paused, expecting Steve to appear with every heartbeat. There was no noise in response. Braver, Eliza walked to the kitchen. Dawn colored the house in shades of gray. But the shadows were distant and unhelpful. If Roan didn't want to see her, she wouldn't call. She could deal with Steve and tell him it was over. His threats no longer held any power.

She'd believed Steve when he told her the blame would fall on her, too scared of him to do anything. But he was just as scared of her and what she would do. His fraud wasn't as thorough as he'd let on. The glimmer of hope that if the papers were found she could be free was all she needed to press forward.

Eliza lifted the slim handset and slid the phone into her pocket. Then she began the long march upstairs. The only door open was the guest room. She moved along the wall and peeked around the door.

Slumped in the chair was Steve. His head rested against his chest. No breath moved his body. Dread crawled down her back, tugging on her skin with its cold-clawed feet.

Oh no.

Steve was dead. Roan had taken her desire to be free of Steve to the extreme and killed him. Her goblin lover had acted in a way no human would.

Why, Roan? The question remained on her lips, unspoken. Because Roan wanted her, needed her, but would never say it. He would do whatever she asked as long as he could hide behind being goblin.

Steve twitched. Eliza jumped back and gulped a breath of air. He lifted his head, saw her, and backed into the chair as if he was seeing a ghost.

He was alive. She released the breath and smiled. Roan hadn't killed for her. If he'd been here, she would've hugged him regardless of what he looked like. Goblin was only the color of his skin. But Steve…she looked at him with eyes that had seen beyond this world. Steve was nothing but a pink-skinned goblin hoarding gold.

"Are you all right, Steve?" His usually immaculate suit was crumpled. The tail of his too-tight tie flopped over his jacket shoulder. One shoe was missing.

His hand crept around the back of his head. He checked his fingers as if expecting blood. But his hands were clean. He looked up at her, a frown clouded his eyes. Then he shook his head as if dislodging a bad dream.

Once she would have run to his side offering assistance. Now she watched. An injured snake was still a snake.

"What happened to you?"

Steve opened his mouth—no words came out. He tried again. "I was waiting for you."

He touched the back of his head again, confused. "I need an aspirin. Where have you been?"

Eliza crossed her arms. "Out. Thinking."

"You left this behind." From his pocket he pulled out her square cut engagement ring. It had been ugly the day he'd given it to her and it was ugly now.

Roan had created a ring filled with the flowers he could never give her in the Shadowlands. A ring she would love. She twisted her hand to hide her new ring from Steve. No sense in annoying him. A wounded snake was more likely to bite and Steve had more venom than a cobra.

She shrugged. "I took it off to shower."

"It was on the floor." He flicked the ring between his finger and thumb. Steve walked toward her, his gait uneven from the missing shoe. He lacked the grace of being born a warrior and the sureness of being king.

"Must have got caught in my clothes." She kept her gaze steady.

Hidden by her arms, her hands fisted. He was going to try to put it back on her finger. She didn't want the ring or Steve touching her skin again. She didn't offer her hand, and he didn't demand.

The smooth lawyer mask he wore broke, and she saw through the cracks to the man she had once loved. She had admired his determination, his desire to reach the top, ruthless, fearless, passionate. Their life hadn't always been a tightrope walk of hate and blackmail.

He closed his hand over the ring and put it in his pocket. "You win. Keep your house, your trust fund." Steve retrieved his shoe from the side of the bed. He tied it up. "I hope it makes you happy while you sleep alone."

Eliza raised her eyebrows. "You're leaving?" *Without a fight?*

What had happened in her absence? She cast her gaze over Steve's rumpled appearance. Had Roan visited Steve's dreams?

Steve loosened his tie so it no longer strangled the collar of his shirt, then he tucked the tail into his jacket. One button was missing. Puzzlement furrowed his forehead, but he let it pass and re-schooled his face. The mask fell back into place. "I'm breaking the engagement. You're not worth the grief."

"What's the catch? There's always a price with you. A penalty. What do you want in exchange for my freedom?"

Steve would've faded to goblin in a heartbeat if he thought it was in his best interest; letting her go would only serve him. Unless it was a trick designed to suck her back into trusting him and handing over control. Never again would she fall under his spell.

"Your silence. I think that works in both our interests." He did his best to smooth down his suit.

Eliza nodded. He'd agreed to end their private relationship, but she had one more request.

"I want your resignation." If she was cutting out cancer, she was going to use a heavy hand to ensure it never grew back and invaded her life. Better to lose the limb.

Steve remained quiet, but she could hear the well-oiled wheels spin. Lubed with money and lies, there was no squeak as the gears changed.

"Fine. I'll even move out of state."

Too easy. "I don't believe you."

Steve shrugged and glanced away. "You never wanted to be a society wife. You played the daughter for your father. But you were never convincing. I want more than a good copy."

Eliza forced a smile. Even now he was trying to save face as if it were her fault they were breaking up. "Good-bye, Steve."

But she knew this was just the beginning. She had to find the papers before he left the state, otherwise they would be gone forever and it would be much harder to face the police knowing she had nothing to back up her claims…and if they failed to find anything pointing to Steve's guilt it would be a risk she would pay for behind bars.

He placed his hand on the door. "I have contacts. If you breathe a word to anyone, I'll know. And then no one will be able to save you." Steve walked out of the room.

His footsteps faded down the hallway. Then there was nothing until the front door closed.

Eliza sat on the bed. The covers were dragged to one side and a pillow lay on the floor. She hadn't left it like that. What had Steve done? Did she care anymore? She rubbed her hand over her face. She needed a shower. Breakfast. And a plan.

<div align="center">~~~</div>

Steven unlocked his office. He hand wrote a resignation letter to Gunn, the only surviving partner of Gunn and Coulter. Eliza had been part owner in name only. He folded the letter, placed it in an envelope, and then stopped.

He touched the lump on the back of his head. He'd fallen asleep while waiting for Eliza to come home and had woken up with a sore head and a vague memory of a nightmare that had threatened to behead him. Steven shook off the feeling that there was something he should remember. He must have hit his head against the wall.

In precise handwriting he addressed the envelope and placed it on the receptionist's desk. Eliza wouldn't be back at work for another month. She hadn't asked for the honeymoon tickets. He allowed himself a smug smile. He'd keep them. He deserved the trip to Europe. She could deal with the wedding cancellation. He nodded as he unlocked his filing cabinet. Cutting himself free of Eliza was already feeling good. He thumbed the files. All but one would stay with the firm. Toward the back, labeled like every other file, was Chiverney. Hidden in plain sight. Like every client there was paperwork and invoices for hours billed. He left all of them. All he wanted was one yellow envelope.

Steven flicked open his briefcase and placed the document envelope inside. Fragments of the dream flitted past, too fast for him to catch. He shrugged them off but couldn't dispel the unease they left in their wake. There was no harm in being cautious. He opened the envelope. Full of paper. He flicked the edges of a couple of sheets. Now he was getting paranoid.

His eyes narrowed. Gravity threw his stomach sideways like a fairground ride designed to make people sick. The papers were blank. He poured everything out. Fresh, white paper spewed over his desk and floor.

"No!" he roared.

He rummaged through the papers looking for anything with writing. Every sheet was blank. While he'd dreamed of something hideous threatening his life, Eliza had been in his office. He'd been passively waiting for her to come home while she was out stealing from him.

"Bitch." He raked his fingers through his hair.

He'd agreed to leave her alone, to quit the firm, to move, to fake devastation over a last-minute breakup.

And all along she had played him. Eliza hadn't even finished her law degree, and she'd outmaneuvered him. He laughed. All this time he'd thought her too weak and too stupid to be a threat. Now Eliza had the documents that placed the fraud at his feet. All she'd ever done was the paperwork to set up the company, the same paperwork she'd done a thousand other times as his legal secretary.

He picked up the phone. He wasn't going away without a fight.

------m------

The water ran clear in the shower without the need for magic. Rivulets spilled over Eliza's skin, drawing Roan's eyes in a hundred different places at once. The curve of her back. The dimple above her butt. The gold handprint that water wouldn't remove. Down the back of her thigh to the crease of her knee. The calf that had wrapped over his hips. He knew he should leave. Daylight filled the bedroom. No shadows would hide him. He eased his camo around the tightening in his groin.

Eliza's head lifted, white bubbles crowned her hair. Roan pulled back so he was out of view, but he could see her in the mirror. She faced the door as if she sensed he was there. She waited a moment, listening. Roan stayed motionless, cursing the beads that announced his presence. If she turned and looked in the mirror, she would see him.

She tipped her head under the water. Her breasts lifted as she massaged her scalp rinsing her hair. The soapy streams circled her tight nipples the way his tongue had. He wanted to be in the shower with her. His hands washing her. Drinking the water perfumed by her skin. Roan fisted his hands and forced himself to gaze at his reflection.

Not in this body.

He sighed...not in this lifetime.

This wasn't a pleasure visit. He looked at the large yellow envelope in his hand. Steve had been more than helpful when faced with a sword-wielding demon invading his dreams and turning them into terror-filled nightmares. He'd begged for his life as he'd babbled the answer to every question Roan had asked, and some he hadn't. These were the documents Eliza needed to be free of that man. Roan smiled. He was getting soft as he got older. It would have been so easy to sever Eliza's bond to Steve with a flick of the sword. But she wouldn't want that. She wouldn't want him killing for her. So he'd let the man live even after he knew what he'd done and how he'd trapped Eliza.

Eliza had traded the greedy bastard for goblin.

With these papers he could cut the ties that bound her to Steve. But was he doing it for her, or for himself because he didn't want to share?

Roan took one last look at the pale, pink perfection that was Eliza. Her eyes closed, and her face in the water. A faint smile on the lips that had kissed him. He wanted to be the man she wanted—that he used to be. The mouth of the goblin in the mirror turned down in an expression that was supposed to be sadness but looked more like a fierce grimace.

He placed the envelope on the floor at his feet. Then he took one dreadlock and worked off an amber bead. He should strip the dread of all its beads for the number of times he'd served Eliza.

The bead screamed in his hand, begging to be put back. He placed the bead on top of the envelope. *Only amber*. Drops of the sunlight he missed. He threw a longing glance at the patch of sunlight by the window. The warmth beckoned, and his skin itched as if the sun was summoning him into its presence. Like a good goblin, he obeyed. Through his boots and clothes, the weak morning sun touched his skin. Slicing like a razor. The burn went bone deep, yet there would be no mark on his skin. Goblins were never meant to see the sun. He closed his eyes, knowing that he could stand here all day and the heat would never penetrate his heart.

"Roan?" Eliza squinted into the light. Water dripped from her hair, onto her shoulders, down her collarbone, only to be soaked up by the pale green bath towel that covered her body.

He stood trapped by the sunlight, the core of his bones boiling. The only shadow to escape into was his, stretching toward Eliza. If a goblin entered his own shadow it was said he would never emerge. Or so Roan had been warned by a man more weathered than the cave he'd inhabited. Today wasn't the day he was going to test the old god-speaker's word. To his left, the curtain made a weak shadow, but it was enough.

Her foot touched the envelope. She glanced down. It was all the time he needed. His beads chimed as he moved from sun to shadow, and then he was gone. What Eliza did with his gift was up to her. Maybe tonight while she slept she would think of him. If she did, he knew he would go to her. This time he didn't care where they met as long as they were together. If she didn't call…he would know the true heart of his queen.

Eliza looked up in time to lose Roan to the dark. Water splashed onto paper. She stepped back and picked up the amber bead, not quite a match to the one on her bangle. The carving was different, the color deeper. A yellow document envelope covered in soggy dots lay on the floor. Steve's handwriting neatly labeled it as belonging to Chiverney Holdings. One of the many companies that used Gunn and Coulter.

A shiver chased over her bare flesh. Chiverney was different. Chiverney must be the company Steve was using to hide the fraud.

Without opening the envelope she knew what it contained. She felt the thickness and the weight of paper inside. The weight of freedom. These were the documents she had spent so long searching for. Always so careful to never raise suspicion. And now she had them.

Her hands shook. She wanted rip open the envelope, to rifle through every page and find out how much, and when and where every dollar had gone. But she couldn't touch the papers. Her fingerprints couldn't be on the documents.

She hugged the envelope. With a shaky breath she whispered, "Thank you."

Roan had visited Steve. That was why Steve had been disheveled and willing to leave. What had Roan said to him? Had Steve looked the goblin in the eye and seen what he would become? No, probably not. And she didn't care. Roan had discovered the location of the documents and retrieved them for her. She couldn't take her eyes off the most precious gift she'd ever been given. More valuable than gold, these papers proved Steve's guilt and bought her freedom. Roan had granted her wish.

Her home phone rang, but she ignored it. Her cell phone rang, so she checked the number. Steve was calling from the office. She let voice mail take the call—and the abuse. He knew she had the documents. There was no time for contemplating what to do or how to do it. She had to make the call she'd both dreamed of and dreaded making.

Stiff fingers dialed the numbers on Detective Griffin's business card. But fear didn't flood her veins and paralyze like venom the way she'd imagined. Fear fed her. It mixed with excitement, and rushed through her body like an electrical current until her skin buzzed. Her mind swam with possibilities.

She could pull the tablecloth from under Steve. One call could cost him his world. Or her, her freedom. But freedom hadn't been hers to sacrifice in many years, and risking it was like visiting the high rollers club with a fake credit card and then winning.

Documents still in hand, she calmly told Detective Griffin everything from the first threat, to finding Steve in her house that morning, to his shock departure, and finding the papers that incriminated him. The words came easily without stumble. She'd had years to prepare them and only this one chance to use them. A grin formed as she spoke. One that made her cheeks ache. She hadn't had a reason to smile since she'd accepted Steve's ring and agreed to his demands.

By the time the police knocked on her door she was dressed and her hair was almost dry. Her cell phone had rung every couple of minutes until she'd turned it off.

Griffin greeted her and put the envelope in a bag, then arrested her as a suspect in the fraud investigation. His words flew around her ears but never landed. She nodded as if she understood what he was saying.

She looked guilty.

It was her name on the documents. Every fear that Steve had cultivated grew a little larger and a little closer as she sat in the back of the police car on her way to the Major Fraud Squad offices. Hands wrapped her stomach, squeezing and twisting until just breathing made her ill.

What if the documents were so well done she was convicted while Steve walked free? She rested her head on the glass and watched the streets slide past.

No.

She closed her eyes. She trusted Roan. She had to trust the police. She had to trust herself.

But without Roan, without him finding the documents, would she have had the courage to place the call? Or would she have kept silent? The knowledge of the crime chewed through each newfound happiness until her freedom was nothing more than an illusion bought with dirty money. This way she would be truly free, whatever the outcome.

She bit her lip and closed her eyes. If only breaking Roan's curse was so easy.

Chapter 14

Dusk was easing its hands around the city, choking out the sun, when the police let Eliza walk free. She leaned against the station wall for support, comfortable to be held by its shadow while she waited for Amanda to come and collect her. Only one day had passed, yet it felt like she'd relived every day of the past five years. Every date, every argument, every word she'd ever spoken to Steve. Every answer videotaped as a suspect.

When the police were done toasting one side they'd flipped her over and started again, waiting for a crack to appear in her story. Always coming back to the one question she couldn't answer truthfully:

How did she come to have the documents?

They were in her house.

Must have been Steve?

What else could she say? Later they'd turned off the tapes and interviewed her as a witness with all the details raked through again. The evidence would determine which interview the police used.

For the moment she was free but under investigation. And so was Gunn and Coulter. If Steve had drawn the company into his scandal, the firm would go down in a blaze of corruption. Her father would be suing from the grave.

Amanda parked and Eliza slid into the brilliant blue sedan. Loud rock pumped through the speakers. Only when Brigit wasn't in the car did Amanda put her speakers to work. The rest of the time the music was little more than background noise.

"What is going on?" Amanda turned the music off. "Why was Steve arrested this morning?"

"Steve was arrested?" She'd relive today again just to hear that news again.

"You didn't know? It's been all over the news. I thought that was why you were at the station." Amanda guided the car through the city clogged with office workers heading home.

Eliza shook her head. Of course the police would bring him in. They'd brought her in. At the moment it was all paperwork. She allowed herself a grim smile. Whatever she'd gone through, he'd gone through. And he had the guilty conscience.

"What for is still a mystery." Amanda looked at her, one eyebrow raised, her eyes momentarily off the road.

"Fraud." It didn't feel like a victory. More like the announcement of war with the battles yet to be fought in the courts, in the news, and in the gossip magazines.

Amanda slapped the steering wheel. "I knew he couldn't be trusted."

Eliza rubbed her fingers into her temples. "Please. I don't want to go through it again." There would be plenty of time for that. Tonight she just wanted to sleep and dream and be with Roan. Tomorrow would come around soon enough, fists up ready to fight.

"I take it my name wasn't mentioned in the news."

"Only as the fiancée," Amanda confirmed. She picked Eliza's hand up. "Nice ring." Her eyes darted from the black diamond to the road. "Never seen anything like it. Gift from a *friend*?"

Eliza snatched her hand back and folded them in her lap, hiding the ring that would never come off. How could she explain she was a goblin's queen? That she'd fallen in love and was going to lose him to a two-thousand-year-old curse?

"Steve and I split this morning." Even the timing of the breakup was suspicious. "That didn't make the news?" she snapped, knowing Steve's arrest had more impact with her name attached. No doubt the press had smelled blood and was moving in for the kill.

Memories of the media coverage after her mother's death, Matt's death, and then her father's death came back to kick her in the guts. The news vans. The endless parade of reporters looking for the exclusive photos of the grieving family. The rumors that had circulated for months afterward about her being the most unlucky spoiled brat. *Cursed* one headline had run. They didn't know the meaning of the word.

Amanda squeezed her hand. "I'll help untangle the wedding preps."

Eliza rolled her head back against the seat. She hadn't thought that far ahead. With the wedding only days away she had to cancel. Once she did, another circus would ensue. She was sure Steve had pre-sold exclusive photos to a magazine.

The Shadowlands beckoned as an escape from the publicity that would poke and pry into every crevice of her life. Was it was too late to tell Roan she'd changed her mind and wanted to stay with him?

Amanda pulled onto her street. It was littered with vehicles, the detritus of the media industry chasing the next headline. They had the Coulter name firmly in their sights. Eliza readied herself for the onslaught. No one was taking over her life without a fight. She wouldn't run and hide.

Amanda slowed. "Are you sure you want to stay here tonight?"

"It's my house and I won't be forced out of it by anyone." Her mother had always handled the press with a smile and a thick pair of gloves. Her theatrical career had ensured the media was never far behind.

Never show fear, they can smell it, her mother had said.

"If you need anything…" Amanda pulled into the driveway, followed by a swarm of cameras right up to the property line. They wouldn't dare trespass.

Eliza hugged her. "Keep Brigit away. I'll call you tomorrow."

She fixed a smile, dug out her keys, and walked toward the house without a backward glance. Amanda revved the engine and sped backward up the driveway, hand on horn. Eliza winced. While not in her mother's guide to press relations, it was an excellent distraction.

Eliza locked the front door behind her. The press would have some nice photos of her back for tomorrow's paper. Unlike her mother she was under no obligation to talk to the press. She turned off the alarm and then reset it in night mode. It beeped, marking the thirty seconds she had to get upstairs. The other panel was in the main bedroom, a room she would never use again. She would have to call the security company in the morning and get a new panel set up in the guest room…and maybe while they were at it they could show her how to set a new code.

The dash was invigorating. She closed the door feeling lighter than she had in years, even though she'd opened Pandora's Box. The truth was out and could never be put back. Silence swelled to fill the house. Deepened with each breath. One step at a time. One day at a time. One night at a time. She would survive.

Eliza stripped out of clothes that smelled like the police station. Steve's corruption had infiltrated the fibers and tainted them. Instead, she pulled on bright yellow butterfly pajamas. The only person who had to like them was too exhausted to care. Never again would she wear a satin nightdress. Ever. For anyone.

She flopped onto the guest bed and closed her eyes. She should have showered first. Her limbs sank farther into the mattress. She should get up and eat something. She sighed. In a minute. She'd just lie down for a minute. Her eyes wouldn't open. Exhaustion claimed her. Sleep pulled her down into its darkest depths.

Her dream suffocated her. She couldn't pull away from the gentle grip that became clawed hands. Peace became panic. She couldn't wake up and couldn't break free. She fell out of the blackness and into gray.

She stood, dust clinging to her pajamas. She swiped at it and frowned. Gray. Around her the endless plains of the Shadowlands stretched.

This has to be a dream.

She pinched her arm with clammy fingers but didn't wake. She let out a slow breath and surveyed the barren landscape. Only Roan had ever brought her here and taken her home. Without him could she get home?

In the distance, huge rocks speared the sky. Roan's caves. It couldn't be that far. Since she was unable to wake up or leave, there was only one thing to do—she would have to walk.

The ground was cold, like walking on gritty ice. She moved quickly just to keep her feet from freezing and sticking. The scenery didn't change and the caves got no closer. The same twisted, blackened trees glowered from her left. Her breathing tightened and caught in her throat. She wasn't moving. She was no closer to safety.

Then she ran.

Her bare feet kicked up puffs of dust. She panted, but the spire remained fixed in the distance. A speck in the twilight sky moved and grew larger...coming toward her. Eliza pushed harder. She had to reach the caves. The speck became a crow, circling high on a magical wind. It dropped and rushed toward her. She was in trouble.

The only crow in the Shadowlands was the druid who had cursed Roan. Was he expecting her to call for Roan? If she did, she could be luring him into a trap.

The giant crow flew straight at her. Head on, eye level. It cried out and her blood became water. Insubstantial in her veins. Her legs cramped. But she ran on, ducking as the crow took to the sky. The steady beat of its wings sounded behind her. Chasing. Sick certainty forced her on.

The crow swept close, the tips of his wings brushing her face. Eliza yanked out handfuls of glossy-black feathers. The crow attacked again, talons outstretched. This time it didn't pull away. The wind beat against her skin while the bird bloodied its claws. Pain seared up her arm, down her back. Warmth spilled from the wounds she didn't have time to stop and examine.

Her skin was no match for the flurry of beak and claws. Forced to her knees, she frantically groped around in the dust. She needed a weapon. A rock, a stick, anything. She wasn't going to let an overgrown feather pillow kill her. Her fingers closed on something hard. She pulled it free of the dirt and lashed out. The impact jarred her arm and rattled her jaw. The crow tumbled through the air, then steadied. Its beady black eyes watching.

Eliza swung her weapon like a batter getting ready to hit a home run. When she saw what she held in her hands she almost dropped it. In her hands was a bone. The length of a thigh. Goblin or human? She forced herself to hold onto it instead of flinging it away. What had Roan said? Something about being one with the sword?

What else had he said? Something about the Shadowlands not being a dream. That if it were, she should be able to control it. She glanced at the bone that had conveniently appeared when she'd needed it. This was a dream…a dream the druid was trying to control with magic. The sneaky bastard. Did he know she'd been meeting Roan in her sleep?

The crow sensed her hesitation and swooped. She ducked and swung but didn't connect with the bird. Blood streamed down her arms burning her skin. Could she die in a dream? Surely there shouldn't be this much blood?

"What do you want, Elryion?" She needed to wake up. Instead of the cold of the Shadowlands she tried to imagine the warmth of her bed. She was in bed, sleeping. The Shadowlands shimmered as if the dream were breaking apart.

The crow flapped and cocked his head as if considering the woman who poured blood into the dust. Adrenaline pounded in her veins. Her pulse became the pulse of the Shadowlands. The ground jumped with each beat. Her legs weakened, threatening to send her sprawling into the red mud at her feet. The dust was slick with blood. Her blood.

Eliza stabbed the bone forward. "Shoo."

The crow seemed to smile and nod. Then the landscape bounced and slid out of focus. Eliza blinked to clear her vision. The crow was gone along with the Shadowlands.

Her heart raced as she lay in the tangled sheets of her bed. The violent switch in realities had been missing. No lurching, spinning darkness. It had been nothing but a dream. A horrible, realistic dream, but she'd never left her bed. Her breathing slowed. She placed a hand over her heart thankful it hadn't been real.

Her fingers were sticky-wet on her skin. Not slippery like sweat. Her heart gave a solid thump and seemed to stop. She raised her hand, but in the dark there were no colors to be seen. Her arms began to burn as if someone had laid a poker against her flesh. Without breathing she reached out and groped for the bedside light. The pale light glistened on the red that streaked her skin. Large spots blossomed where heavy drips fell on her pajamas. She was bleeding. Her heart picked a pace like that of a panicked rabbit.

How could a nightmare have ricocheted into reality?

She used the sheet to wipe at the blood, hoping to find untorn flesh beneath. Deep cuts appeared along the length of her arms and were swiftly filled and hidden. It wasn't just her arms. She turned; where she had been lying streaks of blood patterned the white sheet. The calm she had been holding on to became brittle and shattered. She clamped her teeth together and held the sheet tightly over the most damaged arm. Blood soaked through too fast, escaping out of her artery with each beat of her heart. Her body was hot and prickly, but she shivered anyway.

She should call in the emergency.

Where was her cell phone?

There was too much blood. The edges of the room became fuzzy as it spun around her. The silence was full of buzzing. She was going to die. But if she called Roan, he'd die too. Or suffer a life worse than death. Her eyes closed. Roan. She held onto the dream of seeing Roan again in the Summerland.

Over the din of the attacking Hoard, Eliza's thought swept past Roan. Faint, lacking her usual brilliance and desire. With the castle fortified, he left the battle and went to her, intending to be just a moment. She wasn't in the Summerland like he expected. She was in the Fixed Realm. Dying.

Blood was everywhere. Her skin was ruddy with the smears. Roan pulled her to him, searching for the wound, her blood giving his fingers the only color they had ever known as a goblin. Bloodred on goblin-gray. Another promise broken, but he had to touch her to heal her. What he found was dozens of cuts. Some nothing more than a scratch, others tore deep into the flesh, slashing arteries and veins. He'd seen worse wounds on the battlefield, but his guts still rolled at seeing the woman he wanted to love hurt.

"Eliza." He spun out the magic, healing the deepest of tears, slowing the flow of blood. What had happened? No one hid in the house. Eliza was alone. His gaze scanned the bed but there was no weapon that could cause these injuries and there were too many for it to be self-inflicted.

Her head rested against his chest as he scooped her

up. He'd never wanted to cradle her with these hands. For a moment he didn't know what to do with her. She needed more healing, and he had more power in the Shadowlands…and he didn't want her to wake and see him like this. But his home was under siege by the Hoard.

His lips twisted. Eliza was safer with him than she was here. But Roan heard the lies he was telling himself. He would've used any excuse to bring Eliza back to the Shadowlands to be at his side. He needed his queen, and he wasn't strong enough to leave her in the Fixed Realm. He stepped into the puddle of shadow made by the bed and crossed between realms. His caves were haunted with the ring of metal on rock and the screeching of goblin war cries. Eliza jerked in his arms and her eyes flickered open.

"You came."

"Of course I did. You asked me to." He would come whenever she called, not because he had to, but because he wanted to. He sat with her on his bed, her blood soaking into his clothes as magic seeped from him into her damaged flesh. "What happened?"

"The druid found me." Her words were barely a whisper.

He shook his head. His fingers, moving against her skin. "That's not possible. He can't cross through."

The druid wasn't goblin. He was human and humans never left the Shadowlands. They couldn't, because they couldn't use people's nightmares to pull themselves across the threshold. That didn't mean the druid hadn't been trying.

"In my sleep." She closed her eyes.

Why was Elryion stalking Eliza? Surely he would know that Roan would never let his queen be killed.

"Stay with me, Eliza."

Her eyelids fluttered, too wounded to obey.

Damn you, Elryion.

The druid had never intended to kill Eliza, just injure her enough that Roan was forced to use magic, or watch her die. A piece of his soul for her life. A trade he was happy to make, but he wanted some left to enjoy the bargain. He placed his hands over the cuts. As his finger traced each line the skin healed. Not perfectly, but enough to stop the blood loss. Perfect, scarless skin would use too much magic. They would both have to settle for near enough. A howl tore through the air, sounding closer than it was.

Eliza lifted her head, her body tense as if the noise were preventing her from falling asleep. "What's happening?"

"The Hoard is attacking. I had to seal the caves."

"They're trying to get in?" She peered over his shoulder as if expecting goblins to appear.

"Elryion must have told them we have gold." Roan started on her other arm. Defensive wounds. Her stomach and face were untouched.

She flinched and dropped her gaze to watch his hands move over her damaged flesh.

He paused, torn between causing her more pain and getting the job done to stop the blood flow. "Does it hurt?"

"No. It's just cold." She began to shake again. She was going into shock.

"Look at me, not at the blood, Eliza." He pushed some magic into her the way a doctor might give drugs.

She lifted her chin, color returning to her cheeks. "You shouldn't be using magic on me."

"Who else am I going to use it on?" He tried to smile to reassure her, but every cell that multiplied and closed the gash pushed him closer to the edge of oblivion. This time the edge was lit by one small white star that burned in the dark. He'd never seen it or felt it before, but he took the star as another sign he was losing the battle to hold onto his soul.

"Thank you."

The small cuts he left un-magicked. Roan lifted the skimpy top, ready to trace over the cuts on her back. Her heartbeat echoed in his chest, and her breath was warm against his neck. For a moment, all he did was hold her. If he closed his eyes and ignored the cloying smell of blood, he could pretend nothing stood between them. He gently smoothed his hand over her damaged skin.

"Let's clean the blood off and see what I've missed." Once he would have washed with magic. Now he was becoming almost human, having to wash with water and save what soul he had left. All things he'd once taken for granted he now measured and weighed. Compared to an extra day with Eliza most tasks were better completed by hand than with magic. The cost was too high.

He took her hand and led her down the tunnel. The white and gold bathroom, stolen from a five-star hotel, plumbing and all, still made him smile. It didn't belong here. And neither did he, but they were both stuck here for eternity. Another expensive, beautiful object ripped out of the Fixed Realm on a whim and a dare. Most of his treasures had been lost to the world long before he'd touched them. His castle was a living museum of the forgotten.

The air in the bathroom remained cool, but the water went from black to clear at his touch, then warmed.

Some things required no effort, and no discernible drawing of magic—moving between realms, purifying water.
There was enough of the Shadowlands now within him
that the magic flowed, within reason. Building caves or
healing meant drawing magic out of the Shadowlands
and that had a price. But he hadn't learned that until
much, much too late.

Roan drew his hand out of the water. "You can get in."

Her tongue flicked over her lip. She glanced at the
shower. "Will it stay like that?"

He nodded, beads jumping. "No games this time."

Cautiously she stuck her hand under the showerhead
and let the water pour over it. She stepped into the
shower still dressed in her bloodstained butterfly pajamas. The water turned pink as her arms washed clean.
She ran her hand over the tight new skin. The eyes can
lie, but touch was real.

Her lips parted as she inspected the fresh scars. "You
win. You still have more."

A smile quirked his lips. "Let's keep it that way."

She pulled her arms out of the water. "Can you make
it warmer?"

Roan turned the tap, a smile teased his lips. *Only a
little game.*

"Oh. I didn't think that would work." She adjusted
the tap.

The water wet her top, plastering it to her skin. The swell
of her breast cupped by the damp cotton. With a thought
the water cooled. Her nipples tightened and she jumped
back. The dare of stealing the bathroom was paying off.

"They're both cold." Roan grinned. He needed the
cold shower. Seeing her naked earlier in the morning

and watching her clothed now was more painful than picking a day to die.

Eliza slapped a handful of water at him. "Cheat."

Roan placed his hand under the reheated water. "It's fine now."

"Prove it. You get in." She crossed her arms under her bust, lifting them and giving the illusion of showgirl cleavage. "Do more than watch this time."

"You knew I was there?"

"I always know when you are there." She laid her hand on his arm.

His skin tightened with pleasure, instead of the pain of being forced to appear. She knew that a goblin had stood in the shadows tracking the flow of water over her skin. She'd turned to face him, to tempt him, to tease him. And he'd been unable to move, unable to touch, because his goblin hands could never love Eliza.

Roan ripped his vest off. He'd dressed for war, not rescue. His weapons belt fell on the floor. The goblins were attacking. The druid needed killing. Eliza wanted loving. The wishes of his queen always came first. He couldn't waste magic on pulling off clothing. His fingers didn't move fast enough, unused to crude necessity. He didn't take his gaze off Eliza. The gold flecks in her eyes became molten as she watched him.

He knelt to unlace his boots. She curled her fingers around the edge of her singlet top and pulled it over her head. There was no chance of breaking the curse, and no risk of damning consequences. Nothing existed between them but the simple lust that thrived between a woman and a man. The lump of metal in his chest turned, as if uncomfortable with this new development.

For the first time in centuries Roan pretended he was just a man. He stepped out of his boots and camo, hard, aching for her touch. A need that burned hotter and deeper than gold, but one that could still ruin him all the same. Only a woman could destroy a man where wealth and power had failed.

She slid the pajama pants over her hips, but she never got a chance to step out of them. Roan closed the glass shower door behind him. The water beat down on his back as he knelt at her feet. His hands skimmed the back of her legs, drawing her hips closer. She tugged one foot free of her pants, and he lifted that leg over his shoulder, so her sex was spread before him. Her fingers wound through the dreadlocks that inhabited his head. Beneath his hands, her muscles tightened in expectation. He couldn't remember the name of the last woman he'd tasted.

His tongue danced across the lips of her sex. Sweet like dew. Roan glanced up. Her teeth were pressed tight together. The pressure on his scalp increased. He took a slow taste, savoring the way she squirmed in his hands. His lips closed over the hard bud, his sucking stopped her breath. Her nails carved crescents into his skin. The more she hurt him, the more pleasure he gave her. His tongue thrust into her core. Her legs trembled, tiny moans escaping her lips. Her body went rigid in his hands and the feel of her climaxing around him traveled all the way to his cock.

Roan stood, slipping her leg from his shoulder to the crook of his arm. He lifted her against the glass and entered her. She arched, her hips thrust forward to take more. Hot and wet, she encased him. Her eyes closed, but she knew what he needed. Eliza used his dreads

against him, pulled him close until their lips met with
the taste of her still on his tongue.

When he wasn't quick enough to obey she took the
kiss. And he let her, giving in to her desire. Being a slave
to Eliza was more rewarding than being her king. Her
tongue slid past his lips, soft as velvet. He pulled her
hips down harder. She bit his lip.

"Yes." Her hand cupped his face, foreheads touching.

Her sheath rippled around his cock and the sensations
tickled his balls. She ground her hips against him, her
breathing so rough it almost ceased to exist. He held her
there tight as he came, unable to resist any longer.

The caves shuddered and grumbled around them like
they were in the belly of a starving beast. Roan closed
his eyes and held Eliza close. Her heart drummed, echo-
ing the water. His thumbs circled, pressing into her
muscle. The shower washed away his short-lived joy.
He couldn't hold onto Eliza. Sorrow leaned a heavy
hand on his shoulder.

That may have been the last time.

He eased her leg down, resenting every move that put
distance between them. Water ran down the edges of her
face, his fingertips brushed her cheek. No tears fell, but
her eyes were bright. His burned. Roan leaned into the
water to lose himself with Eliza again.

"You don't know what you do to me." His lips tasted
the water scented by her skin. If he could stop time, he
would. They would be locked away from the world forever in a dream of their own making.

"I know what you do to me." The smile on her lips
was as innocent as a butterfly and as pink as a new day
challenging a night washed clean by the rain.

The beast groaned an ugly cry of metal on stone. Roan growled and pulled away. The Hoard couldn't just give up and go home. He touched the rock wall. Fissures were opening under the onslaught. The caves wouldn't protect them forever.

"They haven't breached the rock, yet." He turned off the taps because leaving them on was an invitation to dally.

She took the offered towel and dabbed at her arms before wrapping up in the thick white fabric. "What if the druid helps them?"

"Unlikely, he will be well away from the fight." Roan squeezed the heavy tails of his hair, but they remained waterlogged. "Elryion will pay for what he did to you."

"Don't go after him if it will cost you your soul."

"Today, tonight, tomorrow, it's gone anyway." He dried himself roughly then slung the towel over the shower. "If I kill him, I could break the curse." He jerked on his pants. His wet dreads slapped against his skin. Getting dressed instead of using magic was annoying.

"But if you fail…" She placed a hand on his forearm.

He buckled on his belt, throwing off her touch. "Then I'd rather be dead."

His words ripped through the afterglow. They glared at each other. Neither could win the argument. Both were right. Eliza's mouth opened as if to protest, but her eyes were dark with something other than lust. He wasn't good with what happened afterward unless it involved payment. His anger melted under her gaze. She deserved better than a king with a death wish.

Roan softened his voice. "If I'm gone, he'll leave you alone."

"I'd rather sleep in constant fear and still have you."

"You say that now, but once I've faded only the vaguest shell will remain." His fingers lengthened and grayed. Images of Eliza taking him as a goblin roiled in his mind. He swallowed hard, but the poison had taken hold. "You don't want these hands on your body."

Eliza grabbed his hand, placed it against her face. "I don't care what you look like."

Roan resisted the urge to pull his hand away. Her skin burned his palm like a brand. Temptation after temptation, he was falling for each one she offered. But not this one.

"I do. I want a soul. I want a heart that beats." His hand returned to man-shape. "I want more than hiding in the shadows waiting for your summons."

Eliza looked at her feet. "I know. And I understand, but that doesn't mean I have to like it."

"I never said I did." He lifted her chin and kissed her mouth again. How many kisses could he steal in the time that remained? "Come, rest for a few hours. Elryion can't harm you here."

"And the Hoard?"

"It should take them a while longer to break in. We made plans for this occasion."

"You planned to be attacked?"

"I have to protect what is mine." The Hoard would never claim what was his. But at the same time he couldn't fight them face-to-face without giving in to the curse and fading. Even now the urge to run outside wielding his sword was pumping in his blood. He and Dai had set up old-fashioned-style defense. The kind castles had used to repel would-be invaders. They'd found a use for the river—it was a ready supply of burning oil.

They walked back to his cavern in silence. He stopped at the door.

"You're not coming in."

If he did, he wouldn't leave and he had to assist Dai and make sure he didn't fade and attack the Hoard. But Eliza didn't need to know the details of the battle they would lose. It was only a matter of time until the Hoard won. Time he didn't have.

"I have work to do. Subjects clamoring at my door." He ran his fingers through her damp hair. The golden strands clung to his fingers.

"You'll be here when I wake up?"

He nodded, unable to speak. He wanted to be there every time she woke up. Every time she lay down to sleep. Eliza had shown him that he was more than the curse. A gift more valuable than all the gold he'd ever hoarded.

Chapter 15

ROAN CLOSED THE DOOR, AND SHE WAS ALONE IN HIS ROOM. Cold numbed her feet, yet her body was molten with the heat of their loving. Her skin ached for his touch but every time he touched her, she changed. The layers she'd built to protect herself fell away, but they hadn't protected her. They'd trapped her and weighed her down with other people's expectations. She'd conformed for so long she didn't even know who she was, or what she wanted. Only that she wanted Roan by her side. When he left she would be lost, cast adrift by her goblin lover.

Involuntarily her fingers traced the partially healed scratches on her arms. Eliza bit her lip. He'd healed her with magic. Magic Roan couldn't afford to draw. What would remain of him if he faded? Would she recognize him, or wish that he'd died like he wanted?

Droplets of water trickled down her back. Eliza shivered. Asking him to live on for her was cruel, but expecting her to move on and forget was worse. Water dripped onto the floor. He expected her to sleep while the Hoard attacked, urged on by the druid. She hugged the towel tighter. If nothing else, she needed to get dry and dressed.

An antique set of drawers sat on one side of the room—heavy, carved, and missing the mirror that should have filled the frame that rested on the top. Instead it had been replaced with a polished sheet of gold. Her image was distorted by the imperfect surface. Her face lacked the pale, pinched look that she'd become accustomed to seeing. Instead the gold gave her a glow her skin had never had. She tore her gaze away. It was too easy to become sucked in by an illusion.

She opened the top drawer, sure even the Goblin King had a change of clothes. As expected there were T-shirts. Black. Eliza slipped one over her head. Too big, but not big enough to cover her butt. She wrapped the towel around her hair. The second drawer had socks and black camo. Roan's choice of clothing was as colorful as the landscape.

Better to blend into the shadows.

His pants were too big. They hung off her hips and dragged on the floor. Eliza rolled up the cuffs. While she knew his socks wouldn't fit, they would offer some protection from the ice that formed the core of the Shadowlands. She gave her hair a quick rub, then hung the towel over a handle on the drawers.

Out of curiosity she opened the last drawer. A brilliant blue and red plaid was folded next to dark clothes. On the plaid lay a gold clasp. She picked it up, recognizing it from the memory Dai had shown her. A lump grew in her throat, swelling like a ripening fruit. These were the clothes Roan had been cursed in. The edges of the cavern blurred as tears filled her eyes. He'd kept them to die in. Eliza carefully placed the cloak clasp back down and shut the drawer, feeling like she'd violated a sacred space by peering into his past.

Their relationship had an expiration date. She was going to have to live with that, but she didn't have to forget. She didn't have to move on. There would never be another man able to take Roan's place.

—m—

"We have a problem," Roan said as he joined his brother high on the rock ledge overlooking what had been the entrance to their caves. He glanced over the edge at the goblins below chipping away at the rock. He hadn't been able to seal the caves as well as he'd hoped. The Hoard would break through—the only question was before or after he ran out of soul?

Dai peered over his book seemingly oblivious to the Hoard below. "I had noticed the rowdy neighbors and that the queen was in residence again."

"I thought I asked you to defend the castle in my absence." Roan snatched the book off of him.

"And I am." Dai picked up an empty wine bottle and lobbed it over the edge. A half full one rested next to him. The goblins started attacking each other, each one wanting to be the first to break into the caves. "They don't know we're up here."

"He does." Roan pointed at a bird circling high on non-existent air currents. The druid was supervising the war he'd manufactured. Killing a couple of scouts was easy, but taking on a goblin army was dangerous. Every fight would bring his goblin to the surface. Would he be fighting to defend his home, his gold, or his queen? After what the druid had done to Eliza, he deserved to die.

Roan drew his gun. One good shot would end it now. Usually he was so busy fending off the druid's magic he didn't have a chance to shoot.

Dai put his hand on Roan's arm. "I wouldn't do that.

If the Hoard realizes we're up here they will start climbing, and I doubt you have the magic left to do any more re-sculpting."

When he'd sealed the entrance he'd opened a crack above so they could watch without being seen. That magic, followed by healing Eliza, had used everything he'd had to spare—which hadn't been much to start with. Dai was right. As tempting as shooting the druid was, it would only draw the Hoard's gaze upward. He couldn't afford that because he didn't have enough magic left to seal the rock. He didn't have enough soul left for anything other than existing and even that was tenuous. One wrong step and he was gone. Roan forced himself to re-holster the gun.

"What happened to the river?" When he'd left the water had been a burning final line of defense.

"Him." Dai pointed up at the crow. "Besides, burned goblin smells bad."

"Great." Roan leaned back against the rock and closed his eyes. They'd been reduced to throwing rocks and empty bottles at the enemy. Close to two thousand years of fighting had come down to a single decision.

Act or wait.

Drag out the final moments or go down with his sword in his hand.

One last kiss, or one last night with Eliza.

Roan sighed, the news just got worse. "Elryion attacked Eliza in her sleep. The wounds appeared in the Fixed Realm."

Dai dropped a rock that looked suspiciously like an uncut ruby at the goblins below. "I wondered why she'd called. How bad?"

"Bad." He didn't want to blame Dai…but if he hadn't taken her back to the Fixed Realm she would've been safe…and here when the attack had started. Two scouts had made it into the caves undetected. If they'd gotten hold of her…Roan fisted his hand and pushed the thought down. Eliza was no safer here than she was in the Fixed Realm.

"How did he manage that?"

"I was hoping you could tell me."

Dai shook his head, a frown scaring his forehead. "She would've had to be thinking of him in much the same way we used people's fear of goblins to cross over at first. I didn't think the druid had that skill."

"Maybe he didn't, until he had someone who would fear him." It was his fault Eliza was in danger, but he couldn't bring himself to regret bringing her to the Shadowlands.

"He could kill her in her sleep, and she'd—"

"Wake up dead." Roan thumped the book into his hand, then paused and looked at the cover. Dai hadn't been reading metaphysics, or an ancient text or anything that might be of use. "You're reading Harry Potter? Now?"

"It's the last one. I'm running out of time." Dai took back the book. "Don't you want to know how it ends? You can't wait around for the movies. I can give you the rundown on the last two books."

Roan straightened. He wouldn't make it to see the next lot of summer blockbusters. And he did want to know how the saga ended. "How many pages to go?"

"Two hundred." Dai slid a gold bookmark in to mark his place. "Why did Elryion attack Eliza?"

"Because he wanted to. Because he can. Because he knew it would piss me off and I would use magic to fix the damage." Roan's hand dropped to the hilt of his sword. The blade was sharp despite years of hacking and slicing through the bodies of his summoner's enemies. Battle lust writhed in his veins. It had been too long since he'd colored his sword hot-crimson.

He wanted to paint his sword with sacred druid blood. If he'd had the nerve to do it when first accused of selling out to Rome, they wouldn't be here now. And he would never have met Eliza. Was a few days with her worth the centuries trapped here?

The answer leaped forward, yet he refused to acknowledge the truth. He would wait another two millennia to see her again. She flowed in his blood, brighter than gold and hotter than battle. And she waited in his bed.

His brother watched. His face blank, only the tension in his hands showed how much he wanted to challenge Roan and indulge his own desire to fight. Once they had kept their skills sharp against each other. Now that was too risky. A mock fight could turn vicious; they could fade and fight to the death like goblins without even realizing it. Every day they trod a wider circle, not wanting to trigger a reaction that would end their humanity. Roan eased his hand away. He wouldn't fight his brother.

But he was craving battle almost as much as he needed gold. He picked up a rock and let it fall onto one of the goblins below. Skewering one on a sword would've been far more satisfying. But killing one would achieve nothing when there were another ten to take his place. Elryion had brought the Hoard here *and* he had attacked Eliza.

Roan frowned. "Because he seeks to push me over the edge and end this dance." Wanting Eliza warred with his goblin desires. He glanced up at Elryion who watched the battle from the safety of the sky. "He didn't have to hurt Eliza to do that. I am within stepping distance."

"What if we're close to breaking the curse?" Dai took a drink from his open bottle of wine. The label was obscured by age.

Roan's breath hissed past his teeth as he resisted the urge to drop the bottle over the edge and his brother with it. Had all of Dai's study of useless magics rotted his brain? False hope would gain them nothing.

"How are we any closer to breaking the curse than we were yesterday or the first day?"

"The druid is throwing everything he can at us. Why?"

"Because we're almost there and he can get his life back." The thought of the druid being granted a second chance at life in the Fixed Realm was like acid in his gut. He hoped the bastard got stuck in the Shadowlands.

Dai shook his head. "No. He's running scared because the answer is in front of us." Dai pulled out a black diamond ring. The one Roan had made for himself, should he need it. "Wear it."

"No. Without the magic we are vulnerable." Over the centuries, Roan had tried to protect his men. The four swords hanging on the wall were a testament to his failure. Was Meryn one of the goblins attacking?

"You have no more magic to use. Buy us the time." Dai tossed him the ring.

Roan caught it one-handed. In his palm it was nothing but a trinket. On his finger the darkness receded, like a cancer shrinking from radiation. The magic barely a whisper in his ear. The silence was deafening, but beneath it was a clarity he'd felt before in the Summerland. The bright magic remained out of reach.

Look, but don't touch.

Feel, but never hold.

He slipped the ring off and handed it back to Dai. The darkness returned. No bigger, no darker, just the ever-present pull that waited to consume what was left of his humanity. He had a little soul left, but not enough to buy the magic needed to destroy the druid.

"I can't defeat Elryion without magic. I can't defeat him with it. But I have to face him." He would win or fade—the druid wouldn't let him die. Either way Eliza would be safe and the curse would be over, broken or completed.

"What if Elryion had no magic?" Dai spilled the rest of the black diamonds on the rock ledge.

Roan stared at the burning diamonds. He knew what his brother was proposing, had entertained a similar fantasy, but had dismissed it as the workings of a desperate mind. Elryion would never willingly sever his connection to the Shadowlands and face Roan as a man.

"What's your plan?" Roan asked.

Dai smiled, but it never reached the golden gleam of his eyes. Seeing his younger brother like that stung like salt rubbed into raw flesh. Whatever Dai had concocted was more goblin than human. But maybe goblins could win where men had failed.

"We use your queen as bait."

Roan's face hardened. His brother was mad. The plan had more holes than he had gold coins. Even as he refused to consider the possibility, he knew it was the only one that would force the druid to fight on his terms.

A fight he could win. But would Eliza agree and if she didn't, would it matter? He cut off the thought.

"No."

"Think. How much longer can we hold out here? A day, maybe two? Elryion wants her to destroy you. Who else could get close enough?"

Roan's breathing came hard as he drowned in his brother's words. Anger, betrayal, hope, and fear swarmed, buzzing in his ears. He couldn't answer because he might agree to risk his queen to win the game.

Roan pulled up the shadows and went inside. He started back toward Eliza, then changed his mind. He couldn't face her when the idea of using her to beat the druid was so tempting. Instead he slunk below to the prison and the goblin that kept a silent vigil.

Gob glared. His yellow eyes didn't blink. His knobbled legs were crossed as if he were meditating. He never moved unless gold or raw meat was brought. Then he would rage and tear at the bars, willing to destroy himself to obtain what he wanted. Today Roan had brought nothing for the goblin.

Roan lowered himself to the floor and crossed his legs. He rested his chin on his hands and let the Shadowlands bleed the color from his skin until goblin faced goblin.

Gob blinked.

Roan let his lips curl—a sneer or a smile, it didn't matter. From what he had learned, social hierarchy was determined by who could use a sword the best. Kill the king and take his crown, rule until someone better stole it on the end of a sword. Since Roan was on the outside, he was automatically higher up the food chain.

"Soon I will be all goblin. I want to know what goes on behind those big blank eyes." There had to be something. Something more than mindless greed. Something worth saving.

Gob spoke and revealed worn, yellow teeth. "Him wants gold and meat."

"Tell me something else and I'll set you free." It was a promise Roan had made a hundred times before without any gains. Gob just sat there, asking for meat and gold. He seemed unaware that his brethren were digging their way in. If the Hoard found Gob they wouldn't save him. They would kill him.

Gob cocked his head. "You free him. Him become king."

Roan sighed. "Don't you want your freedom?"

"Him wants freedom. Kill you and take your gold."

A weight settled on his shoulders. It was heavy like the torque around Roan's neck. There was nothing to a goblin. No remnants of a soul, or remembrance of who he had been. All that had died when Gob had become goblin. The greedy soul had swapped humanity for more. More life, more gold, more power.

Roan changed tack. "What about finding a queen?"

"You have queen?" Gob sat up straight. "Him kill you, take your queen. Queen be tasty and pink."

Roan's fingernails dug into his hand. Killing Gob now would serve no purpose except salving his own need for death. "Love. What about love and happiness and honor?"

Gob blinked. "Him loves gold. Gold make him happy."

If he failed and faded, he wouldn't care because there would be nothing to remember with. Everything that made him who he was would be gone. Eliza would be nothing but a tasty pink queen suitable for eating, or fucking, depending on his mood. His dreams were heavier than his golden heart. Unless the curse was broken he could never be her man.

The body of the goblin fell away until only a lost man faced Gob. What kind of man would risk his woman's life?

One who was desperate enough to do anything to be with her. If he wanted Eliza, he was going to have to fight. He would have to fore the druid to face him as a man.

When he reached his chamber Eliza was sleeping in his bed. So peaceful despite the battle the Hoard was waging to get in. Her eyelids flickered as he lay down next to her. The black clothing masked where one body started and the other ended. Roan placed his lips on hers. She responded, still half asleep. Her fingers wove through his dreads. He tried to lose himself, to want nothing more than this moment to last an eternity. His lungs could incinerate with their need for air. Air he could forgo. The cold burn of gold carved a path through every thought and would never leave.

They both panted. She gazed up at him, the gold flecks in her eyes bright with joy. She stole a tiny kiss. The merest taste of his lips, teasing him more than satisfying. He responded in kind. Their lips meeting for partial seconds. A game that couldn't last and one he couldn't finish. He had to tell Eliza the plan and let her decide his fate.

Her fingers traced over his cheek to the corner of his eye. "You're not here with me. What is it, Roan?"

He kissed the palm of her hand, not wanting to tell her, yet not wanting to keep such a deadly secret to himself. It wedged between them, forcing them apart. He murmured against her skin. "There is a way to kill the druid."

She gasped and a smile broke her face letting all the light in her being shine through. "That's fantastic."

Roan shook his head, still cupped by her hand. The beads rang hollow like old empty bones.

"Killing Elryion may not break the curse. Nothing else has. I could still fade. Or," he paused, for one possible good outcome there were three against it, "if it works, I could be trapped here."

They could all be trapped here. That wasn't a risk he was willing to take. He would have to let his brother take Eliza to the Fixed Realm while he faced the druid alone.

Her body stiffened against his. "With the Hoard? Could you not use magic to escape?"

"When I was a man I had no magic. I was a warrior. Not a druid or a sorcerer." His only chance of escaping would be during the northern hemisphere winter solstice. That would mean surviving six months in the Shadowlands without magic to help feed him or fight off the goblins that would eat him while he screamed her name.

"Surely if the curse is broken, you will be returned to the Fixed Realm where you belong." Her fingers flexed against his skin as if she could reshape the answer into something definite.

Did he belong in her world two thousand years away from his? "I don't know if I would exist in the Fixed Realm. I may break the curse only to die. You need to know that so much could go wrong. You need to know the risks. That even if it works, we may never meet again."

Eliza shook her head. "Do you have to do this?" Her voice was small and fragile, but the dream broke anyway.

"I've always had to do this. Now there is a way to succeed." He took a breath. "The diamond that protects you will also stop Elryion from using magic."

"How will you get him to wear one?"

The words shriveled on his tongue. He couldn't ask her. He had no right to ask Eliza for help. Roan looked away, unable to hold her gaze. But it was too late. She'd seen the truth in his eyes.

"You want me to put the diamond on him." The words were slow and well formed so there could be no mistake.

He waited for the refusal, for her to tell him he was insane and to go to hell. For her hands to push him away. He couldn't force her to assist in his battle. If he did, he was already gone. He swallowed and waited for Eliza to determine both their deaths.

She lay completely still. Her breath hardly raised her chest. "How would I do it?"

Roan lifted his gaze. Like the queens of his time, she was willing to fight by his side. The warrior in Eliza had risen and wouldn't be tamed. If his golden heart could have swelled with pride, it would have burst.

"He must wear it." Roan took her hand and kissed the ring he had placed there, claiming her as his for eternity. With Eliza waiting for him in Fixed Realm, he couldn't fail. "I was thinking diamond-and-steel handcuffs."

Chapter 16

ELIZA LAY ON THE BED IN THE GUEST ROOM OF HER HOUSE. NIGHT darkened the windows. Was it the same night she'd left? How long had she spent in the Shadowlands this time? She rolled onto her side to face the watching shadow. The goblin stood, sword in hand, waiting for her to sleep. It would have been easier to sleep if he hadn't been watching.

Dai rolled his yellow eyes. "Go to sleep so we can get this done."

Eliza propped herself up. She wasn't sure she trusted Dai. While he wasn't drinking this time, his eyes were glazed in goblin yellow, and his skin that had lacked the delicate shades of goblin-gray in the Shadowlands was now mottled. He may not be goblin, but he currently looked like a goblin. A very well armed goblin and his presence wasn't conducive to sleep.

"I'm trying. *You're* putting me off."

He snorted. "If Roan were here, there wouldn't be much sleep happening."

Eliza bit her tongue to keep from snapping back. Dai had kept his distance in the caves, but she could feel spines of jealousy breaking through his skin each time he saw Roan and her together. He might be a condemned goblin, but Dai was a man underneath, wanting what all men wanted.

She lay back down. "Can you please put the sword away? You're here to guard me, not kill me."

The metal slid home with a whisper that glided over

her skin and drew a shiver. Eliza pulled the blanket closer. Sleep groped around the edge of her conscious. Roan waited for her to call him to the Summerland. But she wasn't ready to see him. If she failed, the fight was over. Their chance was gone.

"What do you think about before battle?"

Dai glared at her, never blinking. "Death."

Her fingers tightened on the edge of the blanket. She peered into the dark. "Seriously?"

"The waste of lives." The shadow slid along the wall. "I've seen too many people cut down on a fevered fancy. Blood shed over a disagreement that could have been solved by words, not weapons."

"But if there is no other way, is that okay?" Eliza watched the shadow shrink into the chair.

Dai laughed, high, almost manic. "Don't ask a goblin to differentiate right from wrong. The answer will never be true."

"I'm helping Roan kill."

"Elryion deserves to die." Dai's voice was like a sack full of broken glass being dragged over concrete. Bitterness made sharp edges out of his words.

"His life for yours?" She wanted to believe it was a fair trade. But she didn't want to wake up and look at Roan with the constant memory that she had killed a man to keep her lover.

"Elryion made that deal when he set the curse. Curses require care and commitment. They must be tended. To curse someone is to bind your life to theirs until the curse is complete or broken."

"You've studied magic." Her eyelids bounced as she tried to stay awake.

"I've studied many things."

Eliza nodded and yawned. Dai had had many lifetimes to learn, and then forget, anything he wanted. She forced her eyes open. Roan had kept her awake in the Shadowlands. The one short nap in his bed wasn't enough. The lack of sleep was catching up. She would trade a month of sleep for one more hour of certainty.

"Will this work?"

The goblin shrugged. "If it does, we are fools for not trying sooner. If it fails, then we have lived for as long as we can."

"Roan thinks he will get stuck in the Shadowlands." It was why he'd insisted she leave and have Dai at her side as a precaution. When she'd argued, he told her she would be a distraction. Distraction brought death. They all had their role to play. The stage was set.

Dai had found the diamonds. Roan had spent all but his last fragment of soul on making the handcuffs for the druid. She had to lure the druid close enough to put them on. It all seemed so easy, except she had never done anything so dangerous in her life.

"We don't know what will happen. Nineteen centuries is a long time to be alive and not quite human."

"You aren't worried for your brother?"

Dai sighed. "Of course I am. He is the only family I have."

The sting poked a hole in the fine fabric of sleep. She'd been so busy thinking about her possible loss that she'd not seen Dai was facing the loss of what was left of his family. She'd been there and survived. They would survive together and find a way to get Roan back. She lifted her head. No yellow eyes glowed in the corner.

He'd closed them. Sometimes it was easier to be blind to reality.

Eliza whispered, "If the curse breaks and he gets stuck, you can stay here."

There was silence from the shadow lurking in the corner. She'd offended him. He didn't like her, so he certainly wouldn't want her help.

Then he spoke and his words sounded more like the rustling of leaves still on the tree, soft and full of longing as they reached for the sun. "Thank you. I've spent so long as a goblin, I'm not sure I can live in this world."

"Neither am I." She yawned. A world without magic, love, and Roan would be as colorless as the Shadowlands.

Eliza blinked. She lifted her hand against the sunlight washing the meadow with gentle heat. She'd fallen asleep. She didn't need to speak his name. Thought alone was enough for Roan to appear.

He smiled, but it was tight. He watched the sky for clouds and birds. "I can't stay."

As he spoke, the grass at his feet turned brown. The Summerland dying from his touch. Deer grazed near the trees. They lifted their heads at the sound of his voice as if sensing the coming danger. Roan handed her the handcuffs, his hand clasping hers. The diamonds revealed their true fire as they caught the sun and held the heat in their heart. But they were still cool to touch, and the steel was heavy in her hand.

She lifted her gaze from the handcuffs. Roan's blue eyes challenged the sky of the Summerland in brilliance. Her dreams were tied up with him. Without his touch she would die. She reached up for a quick kiss, yet he dragged her close and she couldn't hold back. Her hands disappeared in his hair. Lips went from gentle to crushing. She needed Roan more than air. His armor was hard against her skin. The thin fabric of her pajamas offered no protection, but there was too much between them and they were out of time.

Roan loosened his hold and ran the back of his hand over her cheek. "I'll see you in the Fixed Realm."

Her lips burned and her eyes stung, but she forced a smile. Then he was gone. Where he had been standing, the grass grew back, breaking through the ground and uncurling in a few heartbeats as if he had never stood there. Among the green blades were tiny pink flowers. They grew only where Roan had touched.

Eliza picked one. The pink flower was no bigger than her thumbnail. She tucked it behind her ear and sat down to wait with the handcuffs tucked under her leg. As her fingers traced the curved edge, she realized Roan had never given her the key. The sun lost its warmth as she realized why—the druid would die with them on. She removed her hand from the cuff and tried to enjoy her surroundings. She was one of the few people who got to enjoy the beauty of the Summerland.

It was the same as it had always been. The same as the day Roan had brought her here to give her the bead when she was sixteen. She understood why now. He hadn't wanted her to see him as a goblin. So instead she'd seen him dressed in his usual black, armed like a warrior. No living man could ever match up with the memory he'd left her with. No man would ever be able to live up to the reality. She wouldn't be able to come back here if she knew he wasn't waiting. Would she ever be able to dream again without him?

No, this had to work. All curses could be broken no matter what Roan said. But a kiss hadn't worked, and her offering to be queen and lying with him hadn't worked. The Summerland offered no hints.

Around her, deer grazed. Butterflies dressed in impossibly bright hues danced over the meadow. The sky remained cloudless. It was like a kiddie cartoon. And she was bored…well, not bored exactly, but waiting was dragging out the inevitable. Did the druid know of the plan?

She swallowed and checked her watch. The hands spun with no regard for the passing of time. Was she really waiting when nothing in the Summerland changed?

Eliza plucked half a dozen of Roan's pink flowers. She could make her own measure of time. With her nail she split the emerald green stem then threaded another flower through it. The wait would be measured by the length of the pink flower chain.

A crown rested on her hair and a bracelet hung off each wrist before she was out of flowers. She ran her hand over the place where Roan had stood, but no trace of him remained. The grass darkened as if thrown into shadow. Eliza looked up. She didn't need to shield her eyes—the sun was a pale disk smothered by gray clouds. The Shadowlands was coming for her.

The crow swooped through the sky, death and decay rolling behind him in a tide of unstoppable gray. The deer lifted their heads. As the wave of death reached them, their sleek, fat bodies thinned so bones pushed hard against their patchy pelt. These were the animals that roamed the Shadowlands, animals that spelled hunger and starvation at the end of a hard winter.

These were the animals Roan and his men had hunted to survive.

The dying grass swept toward her and surrounded her. Eliza forced herself to remain sitting. There was no sense in running from the druid. The crow rushed past. Feathers hit her cheek.

She turned and yelled, "Kill me. I want to die. Set me free."

The words sounded like lies to her ears, but the crow turned sharply. Eliza turned to face the waiting bird. She crossed her bare toes and hoped Roan was listening and really nearby in case the druid killed her before she could snap on the handcuffs.

"The Goblin King has trapped me. He seeks to keep me. Help me…please." Out of her mouth came Roan's words, carefully crafted to appeal to the druid's vanity, his belief in his superior power and his hatred of Roan.

The bird landed. Feathers shook and a man appeared. He wore a white robe and plain boots. He'd never updated his look, or maybe he couldn't since he hadn't left the Shadowlands in nineteen hundred years. His curse had bound him to the Shadowlands, and unlike Roan, he wasn't goblin so he couldn't use people's nightmares as a means to visit the Fixed Realm. She squashed the pang of pity that tried to gain hold on her heart. This man would kill her without thought if it meant he would be free.

"How do I break his hold? I don't want to be a goblin queen."

The druid approached. His face was blank, colder than the gray dust beneath her knees. He squatted in front of her and reached out with his bony hand to grasp her chin. Staring into his eyes was like peering through the empty socket of a skull. Only shadows lurked where once a man had been. Iced nails scraped down her spine, touching each nerve and drawing it tight.

"Only death can grant freedom. Your choice, his or yours."

Eliza swallowed. Her fingers closed on the handcuffs. All she had to do was latch them over his wrist. They would close and lock. Her heart slowed, pumping strange, thick blood through her limbs. Her muscles obeyed but every action was delayed.

"Or maybe he should choose." The druid turned her head as if studying her. "Shall we find out whose life he values more?" He leaned in close, his fingers caressing her cheek, and he whispered in her ear, "He's goblin, so I think we both know the answer."

Her body caught up with her mind. She slid the handcuffs from under her leg and wrapped the metal around the wrist of the hand gripping her face. The cuff snapped closed around the druid's arm and shrunk until it cut into his skin.

The druid yanked his hand back. "What is this? What manner of trickery?" He clawed at the steel. His face twisted as he tried to comprehend what had happened.

Eliza scrambled away. Her feet hit something solid, and she glanced over her shoulder. Sword drawn, gun holstered. She knelt at the feet of her warrior. Roan touched her hair. His hand was gentle, but his fierce gaze remained on the druid. Then she fell until the dream became reality.

Her body jerked awake with the impact. The mattress was as hard as stone. She sat up, her breath burning her lungs. The shadows in her bedroom swelled, taking the shape of a goblin. A sword cut through the moonlight and stopped one inch from her neck.

A scream caught in her teeth. Her eyes were wider than the attacking goblin's.

"What happened?" Dai lowered the sword.

Eliza swallowed. Her throat was rough like sandpaper. "He sent me back."

"Did you cuff the bastard?"

She nodded.

Dai slammed his sword into his sheath. He held his hands out in the silvery light. They both watched, looking for a pinkening of skin that would mark the end of the curse. Seconds stretched out into years as the world held its breath, waiting for the return of the last Decangli king.

Roan swung his blade as he stalked toward Elryion. If he used magic, his soul would crumble into dust. One wrong step and he would be taken by the depthless abyss. If the diamond had failed to work, Elryion would have already flown away. But the diamond held him trapped. For the first time in too many years, Roan had the upper hand. The druid was his for the killing.

He drew in a breath of tasteless air. This was a moment to savor.

Elryion stepped back. Blood welled from the scratches on his wrist. "What magic is this?"

"No magic." The sword was light in his hand. He was within striking distance. One well-placed slice would kill him fast. A dozen well-placed cuts would kill him slow. There were still important decisions to make before the druid died.

Elryion tensed, his face turned red, but no magic came to his aid. "You break the old laws if you kill me."

The laws the druid clung to had died out hundreds of years ago along with the rest of the British tribes. Once he had feared breaking the old rules, believing shedding druid blood would only damn them further. Now he was beyond caring. "I would be a free criminal over a cursed goblin any day of the week." He flicked the sword.

"Your soul will never find peace."

"What other damnation could be wrought on me?" He leveled the sword at Elryion's chest. The blade would slip smoothly past the ribs and rip through the druid's heart—assuming he still had one.

"Free me, damn yourself." Elryion dropped his hands to his side. He gazed calmly at Roan, a smile on his thin lips. "My death will achieve nothing."

The sword didn't move. Calm flowed through Roan.

"I'll take the chance." Roan thrust the sword, knowing the death of the last druid would forever stain his hands.

Elryion twitched. Disbelief stretched his features. He looked down at the sword impaling his body.

"How does it feel having your heart filled with cold metal? An undeserved fate delivering your death?" Roan pulled his sword free. Elryion's flesh sucked at the blade as if reluctant to release the weapon. "I have lived for this moment."

"Then you have wasted your life." Scarlet bubbles colored Elryion's lips.

"You denied me my life." Everything he should've

done, should've been, had passed him by. A future was all he hoped for.

Elryion's legs buckled. Blood splashed onto the gray dust. "I protected our people."

"You damned us all. Every Decangli who died because of Rome is your responsibility." Every one of his people that he was ordered to kill at the command of the Roman general was because of Elryion. Roan grabbed the white robes. His sword fell to the ground and lay naked in the dust. "You cursed the wrong man. I would have protected us. We could've fought back and won."

Breath ceased to move the body of the druid. Roan let the corpse fall from his hand. It bounced softly in the dust.

"It's over."

Blood spilled from the wound. The dirt drank its fill until the ground was sodden and seemed to bleed in sympathy over such a heinous crime. The cold ache in his chest increased. He placed a hand over his heart. No beat stirred his blood. He closed his eyes and sank to his knees. The one death that should've meant something failed to stir even the smallest response.

"It's over." He thumped his fist against his chest as if to kick-start the reluctant muscle. But he knew his heart wouldn't respond. It was still cast in gold. He was still trapped and his soul was sliding through his fingers.

The sweet darkness of a whispered promise offered no more fighting. All he had to do was let go. Let go and he could be reborn as a goblin. He ignored the star that marred the endless night and reached out into the darkness, but what looked like velvet cut like razors. Roan pulled his hand back. There would be no peace in giving up, only an eternity of denied fulfillment. A craving never satisfied. The only desire he had was to feel Eliza's skin beneath his fingertips one more time. Let her warmth encase him and her smile free him. The white star bloomed like a supernova on the horizon so bright he had to open his eyes to escape the glare.

The body of the last druid lay sullen in the dirt. If the gods still cared, they might forgive him. If they didn't, he no longer cared. His fight was over. There was only one way left to avoid fading. Roan picked up his sword and wiped the blade clean on the edge of Elryion's robe. Then he stood and sheathed the blade. Never had a death achieved so little.

"May you drink in the Hall of the Gods." He took a handful of dirt. "I doubt there'll be a place for me." Roan threw the gray dust over the corpse in a token burial. He refused to use the magic that would damn him to burn the man who had tried.

He would have the last victory.

He would die when he was ready.

He would love Eliza one last time.

Then it would be over.

Roan turned his back and fell into the Fixed Realm. He didn't see the pale green shoots that peeked out from the gray dust, marking where he had knelt. And he didn't see them die when he left.

Chapter 17

THE SHADOWS BENT TO HIS WILL AS ROAN MOVED BETWEEN the realms on a whim. His heart remained silent, a fist of gold that wouldn't melt. Stepping into the bedroom where Dai and Eliza waited took more courage than facing an entire Roman legion.

The beads in his hair whispered his failings in his ear. His queen and brother turned. They may not be able to see him, but they knew he was there, wrecking the dream and bringing despair. Their desperate hope was etched on their faces. The unanswered questions that pulled their lips tore at his innards with wounds that would never heal. He had failed.

Roan released the shadows. He would be seen while he faced the jury. He would tell the truth and pay the penalty.

Dai severed the silence. Their language was twisted by the rasping goblin voice. "What happened?"

The words bled out, smothering the dream of life after curse. How could he tell his brother it was over? That Elryion had spoken the truth. His death had only bought their death.

Roan looked at Eliza. She had risked her life to help and he could never repay her. He spoke in English because she deserved to know, even if she didn't want to believe.

"Elryion is dead." The sweet metallic scent of sacred druid blood clung to his sword, his skin, his soul.

Neither moved. His announcement had turned Eliza

and Dai to stone. But he knew what they were thinking. They knew what it meant. The choice was very simple—fade or die. Goblin or suicide. He wanted a third option. Any third option would do. He had a cavern full of gold and still he couldn't buy the correct answer.

"But nothing happened." Eliza's forehead creased. "You're still—"

"When?" Dai cut her off.

Roan closed his eyes and took a breath.

When? When was a good time to die? Today? Tonight? Next week? A year from now? When would he be ready to leave Eliza? He would fade before he was ready.

Roan gave Dai a pointed look. "I would spend some time with Eliza first."

Dai nodded. His wide, yellow eyes still understood the human need to say good-bye. Shadows engulfed him as he withdrew to the Shadowlands. Then Roan was alone with Eliza.

She slid off the bed, dressed for sleep but wide awake. "What now?"

Roan stood his ground even though he wanted to retreat into the shadows and hide his face from his queen.

"Nothing." His fingers reached out. He touched the tangled strands of her hair. It was softer than silk against his skin. He was caught in a web of broken dreams and desire.

She shook her head. He let his hand drop. His skin craved her warmth, the softness of her body, the sigh of her breath against his ear.

"There can be no tomorrow, Eliza. It's over."

"It can't be over." She gripped his hand as if she could stop him from leaving "There has to be a way."

He flinched but didn't pull away. He couldn't pull away from the person who had held his gray hand and not recoiled in fear. The heat from her skin seeped through his flesh, searing deep. But it still couldn't soften his heart.

"I don't have the time left to keep looking." He touched her cheek. "I don't want to quit. But the alternative is worse. The goblin I become won't be me." No matter how hard he tried to believe otherwise, none of the goblins he'd studied had held onto even a glimmer of humanity.

"How long?" She gazed up at him. The gold in her eyes shimmered.

"Not long." The darkness was breathing down the back of his neck, so close he could feel the tips of its jagged teeth. So he looked forward, only to be blinded by the bright star that now blotted his familiar darkness. If he reached for the star, he would burn or fall. "I can't take you with me to the Shadowlands. It's too risky."

His home was besieged. His universe was imploding and all he could do was watch the shock waves spread, hurting everyone they touched. Chaos everywhere he looked.

She pressed her lips together. If he were a man, she wouldn't have hesitated to place her mouth to his. If he were a man, he wouldn't have hesitated to take her on the bed.

"Eliza…" Roan leaned in. His lips touched her hair, not her skin, not like this. Not in this gray, ugly body. He inhaled her scent. Fresh, female, flowers. All things he missed in the Shadowlands. Would they haunt him in death?

"I will go back to sleep. We can be together." She

fisted both her hands around his.

Her grip crushed his swollen knuckles. He knew what she was asking. He should refuse to meet her in the Summerland, but he couldn't. He wanted to spend every last second he could eke out of his soul with her as a man, not a goblin.

"You have a life." One he couldn't be part of. "You cannot live in a dream, waiting for me."

She spoke in a whisper, begging him to stay. "Please. Don't leave, yet. I know…I understand what you have to do. I just…I'm not ready to say good-bye."

Roan wrapped his arm around her. The cold of his metal heart spread, taking over all space in his chest. "Neither am I." The truth didn't set him free. It caught in his throat like a burr. "I will come tonight."

To keep his promise, there would be no more use of magic for anything other than moving between realms. An instinct he would have to fight or wear the black diamond ring that weighed down his pocket waiting to be used.

He kissed the top of her head and let the shadows swallow him. Cutting out his heart would have been less painful. It didn't beat. It served no purpose except to remind him of what he wasn't, and what he would never be again.

A man.

Roan's sigh filled the glittering cavern. He felt every one of his one thousand nine hundred and seventy-one years as he sat on an iron-bound chest filled with Spanish gold. He had thought he'd get one more birth-day, but now he wouldn't even be able to last the couple of weeks to Dai's. Around him the rock rumbled as it gave into the greedy hands of the attacking Hoard. They would break in and steal his gold. And he should give a damn, yet all he could think about was the queen he'd left in the Fixed Realm.

In his fingers he worked a dread, rolling the clump of hair. He'd spent many hours creating and then maintaining the headful of bead-dressed snakes. He'd always had time to waste. His fingers smoothed over a bead. Gold. The geometric pattern carved into its surface once had offered comfort. A reminder of the hard won control. A reward for disobedience. A show of wealth.

Worthless.

His life amounted to a pile of gold that no one would ever see. Gold was nothing but a shiny yellow metal. Too soft to be a weapon. Too cheap to purchase a soul.

The rock walls were coated in its sickly sheen. But in here Eliza had glistened, her skin had been damp with sweat, and the gold in her hazel eyes was brighter than any coin he had claimed. He sighed. If he'd never taken her as queen, death would have been a welcome reprieve and not a cowardly escape.

"Where's your queen?" Dai leaned in the hole in the wall. His gaze roamed over the piles of coins and death masks of leaders long dead. Their memory was cast in gold like they could buy immortality with a shell that bore their likeness.

He watched as his brother became mesmerized, his eyes changing from blue to yellow. The curse finally showed its strength in the one he had thought immune. And it had moved quickly once it had caught him, dragging Dai into its viselike grip. The black diamond didn't return what had already been lost. It only slowed the gradual digestion of the soul. Of all the men who'd passed, watching his brother fade was the hardest.

Roan stood. "I can't bring her if I can't guarantee her return."

They needed to leave this place before Dai lost his battle. He wasn't sure he had the fight left to kill his brother. Dai was all that remained of his family, his people, his kingdom.

He put his arm around Dai's shoulders and drew his brother from the cavern. Dai followed without fight. His eyes returned to blue away from the golden lure. Magic tingled in the ends of Roan's fingers and ran cool in his blood. He could seal the cavern to prevent Dai from staring at the gold, but he would pay a pointless price and they would both fade.

"I'm sorry you couldn't lie with her again." Dai shrugged off Roan's arm.

Roan shook his head. He wished he could believe his brother's words, but they were too close to goblin for them to be real. "No you're not. How long until you would have challenged me and tried to take her?"

Dai rubbed his hand over his chin. "Sooner rather than later. You've fought this battle for centuries. But I am falling fast. Without the diamond I would be gone already."

"The curse took us all differently." Some never got to feel the lust for gold. Fane had taken his own life. His spirit crushed by the harshness of the Shadowlands and the starvation rations of bony animals and bark from stunted trees. In desperation they'd killed a goblin. But none of them had been able to eat what they would become. Learning to enter the Fixed Realm at will through nightmares had saved them for a worse fate. Hope that they may succeed and be free.

"How goes our defense?" Roan said as he stepped over the rubble left over from his temper tantrum.

"It should hold until we are dead."

Then the Hoard would have the run of the caves. His home. His chamber where he had brought Eliza. His bed. Roan pushed aside the bitter thoughts. There was nothing he could do. In his mind this moment hadn't been flavored with bitterness and regrets. He'd had years to make peace with death, yet he couldn't bring himself to face the end.

In the dining room, the four swords hung on the wall. Roan pulled them down. The sword they'd hung for Meryn was a stand-in. If he was still alive, he'd be running with the Hoard and his sword would still be in use. Roan allowed himself a grim smile. The sword had never been Meryn's favorite weapon. He laid each blade on the table so they could dine together again.

"How long are we going to tread the edge?" Dai ran his fingers along the edge of metal.

"Are you so keen to die?" Before Eliza it had been him ready for the bullet, only holding on to give Dai more time. Dai had always had hope. The man on the other side of the table was a sad copy of the man his brother had been. Even when taken by Rome for educating he had remained true to the Decangli, encouraging the rebellion at every turn despite the risk. Now the curse had finally broken him.

"Are you so driven by desire you will risk becoming Hoard? Will you honor the pact?" Dai lifted Fane's sword so the tip rested against the flesh beneath his chin. His blue eyes darkened. "Or should I take care of myself?"

Roan looked away. He didn't want to see his brother's blood on the table. "Stay your hand. I will. But not today. Enough blood has been shed." Roan laid his sword on the table. "Let us dine with the ghosts today. Tonight I will see Eliza in the Summerland. Tomorrow will come soon enough."

Dai let the sword bang into the table. "If you return to find me gray and one with the Hoard don't let me live like that."

Doubt and a decaying lack of trust strung between them as fine as the silk spun by spiders and twice as strong. Bound together until the end tore through and burned all ties that made them human. Roan placed his hand over his frozen heart. "You have my word. You have always had my word."

But did he have the time to see Eliza when his castle was crumbling and his soul was disintegrating?

Dai's fingers circled the hilt of his sword. He nodded. "Then let's save the last meal until we are truly dead. Let the ghosts come to show us the way to the Hall of the Gods."

"And until then?" There were hours to fill until Eliza would sleep. Here they would be rationed out like grains of rice to a starving man desperate for sustenance. He'd hoped to pass his final day with his brother, but his brother was fading away.

"Until then I have things to do. Distractions to find. Gold to hoard."

"Don't make light of the shadows nipping at your heels."

"I speak the truth. I have centuries to make up for. So while you plot your death in fine detail, I will go out. Just make sure you include me." Dai smiled and for a moment the old humor was back in his eyes. "Maybe Gob could light the pyre and send us off."

Roan picked up his sword and slid it home. Gob wouldn't do anything that didn't benefit Gob. Burning the dead served no purpose when goblins had no spirit to send off.

"Happy looting. Keep your eyes out for a book on curse breaking."

"Unless it is made of gold, I have no longing for books. My head is full, and my heart is empty." Dai became a darkened outline, then he was gone. Finding a nightmare and sliding away into the Fixed Realm.

Roan stared at the empty table. They had never all sat at this table. But the memories of his men had always been welcome. Today they crowded around, leaving no room for the living.

Through the rock walls he heard the howls of the Hoard as they worked their way through the rock he had sealed the entrance with. He would have to add more or they would break in. He looked at his hands and sighed. He would have to do it without magic. One rock at a time the way any man would.

His anger hadn't been wasted. If he hadn't torn the walls up, he wouldn't have anything to block the entrance with. At the moment any extra distance between him and the Hoard was a good thing.

When his hands ached and his skin was rough, Roan stopped. He admired his drystone wall, and while he knew it would be broken down more easily than solid rock, it was a start. His back ached and for a moment he felt almost human. It had been a long time since he hadn't used magic for everything. He flexed his fingers. A smile spread on his lips. He was at the end of a dead end road, and yet he hadn't been this human in centuries.

He climbed up to the ledge to check on what was happening outside. The number of Hoard goblins had been swelling as word got around. As they gathered, fights broke out. Now it was a pitched battle with each faction fighting for digging rights. They would dig until defeated and another mob would move in. Their own greed was slowing them down. Out of habit, Roan checked the sky for the druid's crow.

It was empty.

He turned away not wanting to watch the battle and deaths. Inside he walked back down the tunnel, winding deeper into the rock. On his way he dropped into the Fixed Realm, and back, without breaking his stride. Somewhere, someone was always having a nightmare and it was enough that he could flit through to anywhere he wanted. It hadn't always been so easy. It hadn't gotten easier because he'd gotten better. It had gotten easier as his soul had shrunk and the Shadowlands had become part of him. Once his soul was gone he'd be like Gob. Soulless and trapped, existing only for gold. In his hands were two plates of steak and fries. Someone would be waiting for their orders a little longer.

Gob stared at the wall unaware of the attempts of his brethren to break into the caves. His eyes were bright with the same luminescence as a glow-stick, and he had as little substance between his long pointed ears. Roan placed one plate at the edge of the bars. The goblin went from comatose to beast in less than a second. His long fingers scooped meat and carrots, pouring them into his wide mouth like he wouldn't eat again.

He wouldn't.

Roan picked up his knife and fork. While Gob slurped and chewed like a pig digging through slop, Roan ate without tasting. He'd hoped to find something within each goblin they'd caught that resembled humanity, or at least remembered it. Never had he found such a creature. He wasn't vain enough to think he could be the first.

Gob picked up his plate and licked it clean through the bars. Then he did something unexpected. He slid the plate into the cell.

Roan swallowed and placed his cutlery down. "Why do you want the plate?"

"Him likes the plate. Has gold." Gob's hand caressed the edge of the plate.

Like Roan's, it had a thin line of gold around the rim. He'd failed to notice something that should have brought a little joy to the meal.

"Did you like your meal?"

"Gold on the plate." Gob licked the plate again like he was trying to remove the gold foil with his tongue.

Was Gob less human than all the others, or was Roan less goblin for knowing Eliza? Not that it mattered. Gob and he would share the same fate. While the previous goblins had either been killed or had killed each other, Gob was trapped under the mountain. Without magic Roan couldn't open the rock or the bars. Because Gob was goblin he couldn't exit via the Fixed Realm. Goblins could only pass through during the winter solstice. Locked in the cell, Gob had missed the Wild Ride.

Roan pulled a coin out of his pocket. It flashed yellow in the candlelight—bright enough to draw Gob's eye from the plate. Roan flicked it onto the floor. It spun a foot away from the bars. Gob lunged for the treasure. Roan drew his sword, willing Gob to see the trap and pull back. Gob flung his body onto the point of the blade to reach the coin.

The goblin never looked up, even as Roan twisted the sword, his yellow eyes remained fixed on the coin. His fingers scrabbled on the floor while his body died. Roan remained still, unable to move. The sword became heavy with the weight of death. When the numbness receded Roan pulled the bloodied blade free. Black grease smeared the surface. Goblin blood. He wiped the blade on his black camo and sheathed it. Then he placed the coin in Gob's hand, closing the gray fingers over the metal.

"It wasn't even gold," Roan murmured, careful not to wake the newly dead.

A golden-colored alloy had been all it took to drive Gob into a frenzy worth dying for. Roan closed the goblin's eyes so he wouldn't have to stare at his rock prison while he waited for the Shadowlands to reclaim his body.

Hopelessness rode Roan's back like a demon. Whipping and shrieking to drive him on and over the edge of the abyss. The last of the Decangli would have to light their own pyre and then find the courage to climb aboard.

An aberration of history, a glitch in the nightmare, a fairy tale best forgotten. Only Eliza would carry his memory forward. How long would she hold on to something more fragile than a dream conceived at dawn?

—m—

Without the goblins, the bedroom was lighter and emptier, like the air had been sucked out by the vacuum of Roan's departure. Eliza crumpled onto the bed and wrapped herself in the quilt. She'd helped kill a man for no good reason. The murder had chewed up the night and spat out the morning, leaving a bitter taste in her mouth. Roan was still on the verge of fading, and she couldn't let him go to find peace in the ever-open arms of death.

She was convinced she could love the gray-skinned monster that stalked the shadows of her room. But could she really welcome him into her arms, knowing his heart would never beat for her? Without a soul, was he really Roan or just another goblin? She didn't have the guts to find out or the cruel streak to demand he fade and test the theory. Every goblin she'd seen had been killed by Roan, and that should've been enough of a warning.

From the bedside table she picked up the half-read book, *Goblins: Myth or Truth?* She pulled out her bookmark and continued reading, needing to understand, to absorb, that a goblin was less than a gray and twisted human. She was looking for anything that would make separation easier. She wanted to read of the evil that goblins brought to the world. The folk tales that warned children of being greedy in case the goblins claimed them as their own. As a child she'd always left a coin in the garden on winter solstice so the goblins would be too distracted to look inside. And she slept with a light on to keep the shadows at bay.

One small section referred to a group of warriors who

were cursed and forced to answer all summons. Their crimes were not their own. Her lips twisted. That wasn't a random passage. She flicked to the bibliography. *What is a goblin?* A small unpublished volume of work by an unnamed author that presented an alternative to recorded history. It had been found during library renovations at Oxford. Had Dai written a defense for the actions they'd been compelled to take? The rest of the page was dedicated to warnings about summoning the Goblin King; he didn't always obey and the summoner would often find themselves tricked out of gold.

Eliza read through a few more pages of historical accounts of misdeeds and solstice mayhem that made no mention of queens, or the eating of humans, or any act of goblin kindness. But each new revelation failed to squash her hope. Roan was still human. He still had a chance.

An ink sketch drew her attention. Taken out of a retired harlot's diary it was a picture of a goblin wearing the dress of the day, long coat and breeches, so he looked the part of a rich man. But the head had a hooked nose and the eyes were too large. His long, curled ears were covered by shoulder-length dreadlocks, decorated in beads. Eliza kicked off the covers, suddenly too hot. Roan.

The whore claimed to have been at his service and had been made rich for her efforts. She made no mention of being in the Shadowlands, or of seeing Roan as a man. But her tales of goblin sex had titillated and horrified the town. She'd been burned at the stake in an attempt to drive out the demons that possessed her. Eliza's stomach turned. She slammed the book closed.

She didn't want to read about her lover's previous flings or how much he had paid. He must have been so terribly lonely in the Shadowlands.

Her legs cramped as she unfolded them and moved for the first time in hours. She stretched, readying herself for the sprint downstairs to turn off the alarm. She couldn't bring herself to enter the room where she and Steve had slept. Not yet. Her racing footsteps were muffled by the carpet. The alarm started its countdown. The steady beeps warned of the impending screech. She was going to have to get the security system rewired. This was not a good way to start the day.

She typed in the code and held her breath. The house went silent. Her heartbeat was too loud and seemed to echo off the walls. She stood alone in the foyer of her parent's house. The house she'd expected to leave when she married, but come back to visit with her husband and kids. Family dinners with Matt, Amanda, and Brigit. Steve had never been in the picture. She'd never thought of him as her husband. He'd just been there like a boy-friend of convenience, meeting her father's approval while she studied law.

When had she outgrown him?

Maybe if she'd loved Steve more, he wouldn't have needed to steal the money to feel worthy. She wandered into the dining room. She could see Roan at the table. Could see him talking to her father. Telling tales of ancient battles. He'd smile at her and wink, their secret that he'd actually been there. He'd be friendly with Matt, but he'd never forgotten the danger Matt's drunken friend had placed her in. If not for that party, she would never have met Roan. If he hadn't helped her then and scared away

Matt's friend, Ben, she would never have called him
again after Steve's betrayal.

What good was meeting a frog-prince when a kiss
wouldn't break the curse? Eliza crossed her arms and
laid her head on the table. What point had any death
served? Only Steve had benefited, using her grief to
bind her to him. Even that had come back to punish him.

Nothing had worked out the way it should have. She
was supposed to be a lawyer, the Coulter in Gunn and
Coulter. Her life had skidded so far off the track she
didn't know how to find her way back. Without Roan
she was lost. After tonight, no matter how much she
called he wouldn't answer.

Another useless death.

Her breath became thick like a wet towel. Tears
clouded her vision, then spilled on the table. Fat drops
splashed her scarred arms as they broke on the table.
But she didn't care. It was better to get it out now
rather than later. There was no sense in making Roan's
death harder than it had to be for him. If it were her
in his boots, she doubted she would have the strength
of will to go through with it. He had a gold heart and
titanium balls.

She choked on her tears, coughed, and sat up. He
wasn't dead, yet. Eliza wiped her face with her hands,
then her wet fingers on her pajamas. No more crying.
She tried to shake off the misery that had tied itself to
her limbs. But the knots had swollen with her tears. She
knew it would be weeks until they dried enough for
her to live again. Months until she could unravel them.
Years until the chaff marks faded and the wound was
nothing more than a memory that twinged and tugged

when the weather turned. Without Roan, she would just be going through the motions of living.

Eliza pushed back her hair. She had things to do. She made a mental list. Ring the security firm. Ring Gunn and make sure everything was okay. She should cancel her leave since there wasn't going to be a honeymoon. Being back at work would give her something to do. She would be living each day, only to die each night when Roan haunted her dreams instead of being her dream.

For there to be no honeymoon there had to be no wedding. She had to call WPD and cancel the society drama she never wanted. A church filled with celebrities she knew through her mother. Kiss, kiss, is this the right place to be seen? Or politicians keeping ties, asking if she intended to keep her father's legacy alive and stand as a candidate.

All she'd ever wanted was her friends and family to attend. There were precious few left. Many had edged away as Steve had pushed and inserted his own people. Cardboard stand-ins he thought would enhance his standing.

Calls she didn't want to make. She picked up the phone and it rung in her hand, lighting up, demanding she answer. *No comment* hovered on her tongue.

"Hello?"

"Ms. Coulter." Not the press. The voice was too slick and sure of itself.

She responded, guard up. "Yes."

"Andrew Timms. I'm representing Steven Slade."

And so it began. Steve would've had a lawyer ready to meet him at the police station. He wouldn't have breathed in front of the police without recommendation.

"I'm not sure how I can be of assistance." *I don't want to be of assistance. That man may have destroyed my law firm.*

"I'm sure you're aware that to be released from custody Mr. Slade requires surety bail."

Eliza paused with her mouth open. This had to be a prank call. Not even Steve would be so audacious as to ask her for bail money. Stunned silence was all she could manage in response.

"Ms. Coulter, without bail Mr. Slade could spend six months in jail awaiting trial."

The breath she'd been holding escaped. Six months of knowing exactly where Steve was. He wouldn't come knocking on her door or ringing at all hours. There was no way a judge was going to let him walk with time spent. On the flip side it was a first offense so he would only get two years tops with parole after one. She would have one year to rebuild and move on.

One year would have to do. He may not be going to jail for the five years of torment he put her through, of never being safe or sure of herself, but she would take the reprieve and be grateful he'd get something. The other inmates would ensure he'd never forget.

Eliza smiled but kept her voice cool. "I'm sure he'll be just fine." Lawyers were never fine in jail. He'd threatened her enough times, Steve deserved a taste. "Good-bye, Mr. Timms."

She hung up before he could argue the point. Now she had to call Gunn. If anyone posted bail for Steve, the firm was done. And she was sure he had at least one supporter who would help him. One rotten apple poisoned the whole barrel. This would shake even her father's old clientele. She tapped the phone against her lip.

She needed to know if this went beyond Steve and was, she shuddered, endemic. If Steve's cruel taunt about her father's dealings had been the truth, there would be nothing left to save out of the ashes and shattered illusions that were her life. A phone call wouldn't cut it. She had to go in to show who owned the firm.

Chapter 18

ELIZA KICKED OFF HER SHOES. THEY ROLLED ACROSS THE foyer and landed upside down against the wall. No one demanded they be moved or placed out of sight lest someone should see the abandoned heels and be offended. For half a second, she considered picking them up and placing them neatly to one side. Then she turned her back. If a shoe lay on the floor and no one was there to see it, was it really untidy?

Outside of her house, a few reporters still hovered looking for a line. If she said *no comment* one more time today, she was going to scream. She flopped onto the sofa and flicked on the TV. As a second thought, she swung her legs up so her feet rested on the arm of the cream sofa. It was hers and if she wanted to put her feet on it, she could. The TV babbled on about Steve, the implications of his arrest, and the possible depth of the fraud. Eliza muted the sound. There was nothing new to hear. She reached for her cell phone. There were four missed calls. One from Amanda, the others were from WPD.

She called Amanda, delaying calling the overbearing wedding planner.

"Eliza, have you been following the news?" A true Amanda-style greeting—straight to the point.

"I am the news." Eliza waved the remote at the television. "Look, there's me on channel seven going to work." She shook her head. Really, did anyone care? If she hadn't been Bill and Sandra Coulter's daughter, no one would have cared. She wouldn't have rated a second mention. This whole event would have been page ten news. Not the leading story.

"How bad's the office?"

"Disaster zone. The police executed their warrants. Steve's office was stripped. My desk, stripped." But their warrants had only extended to Steve. The other lawyers weren't being touched. The police weren't digging deep. And she could guess why. The current state premier wouldn't want his party tainted. There would be pressure coming down on the police to close Steve's case without dragging the Coulters and the party into it.

Eliza closed her eyes. But the day replayed on her eyelids. No rest for the associates of criminals. "Several of the younger lawyers are resigning."

"Trying to escape without taint."

Too late for that. Client confidence was gone. Some were already talking legal action. Her pulse shook, her skin had alternated between hot and clammy all day. One hit after another. She wasn't rolling with the punches. She was on the ground being kicked in the ribs. She took a breath and released the worst news. "Gunn is retiring."

"Shit."

Neither of them spoke. It was Gunn who had held the firm together after her father died. It was Gunn who had encouraged her to resume her studies while Steve argued against it. Now Gunn was telling her to walk away and not look back. Find another career. Eliza massaged her temples one-handed. Everything she knew was rupturing, expelling the venom that had held her paralyzed. Once it was spilled she would heal. The firm wouldn't.

"What are you going to do?"

Let it go.

Fighting to keep the firm alive would take everything she had, and more. She had to let her father go. Let his dream die. But she couldn't bring herself to say it. The words balled in her throat and stuck to the breath she tried to take. She coughed to keep from sobbing. If she started to cry now, she might never stop. Today she would lose more than her law firm.

At the edges of her mind, Roan had never been far away. For all she knew he could have lost the fight and already be gone. Her final night with him stolen by goblins.

"Is there anything you need me to do, Eliza?"

"No." There was nothing to do. Everything was in play. All the evidence was on the table. Only the sentence waited to be dealt. The edge of the sword brushed the hairs on her neck.

The only light in her day had been the news that Steve was to be remanded in custody until trial. The magistrate had thought there was a good chance he'd tamper with evidence or try to flee. Mr. Timms's earlier call had been preemptive, trying to secure ties with the ex-fiancée to keep his client out of jail. If she'd been Steve's lawyer, she probably would have done the same, although she'd have never slept at night putting the guilty back on the streets. Eliza changed topic the way a learner driver grinds gears.

"I have to ring WPD. Call it all off."

"You haven't done that yet? That would have been the first thing I'd have done."

Maybe she should've done it sooner, but she'd had other things on her mind and Amanda didn't know the full story. Amanda knew nothing of Roan. Aside from a few details, neither did she. He spoke little of his past, less about his previous lovers. If she knew more, would she love him less? Did she need to know more when they had so little time left?

"You know what she's like. This is going to be a major production. It will be all about her." Eliza forced a light laugh like it no longer mattered. It did. Every tie she cut to her old life snapped back and stung. Walking away wasn't as easy as it seemed.

"Have the guests started arriving?"

"I would think so." There were quite a few coming from the eastern states, and with the wedding only three days away there were bound to be a few early arrivals.

"If you need help ringing people…"

Eliza shook her head. "I have to pay WPD in full. She can do it. Ninety percent of the people I don't know except through family connections. They aren't my friends."

"Well I feel very special that you told me it was over in person. Brigit will be devastated. She was looking forward to being the flower girl."

"I'll have a party when Steve gets sentenced, so she can wear the dress and throw rose petals." Even as she said it, she knew she wouldn't give Steve that much attention. No. Walking away meant not looking over her shoulder.

Amanda laughed. "It just won't be the same."

Brigit was expecting a wedding.

"Well, unless I can find a new groom at short notice."

"What about the guy you met?"

Eliza wound a lock of hair around her finger. What

could she say? That fantasy was never going to come true. "It was a fling. He has other commitments."

"Is he married?" Amanda whispered the question.

Eliza could imagine her turning her back to Brigit and cupping the phone.

"No, he doesn't live here. Long-distance relationships never work out." Not strictly a lie, but it tasted wrong on her tongue. She wanted to tell someone about Roan just so he could exist beyond her dreams and be a part of her life if only in memory.

"Um, you could always move. Not that I'm trying to get rid of you, but sometimes you've got to take a jump."

Amanda knew all about jumping. Eloping with Matt before anyone could discourage them against marriage and a baby when they were both at university. Their love had been short and intense. But at least Amanda had been loved. Roan didn't love her, and even though he was trying, he couldn't.

Eliza sighed. "Not this time. Trust me, it was never built to last, but I wouldn't take it back." Not a single second no matter how bad the memories bruised.

Brigit called out in the background.

"I'm being summoned for homework help. I'll call you later."

"I'm having an early night. Catch you tomorrow." If she had the power, tomorrow would never come. It would be night forever.

"Okay. See you." The line died.

One more call, then she could go to bed and find the safety in her sleep that had eluded her during the day.

WPD picked up on the first ring. The conversation went as badly as expected. To a listener, like the police if her lines were still tapped, and she was sure they had been, it was Donna who was the bride with a black dress and no wedding to attend.

"If you cancel now, you will have to pay. If you re-schedule, everyone will understand what with the court case." WPD's voice got higher with each word. This was supposed to be her breakout wedding, the one that would put her back among society. It had done that, but for all the wrong reasons.

Eliza wanted to snap, but instead she broke the news as gently and as simply as she could. "Donna. It's over. We split up. There will be no wedding."

Silence. Paper shuffled in the background. She could just see WPD reaching for a paper bag to stave off hyperventilating. "Donna?"

"And the cake, and the reception, and the church, and the musicians?"

"Cancel them. I'll have to pay for the reception given the late notice, so give the dinner to charity."

"What?" Donna said in a pitch more suited to dogs than humans.

Eliza stretched her fingers and kept her voice calm. "Let St. Vinnie's take the food."

"What? You can't do that."

"Why not? I have to pay. The food can be cooked and donated." Steve would hate that. Eliza smiled. Some good could come out of this mess. "And give the cake to a couple who needs it." Someone should get to enjoy the white-chocolate-black-lace-five-tier monster.

Donna said nothing. But Eliza could hear her lips moving. The horror of the aborted wedding sinking in. She pushed on not waiting for agreement.

"And if you could notify all the guests that would great."

"Are you sure about this? It seems like such a sudden change. Do you need some time to think? Maybe I should talk to Steven."

Eliza fisted her hand. If these instructions were coming from Steve, Donna would have jumped through hoops to please. "He's in jail, awaiting trial, but go for it. He'll tell you same thing. There will be no wedding."

Even though she'd never wanted to marry Steve, canceling the wedding wasn't as much fun as it should have been. It was like stripping away old bandages only to find the wound unhealed and weeping. She didn't bleed for the loss of Steve but for the loss of what might have been had the curse broken. If the curse had broken, she could be marrying Roan. She wanted the fairy tale—the fairy tale wedding didn't matter. She sighed. All delusions must end.

Her voice tightened. "Thank you, Donna. None of this was expected, and I realize it has put you in an awkward position."

Donna became almost human. "Not at all. Just keep me in mind for when you do decide to marry."

Not a chance in hell. If she'd been more active in the planning, then maybe it wouldn't have gotten so out of hand. It wasn't Donna's fault none of this was what she wanted.

"Sure, you've been so helpful," she said, hoping she sounded honest.

"I'll be in touch, Ms. Coulter."

And it was done.

No more wedding.

With a grunt she peeled herself off the sofa. She couldn't waste any more of the evening. What if she got to the Summerland and found it empty?

Eliza set the alarm and ran upstairs. She stopped at the door to the master bedroom. Instead of rewiring the security system, she should cut out the last piece of Steve. Gut the room and start again. Redecorate, paint, and carpet and tile over every memory he'd ever created. She nodded to herself. She would need the distraction. Tomorrow she would begin building a new life, starting by reclaiming the bedroom.

She brushed her teeth and showered in record speed, then slipped into the white sundress. A million tiny butterflies fought to escape her chest. She swallowed to keep them in. She had to find out if he was waiting.

If the Goblin King was still in residence.

Sleep came easily. Eliza barely lay down and closed her eyes when she opened them to the eternal summer dreamland. She'd expected a battle from her body for going to bed too early and for wearing the wrong thing. She ran her hands over her stomach and the thin, white fabric of the sundress. The breeze teased, lifting the edges of the dress. The grass tickled her legs like a sweeping green ocean in which she could easily drown.

"Roan."

On the horizon storm clouds formed, bubbling out of nothing. She tucked a strand of hair behind her ear. Once he arrived the colors would fade. Once he was gone there would be no color worth seeing.

Beads chimed in the breeze. Music she would never hear again. She turned to face him. Roan swept her up into his arms.

"I wasn't sure…" She kissed him. He felt real, cool against her skin, his muscles hard beneath his clothing. This time he wore no armor, just the sword and gun. He had no life left to protect.

"I wouldn't go without saying good-bye." Roan set her feet down.

Eliza stepped back still holding his hands. She raised one brow. "Is that all this is?"

Roan smiled. "I didn't come all this way for words." He tugged her close. "Unless pretty words is all you want?"

Her tongue moistened over her lip. "I want you. I've always wanted you."

The heat in his eyes burned all the way to her core. Her heart burst into flames. She would never be the same again. No other man could fill the gap that Roan would leave or fix the damage left by his passing. She tugged on his hair and caught his mouth, but he was ready. Fueling the spark.

Their lips touched and opened. A hungry, harsh, and desperate kiss that wounded. Neither could let go. His hands gripped her bottom, pressing her close. She moved against the hard length of his shaft. Like sunburn from the inside out, every touch was too much, but too little. Roan made her burn, and only he could cool her down.

"I've waited all my life to find you." His forehead rested on hers. Kisses landed on her lips, stealing tastes.

The fabric of her dress bunched in his hand. His cool fingers skimmed across her bottom. "You're not wearing underwear."

"And you are overdressed." Eliza pulled at his T-shirt.

He released her just long enough to slip out of his clothing and drop his weapons on the ground. She palmed the smooth planes of his chest. The scars were a part of the cloth that made Roan who he was. She kissed the one over his heart, knowing she would never hear it beat. His heart would never race as they made love. Would never allow anything but the love of gold inside. He took her down into the grass. It bent, a soft green mattress cradling her body.

Rain splashed on her skin, warm summer rain, not the acid of the Shadowlands. Roan glanced at the sky. Clouds had gathered in honor of the occasion, blocking out the sun. The last fling of the Goblin King was cast in shadows.

"The land is changing." Roan placed his hands by her shoulders.

Beneath him she was dry. But the grass turned brown and wilted from his touch until she lay on bare dirt. "I don't care where we are."

Water dripped from the end of his hair onto her face. He kissed it away, tasting the water that fell on her skin. He rocked back onto his heels and turned his face to the rain. His lips curved. When he looked back at her, it became a grin. She glanced down and saw why. The sodden dress clung to her skin, revealing more than it hid.

His fingers traced the shape of her breast, circled the pink peak pressing against the fabric. She held her breath and waited as he undid the buttons down the front. His skin glistened in the rain. Raw and powerful. A Celtic god made mortal. Lightning streaked across the sky chased by an unseen, growling monster.

Roan lowered his head to the newly exposed skin. His tongue lapped the water from her nipple. Her fingers threaded into his hair and became lost among the dreadlocks and beads. She tipped her head back, arching toward him. Her body tight, charged, and ready burst. His hand glided up her thigh, over her hip, lifting her.

She worked her hands free. There was too much between them. She needed to feel his skin on her, in her. The button and zip of his camo separated between her fingers. He groaned as her knuckles brushed his shaft. So she did it again. The barest touch made him shudder. A king on his knees, between her legs, asking for more.

They fought over his pants, shoving them away, smearing rain-slicked skin with the gray dust that had taken the place of the grass. Roan lowered his hips. She held him close, taking him into her core. The heat in his eyes warred with something else. Seeing pain and loss drawn so clearly in eyes that had always been sunny brought back the reality. Reality had no place here, this was dream. Their dream.

Wrapped tight in Eliza's arms, her hips moving in perfect rhythm with his, Roan tried to remember the moment when his heart would race like it would break. Searching for that perfect moment to be free. But he had been too numb for too long, with only gold fueling his desire, that he couldn't fake being human.

For Eliza he tried, kissing her as if he could feel desire urging his heart faster, racing the rain that beat on his back. She responded, nipping at his lip, gasping as her sex tightened around his cock. His body wasn't immune. But he didn't want it to be over. Because once Eliza left him there would be nothing left of him. He nuzzled into her neck. She squirmed, but he held her still, drawing out every thrust into something he could carry with him, if not in his heart, then wrapped around the withered, gold-plated muscle.

The darkness in him retreated, backed into a corner by the bright star that now took up most of his horizon. It scorched and blinded. Knowing the familiar, cold black was behind him waiting for him to step over the edge and into the abyss was all that made him stand his ground from the new invader.

Eliza's nails dug into his back. He buried himself in her. She came again, taking everything from him. And he let her. Everything he had, or was, was hers and had been since he'd first seen her all those years ago. Even then she'd kept him human. Behind him the abyss screamed as it faced the light, and he saw the bone-riddled edges. The remains of those who'd jumped. It chomped at his heels, the maw of the curse that wouldn't let him rest.

But he rested over her. Their breath mingled as one.

Her hand cupped his cheek. "I love you." She blinked too fast and forced a smile. Her finger lay over his lips. "I know…you can't."

His hands dug into the dirt. He wanted to respond, but he couldn't lie to her. Roan kissed her finger. "I want you more than gold. I would trade it all if I could love you for just one breath."

Beneath his hand something stirred, tickled his palm. He lifted his hand, and Eliza turned her head. Pink flowers broke through the dead grass and gray dirt. The ones he had tried to create for her now grew without effort. He plucked one out of the ground and tucked it behind her ear. The petals were the same shade of pink as her mouth. Their lips barely touched in a kiss more delicate than the strange magic at work around them.

"They were here last time." She snapped a stem and pushed it through one of his beads.

"You had them in your hair last night." In his hair the flower wilted and died.

"They only grow where you touch."

He pulled back. She moaned as he left her body. He stood and pulled up his camo. Eliza was right. Any place he had touched was now filled with pink flowers. Flowers that died when he touched them, even though he'd created them. Around them the world was colored but bleached, as if the rain had stripped away the bright shades of the Summerland and left the land confused. Was it a nightmare or a dream?

"Look behind you." Eliza sat up.

A ghost of a rainbow colored the gray sky. Roan frowned. None of this right. The icy magic of the Shadowlands still flowed in his blood. The heat of the Summerland ran just beneath the ground but too fast and too hot for him to touch. All magic would damn him. He sat back down in the dirt next to Eliza.

She leaned her head on his shoulder and smoothed her dress over her legs. He flicked the dirty hem up revealing more of her smooth thigh. She pushed it down, smiling, a dare in her eyes.

"Are you tempting me?"

"Is it working?"

He hauled her over so she straddled his hips. He lay back on the ground. Against his back tightly packed buds broke through the ground. Each petal that unfolded tickled his skin. Her dress gaped open around her breasts. He traced the neckline, drew her down for a kiss. She lay on his chest, her heart beating for both of them.

"Tell me about your life." She twirled a dread around her finger. Her fingers danced over the beads.

Roan smoothed her hair. "What do you need to know? What do you want to remember about me?"

"Stay here until you've told me everything."

"If I could hide here I would. But I can't. Dai walks ever closer to the edge, and I can't escape my fate. I gave up too much in the search for power to kill Elryion."

She titled her head. "Did you have a family?"

"One brother, one sister. Both younger." He sighed. She wanted to remember him as a man. She wanted to know his life before the curse had taken everything from him. At one point it would have chafed, but being remembered as a man was more than he'd ever thought possible. "She didn't survive the rebellion."

"I'm sorry."

"Don't be. It was too long ago for that wound to still weep." Like everything he'd known, they were long gone. The world had spun past him in a brilliant parade of history, marred only by the shadows of the goblins that watched, wishing they could take part. Eliza would selectively excise the memory of him as a goblin. A luxury he would never have.

"Did you have a wife?" Her voice dropped like she was afraid of being heard, or maybe she was afraid of the answer.

He shook his head. "No. I refused to marry a Roman woman under Roman law."

Eliza's pale brows drew together as if she was trying to understand, and failing.

"Life was different. The rules were different. Men were judged differently."

"No regrets?"

"Not anymore." He'd seen more than any man should. "I couldn't have asked for a better queen." He lifted her hand and kissed the ring. It slid off leaving her skin unmarked. "I'm releasing you of any obligation."

She gasped and tried to take the ring back. "Please."

"I have to let you go. No ties." Her face would be forever held in his memory. He would stand by the door to the Hall of the Gods, waiting for her to pass through on her way to her next life just to see her again.

She gritted her teeth and sat up.

Roan pushed himself up so she sat in his lap. "We've spoken about this. Please let me go."

"I don't want to. I would rather be here with you than in the Fixed Realm."

"If you do not wake and eat, you will die. And I cannot die in peace knowing I have dragged you with me. Bad enough my brother shares my fate."

Eliza looked away, studying the grass. Her face was set with the pouted lip of a child not getting her way but understanding why.

He cupped her cheek so she had to look at him. "Don't leave in anger. Wish me well, as I wish you well."

She sucked in a breath and heaved it out. She was trying so hard to keep together, to not cry in front of him. Part of him was glad; already he was torn into a hundred fragments. The rest of him wanted to see her tears so he would know what his death would mean. How fast would she leave him to chase her future?

"Grant me one final wish…if you can."

Roan dropped his hand. His heart ached, the gold colder and tighter as the darkness blackened, trying to erase the blot of brilliant white that had invaded his being. He fisted his hand tighter around her ring.

"I can't use magic." He bit each word out. The cold current that flowed thick as blood rushed to his fingertips, pleading to be used. The heat from the star faded under the pressure of giving her what she wanted.

She swallowed and leaned back as if sensing the rush of power that wanted to consume him. "No magic."

"What then?" He eased his hold on her ring.

"Come to my house for dinner."

Roan opened his mouth.

She covered it with her hand. Her eyes widened. "It can be a farewell party for you and Dai. A gift from me. Don't die alone in the Shadowlands." Her words poured out on top of themselves in the race to be heard.

And he gulped down each one, water to a man dying of thirst. But the temptation of another day was tainted by the body he would wear. Her last vision of him would be as the Goblin King.

"Say yes. Please say yes." She slowly removed her hand and sat back.

Even disheveled and dirty from lying on the ground with him she was still the most beautiful thing he'd ever seen. When he blinked, a perfect impression of Eliza was painted on his eyelids. The sun was well risen where she lived, night had moved on. Mere hours separated them from another meeting. Would the caves hold or would they have to abandon them and the gold they contained? Could he eke a half day out of the tattered remnant of his soul? If it were just him, he would fade trying to be there. Dai would argue against any further delay. He couldn't refuse his brother a warrior's death.

"I can't promise." He lifted his knees.

Eliza stood. She held her hands out to him. He took the offer not because he needed help, but because he wanted to touch her again. They held hands lost somewhere between the Summerland and Shadowlands. He couldn't spoil the night with a final farewell.

"I will come to say good-bye if I can't be there for dinner."

She nodded. "It's time for me to wake up."

"I wish it wasn't so." He leaned down to kiss her one last time. "Dream of me." He gently eased her into waking.

Her sigh lingered on the breeze. He picked his belt up and refastened the weapons. Where he had lain on the ground the little pink flowers sprouted. He stepped to one side and squatted down. No flowers sprang out of his new footprints. Only the ones made with Eliza had any life. She was the key, but he had no idea how to use her to unlock the curse and no time to figure it out.

Chapter 19

COLD ROLLED OFF THE RIVER, EVEN IN SUMMER. THE LIGHTS from the city and boats reflected on the surface as if another city dwelled beneath her waters. Roan leaned against the bridge. His fingers worked over the dreadlocks, twisting the snakes of hair from root to tip. The habit of an unnatural lifetime. The river smelled. Polluted by rubbish and noise, but this was his home.

Or had been.

The ruins of his town lay buried under centuries of life. But if he closed his eyes and ignored the engines of the cars racing by overhead, time fell away. He slid back to before the Roman invasion, to his childhood. His father had taught him to fish in this river. As king he would have to feed his people as well as lead them.

He'd fought mock battles with wooden swords and later real ones that left the river running red with blood. Roman or Decangli, the one thing he had learned was people all bled the same. All screamed the same. All died the same. A look of surprise that twisted to agony as they clutched at the wound. He'd been no different as blood poured from his chest. He'd watched the crows circle after the battle ended, but had woken with his eyes intact, his wound clean and dressed. His father was dead and he was king, handed over to the Roman general as a political prisoner. The freedom Dai had been allowed was removed, so he truly was a slave to the general.

Roan walked a little way up the river, careful to stay in the shadows where his skin and clothing hid him from sight but not the damp in the air. Each time he came, the town had changed. The garrison was little more than preserved rubble. But he knew, even now through the maze of streets and lights, where it had once stood. An open sore on the landscape. A tumor that fed off his town, corrupting his people. Three hundred years later it was gone. The Romans, the language, and the memory of the cursed king.

The legend of the Goblin King had lasted longer. Teenagers had dared each other to call the Goblin King. Depending on his mood he would either ignore them or scare them. Their faces white, their lips moving without sound or thought. Some ran, some fainted. At least they didn't order him to kill as so many had done. Well, one had. Roan smiled, his wide goblin mouth flashing too many teeth. A night tied naked to a gas streetlight had sorted that young man out.

Not all who had seen him had been so lucky. The death of one young woman was on his hands, no summoner to be blamed. She'd come for silver and paid with her life. As a trained courtesan she'd been good company, both getting what they wanted and nothing more. Gossip and jealousy among her rivals along with her drawings, the ones he'd told her not to make, had brought her before the church. They had been less than forgiving of her profession and her dealings with *demons*.

She had been the last woman before Eliza. In that five-hundred-year gap, he had lost more ground than in all the previous centuries. He sucked in a breath and released it slowly. The anger that had fueled him for so long was gone. The scales were almost balanced. Because of the curse, he'd met Eliza. For someone like him it was enough. More than he'd ever thought possible.

Behind him the shadows rippled and tore. The hairs on the back of his neck spiked. Roan remained facing the ruins. "Greetings, brother."

"I thought I'd find you here longing for the past."

"Making peace with it." He turned, his beads silent for the solemn occasion. The sight of Dai's face rearranged to be goblin cut every time he saw it. He looked away. "There is little else to do. You?"

"I am done."

They stood in silence as a boat glided over the inky water powered by machine, not man. He'd watched the world change in ways one man should never see. The world he knew was long gone. While he'd watched the changes, even caused a few of them, he had never been part of them. Never lived in the moment or experienced the dawning of a new era.

"Could you step back in and join the flow of time?"

Dai scuffed his boot in the mud. He folded his arms and shook his head. "I would try, but men like us no longer exist."

"*Men* like us are everywhere. Have you not noticed how many more goblins fill the Shadowlands? Men fight for money, not honor. War for wealth, not survival." The world was obsessed with gold and its lightweight paper sibling. Men like they used to be no longer existed.

"The spirit of Rome lives on." Dai's face was grim as he stared across the river. His eyes were seeing something else. He dropped his gaze and looked away. "You know where to find me when you're ready."

Roan reached for his brother's arm too late and grasped nothing but air thickened by the night. He took one last look at where he had been born and then followed Dai into the shadows.

The shelves were bare. Not a scroll. Not a tablet. Not a book to be seen. Dai had emptied his library. Roan blinked and turned, hoping he'd mis-stepped and ended up in the wrong cave. Odd golden artifacts littered the floor. The polished desk usually hidden by maps and texts was bare except for the gold-rimmed spectacles.

Dai reclined in his leather chair, his fingers pressed together. "I wasn't expecting you to follow so fast."

"What happened?" While Roan lacked Dai's expertise in the written word he'd appreciated the volume of knowledge stored in one room.

The time spent deciphering and then the thrill of the wild goose chase as they'd hunted for a mythical cure only to find it useless. The hair from a dragon. Amulets. Spells. Prayers to gods that no longer listened. Holy water. Penitence. Confession. Pilgrimages. Voodoo. Witch doctors. Poison. If they hadn't tried it, it didn't exist.

"I cleaned up. Dead languages held little appeal, but I felt guilty about leaving them to rot here so I added them to the vault at Birch."

"They were your life's work." Roan dropped into the other chair. For Dai to give up everything he'd collected…he studied his brother in the glow of the candlelight. His skin was paler, but not gray. His eyes were blue, but yellow burst around the pupil.

Dai smiled and leaned forward. "Are you looking for goblin?"

"Do I need to?"

"My latest finds have appeased the greedy golden-eyed monster. I didn't even feel the bite taken from my soul in payment." Dai touched his pendant. He reached into his drawer and pulled out two books. He laid them on the table. "I kept these for you. Shall I?"

The last two in the Harry Potter series. Listening to Dai's summary would be the same as admitting he wouldn't live to see the films. He wasn't ready to concede defeat. Not while there was still time. Still a chance to pull victory from the jaws of defeat. Battles could turn in a moment. The clanging of axes on rock mocked his hope. The only reason his cave hadn't been invaded yet was because the goblins kept attacking each other.

Roan eased back in his chair and feigned relaxation. "Tell me over dinner."

"Dinner?" Dai tapped the cover of the final book. "Why dinner?"

"Eliza has asked—"

"Eliza." He swept the books off the table. "How long will you dance to her tune?" Dai ran his fingers through his hair. He frowned at the books on the floor then checked his hands, looking for the gray stain that announced the fade. Dai had lost his distraction. His love of learning for learning's sake was gone, and with no buffer he was vulnerable.

The daily battle was one Roan was familiar with, but since taking Eliza as queen the darkness had slowed its attack. Or maybe his defense had gotten better as gold had lost its lure and was replaced by lust.

Dai's breath hissed out, but his skin didn't change color. The black diamond held him safe from the darkness of the Shadowlands. He was as human as he would ever be unless the curse broke or Roan succumbed. Roan knew which side the good money was betting on. Hell, he knew which he was betting on and it wasn't the outcome he wanted. The only way to spare his brother becoming goblin was death.

Roan spoke quietly. "I will not let you fade. But I do not wish your death either." He stood. "She has offered a farewell dinner. I didn't accept. I did promise to say good-bye."

He clenched his teeth. He wanted dinner, knowing it wouldn't ever fill him. It wouldn't be enough, but they were standing on the edge listening to the rocks break away and bounce down the cliff into the abyss. The grip he had on his brother was slipping.

"The decision is yours, Dai." Roan turned and left his brother in the empty library. If his brother was forced to hold the life of others in his hands, to feel the weight of care, maybe he wouldn't rush to extinguish what little spark remained.

Only a few brave photographers camped outside Eliza's house. The rain had forced them into their cars. Their telescopic lenses peeked over the tops of windows like one-eyed sightless monsters. They'd got some photos of her going grocery shopping. If that made it to print, there was something truly wrong with the media.

Eliza shut the curtains and turned up the music. The shopping bags bulged on the kitchen floor. She'd bought too much. But she didn't know what to buy. What did one serve as a king's last supper? Seafood? Steak? Roast? Delicate canapés?

Everything.

The ten-course menu sat on the marble bench waiting for action. Roan might not come. He might have already gone and she hadn't noticed. She bit her lip and sniffed. She would know. She would feel it. The separation would burn like a hot knife pressed against her palm. She snatched up the first bag and unpacked the shopping bags with too much vigor. Then she arranged the food by recipe, busywork to keep her hands moving and her mind silent.

Roan wouldn't go without saying good-bye. He had promised.

The ingredients sat sullenly on the bench-top. On another occasion the food would have become a dinner party, a celebration, not a wake for the soon-to-be-dead.

One uninvited guest watched her cook. His scythe propped in the corner, the harsh white planes of his face half-hidden by the folds of his shroud. She shivered. Not even the heat from the oven could take the chill out of the air. No matter how long she stalled, or how long the dinner went, there would be no escaping Death.

Roan opened the bottom drawer and ran his hand over the blue and red cloak. In his time it had been finely crafted. Now the weave was rough, the dye dull. He lifted the clothes and inhaled. Did they still hold traces of wood smoke, or was his memory playing tricks? These were clothes he'd hoped never to use.

He peeled off the black T-shirt, removed his boots, socks, and camo. Over the years he'd worn different uniforms, the clothes of the times as if he could drop into the Fixed Realm and participate at any given moment. Always ready. He folded the clothes and placed them at the end of the bed. His boots were tucked just underneath like he would be coming back.

The only concession to modern life he would take would be the Colt. He still hadn't decided what to do. If he died in the Fixed Realm, what would happen to his body? He'd never seen a goblin die in the world, although he was sure some did during the solstice Wild Ride. Maybe it was their corpses that filled Area 51. A place so secure that not even he had found a way in—and there weren't many places that kept him out. He didn't want to leave a body for Eliza to deal with. On the other hand, dying in the Shadowlands held no appeal.

Roan picked up his clothing and strode naked to the bathroom. He took his time as if it meant nothing. The water coursed over his skin, but he didn't feel its cold fingers—he didn't waste magic heating it for himself. With his eyes closed all he saw was Eliza naked, and it was too easy to fool his flesh into thinking she was there. He rubbed his hands over his face. Without magic he needed to shave. He hadn't put a razor to his face in centuries. Today wasn't the right day to relearn. His fingers wrinkled like grapes left in the sun, but he stayed in the shower, rinsing the rock dust from under his nails as if Eliza would notice the gray dust on gray skin. Anything to delay. One less thing to do. One less thing on his rapidly shrinking list. One more last time finished.

The weight of the end settled on his shoulders. A sodden winter wool cloak that he'd ignored, until now. The darkness whispered of life. Life was life regardless of how it was lived. What good was a soul when the body burned to ash? Roan wrenched himself away from the edge. Its promises made by the gray of a false dawn didn't tempt him. Better to be incinerated by the growing white star. He turned off the shower and forced himself to dress.

Usually magic meant his hair would be clean but not wet. Wet, the tails of his hair were heavy. The beads didn't dance. He did his best to dry them, but what suited a goblin annoyed him as a man. He had no need to show his wealth in gold and amber anymore. He should cut the dreadlocks off. Hack through them with his sword and leave them to rot in the Shadowlands. But Eliza's fingers had tangled in the snakes. She had rolled the beads in her fingers. It was how she recognized him as a goblin.

In the mirror very little had changed since the night he was cursed. He looked no older, no wiser either, just a little more scarred. A smile crept over his face. The king in the mirror he knew. He was Roan, the king of all that remained of the Decangli. Nothing would ever take that from him. He hung the towel over the rack. The sun was slipping to the other side of the earth. Night was encroaching on Eliza's house.

He needed an answer from Dai.

Roan placed his hand over the candles in the bathroom. The flames tickled his palm but lacked the heat to burn. Like everything else in the Shadowlands they drew on the magic that tainted the air for survival. The green fire died without a splutter. As he walked down the tunnels to his room, he extinguished each candle he passed. They had lit the caves for six centuries. Their service was done.

Dai sat on the edge of Roan's bed. He'd changed clothes. Gone were camo and the military styling. Instead he'd chosen a jacket and trousers that belonged to someone who spent their days marveling over the change in language and writing styles over the centuries. It was enough to make Roan pause at the door and wonder who had taken the almost-goblin and brought back his brother. The only giveaway was the gold accessories. Buttons, belt buckle, earrings.

"You've found yourself again."

Dai shook his head. He studied the gold rings on his fingers. "No, but I know how I want to be remembered. I thought those clothes were ruined."

"I lugged them around for centuries before learning how to mend with magic." Before he'd realized what the magic took it had become second nature. Magic could fix, or change, anything for a price.

"I wondered why your pack was always so bulky." Dai spun the ring on his finger as if contemplating removing it. "I have been thinking," his lips twisted in a wry smile, "about something other than gold." He looked up at Roan. "Dinner would nice."

Roan relaxed his shoulders, releasing the tension he hadn't realized he'd been carrying since giving Dai the power of death. He nodded, about to speak, but Dai raised his hand, asking to be allowed to continue.

"If I were you, dinner is all I would be thinking about, even though we haven't needed to eat in a long time. I couldn't have handed the decision to another."

"You are my brother. I trust your decision." Not entirely, he could've ordered Dai's attendance and risked a fight, but it was better a man make up his own mind than be forced. He'd hoped Dai was still human enough to feel the weight of responsibility, and understand his death wish could wait an extra hour or two while Roan pretended to live.

"A risky strategy. What plans have you made?" Dai ran his palms over his thighs.

Dinner was only a temporary reprieve. Roan's blood chilled without touching the magic of the Shadowlands. A single self-inflicted head shot. Not a glorious death, but a bullet was all that was required to kill a goblin.

"Options are limited. Here or there. My preference is the Fixed Realm."

Dai frowned. "And the bodies?"

"There is an active volcano in Hawaii. It is beautiful. We could time it for sunrise." Let the force of the shot carry their bodies over the rim and into the fire that would take them to the Hall of the Gods.

"That solves the problem of the pyre. We can take the swords and torques of the others."

Roan's throat was too tight to speak. It was one thing to plan and prepare, but another to participate. His desire for life was getting in the way of his need for death.

Goblin battle cries rattled off the walls. The extra barricades Roan had spent building to waste the time between seeing Eliza had given way. All the rocky debris from his anger had been put to good use. It had bought them the time they needed. Both men turned to face the doorway. The Hoard had arrived. Roan's hand slid to his gun. They were out of time.

Dai frowned. "That held for longer than I thought it would."

"I reinforced it while you were gathering gold."

"I should have helped."

Footsteps pounded down the tunnel. Dai stood and removed the platinum and black diamond pendant and placed it on the bed. "I wouldn't want to keep your queen waiting. Shall we go?"

Roan nodded and wrapped them in shadows. He didn't want to see the blood as the goblins found the gold room. And he didn't want to watch Dai defending the treasure…and he was sure he would succumb if he stayed. Together, the brothers left the Shadowlands for the last time.

They stepped into a house lit with candles. They burned on every surface and melted. Tears of colored wax slid down their sides, escaping from the heat of the orange flame. Roan passed his hand over the tiny fire. It flickered. He lowered his hand over the flame. His gray-skinned palm heated. Pain sliced through his hand. Roan pulled his hand back. He rubbed the tender, burned skin. He hoped he would be dead before he hit the lava.

Around the two goblins, the house was silent. He sniffed. It wasn't the candles that perfumed the house, it was food. For the first time in centuries he was hungry. Not just wanting to eat out of an obsolete human habit hungry. But really hungry. He stomach tightened and gurgled. Where was Eliza? Roan looked at Dai. Dai shrugged. His hands were full of the swords from the fallen and faded.

Roan walked through the house toward the kitchen. It hadn't changed much since the first time he had visited. That night music had poured through the house and flooded the garden. Teenagers had run amok with beers clutched in their hands. Upstairs a frightened child had hidden from the boys who dreamed of being men without understanding what it meant.

He changed direction. Eliza would be upstairs. He signaled to Dai his intentions, unwilling to break the silence that protected them. Roan moved through the shadows that cloaked the stairs. His beads chattered around him, and he didn't expend any magic to silence them.

"Roan?" Bare feet raced across the landing to where he stood at the top of the stairs.

"I am here." In spirit and the wrong body, he remained in the shadows, content to watch her.

Eliza had pulled her hair up, put on makeup, and dressed for the occasion in a knee-length gold evening dress. He didn't need any light to know she was tempting him into living. And it was working.

She stopped three feet from him, suddenly awkward. "I wasn't sure, I've cooked. It's ready." Her hands fiddled with imaginary strands of hair.

"Dai is downstairs."

"Yes, of course." Eliza nodded. She peered in the shadows, searching for his face.

She would never like what she found. Roan released the shadows anyway. There was no point in hiding, and slinking through the dark, pretending he didn't exist. He heard her swallow, then she reached out her hand. He wrapped his long gray fingers around hers. She was warm against his cool flesh. Hot enough to burn, if not his skin, then what was left of his soul.

Together they walked down the stairs. King and queen. Dai waited at the bottom. He inclined his head and let them pass to lead the way into the dining room.

Four swords lay on the oval table, three with bronze

torques. Meryn still wore his, the curse locked around his neck where it would remain forever. Three places had been set with cutlery. At the center of the table were flowers, an ornate silver candelabrum, and two bottles of wine, one red, one white.

Eliza stared at her distorted table setting. Her fingers squeezed his hand. "Did you want me to set the other places?"

"No. It's enough they are remembered."

For a moment none of them moved, afraid to take a seat and start the last meal they would share. Roan eased his hand free. "Would you like any help in the kitchen?"

Eliza came to life, the spell that held her frozen had broken. She shook her head, her golden hair shining in the candlelight. "I'll bring out the canapés. Have a seat."

Roan watched her leave, his feet wanted to follow, but he sat. He drummed his long fingers on the table, the yellow nails clipping the wood. They were wasting seconds they could be together.

"That wasn't uncomfortable at all." Dai leaned forward with his elbows on the edge of the table, and he rested his chin on his hands.

It was a pose Dai often took when thinking, but it was at odds with the body now performing as his brother.

"What if I've missed something? Something obvious that would free us." At the edges of his mind the bright star whispered, but its voice was drowned out by the screaming darkness. All he needed was silence to hear the answer—if that was what was being whispered. For all he knew it was a trick of the Shadowlands designed to tear him apart faster. Except it wasn't. He hadn't been this stable…ever.

Dai clenched his teeth. His face pulled into a snarl. "What haven't we tried? What else is there? What is left that could break the curse? Even your queen loves you, and still nothing changes."

Roan frowned. "What do you…"

Eliza walked back into the room. "I didn't know what you'd like." She set two platters down. "So I made California rolls with smoked salmon and mini quiches with bacon." She glanced at Roan.

The need for approval widened her eyes. The candlelight danced in her pupils until her eyes glowed as if lit by their own fire. Brighter than any black diamond could hope to burn. She was in love with *him*. Not just Roan, but the Goblin King. Her pleading *I love you* was more than just words spoken to sharpen his decision.

His tongue traced his lip as he tried to find something to say that would be worthy. He found nothing. "It all looks delicious."

At that moment he wouldn't have cared if Eliza had served salted rats on a stick. Eliza loved him, yet the curse remained. No matter how hard he tried he couldn't force any emotion out of the gold that had taken the place of muscle and become his heart.

She smiled and sat. There was enough food to serve all six of his men had they been there. Roan filled his plate. Leaving leftovers would only serve as a reminder tomorrow. Silence descended on the table while they ate.

Dai poured wine. He had a sip and placed his glass down with such care Roan knew he was about to ask a question more prickly than a briar. His leg wouldn't reach to kick his brother, and he knew Eliza wouldn't appreciate the disruption to dinner.

"Roan mentioned you were on a break from studying law. Do you intend to continue?"

She took a drink before replying. "I don't know. I don't know what I'm going to do after this. It's changed my perspective." She touched her cheek and forced her mouth into a smile, but her eyes were in disagreement. "If you're done I'll bring out the entrée."

She'd gathered the plates before anyone could disagree and vanished into the kitchen.

"Leave her alone. This can't be easy for her." It wasn't easy for him to sit with Eliza and have her look at him as if it didn't matter what color his skin was. She loved his soul. When that was gone it couldn't be brought back.

"I was making polite conversation."

"You were digging for information. Like you always do." He couldn't protect Eliza, not from his brother's curiosity, from death, from life. After tonight she was on her own, no matter how hard they rallied against the heavy hand of fate.

Dai shrugged. "Better than sitting here in silence."

"There is nothing I can say." Roan pulled at a dreadlock and worked the rope of hair through his fingers. Annoyance tugged at his scalp as he worked.

"Have you tried?"

"How can the curse be broken by something I can't feel?" Roan spoke through clenched teeth. The ache in his chest around Eliza was brutal. Like someone was trying to split his ribs to inspect what lay beneath. Blood eagled, one of Rome's favorite punishments.

"But would you mean it?" Dai waved his hand as if he was pulling the answer to their wishes out of the air. "Magic is about intent."

Magic might be, but love wasn't. Did Dai even understand the difference, or had he spent so long in his books he'd forgotten how being human felt?

"I won't lie to her." She knew he wanted to love her but couldn't. There was no room in his metal heart for anything but unwanted gold.

"It wouldn't be lying. It's the thought that counts."

"If that were true…" Roan raised his hands. They were gray, not flesh-colored. Look at them. They could barely be civil. Another day and they would be at each other's throats over the pile of gold buried under rock.

"If what were true?" Eliza had glided barefoot back into the room. Bowls of soup balanced on a tray.

Roan wanted to stick a sword through his brother. Nowhere that would kill him, just enough for his tongue to be too busy moaning to speak. "Nothing."

"That a wish may break the curse." Dai grinned. What should have lit his eyes with humor turned his crooked goblin features sinister as he reveled in Roan's discomfort.

Eliza set the bowls down. She avoided eye contact with either of the goblins. "I could ask the wish, if you don't mind, Roan."

"Nothing would please me more than obeying that command." Roan placed his hand over hers.

Her face lit up with hope. "Do I just wish?"

Roan nodded even though he knew it wouldn't work. He'd tried it before. Held a summoner on the end of his blade and made him wish. The compulsion had been there, but he'd had nowhere to send the power. He didn't know how to break the curse. If he did then, maybe he could have used the curse's strength against itself. Now, he didn't have the magic to expend on saving his soul. This was a cruel jest to force him into saying words that weren't true no matter how much he wanted them to be real.

Dai leaned forward. The candles held their breath, static flames frozen in the moment.

Eliza chewed her lip, her eyes narrowed as she thought. After a few elongated seconds she spoke. "I wish the Goblin King would break the curse that binds him."

The pull of power was there, spiking his blood with the poison that was killing him. But this time in the mucky river at the bottom of the abyss he glimpsed the bonds of the curse, illuminated by the star. Old and frayed, the ropes barely held his soul under water. If he had magic to command, he might have been able to sever the curse and avoid drowning. His chest ached from the gold that weighed him down and prevented him from drawing in the air that would save his life.

He squeezed her hand and forced a smile. She was the answer to every question, written in a language he couldn't read. "Not that simple." He glared at Dai. "No more talk of curses or wishes."

"What if I said the words wrong? Um…I command you to break the curse. I wish you were free of the curse."

Her pleading raked the surface of his golden heart. He couldn't bleed even though the scratches ran deep. Roan placed his hand over his chest, but the wounded metal wouldn't heal.

"Enough. There is no hope of a deathbed pardon."

Eliza gasped. Her eyes watered like he'd slapped her face. His words had hurt her more than the failed wishes. She'd always had hope. Hope that something they did would break the curse. One true desire they both shared.

Dai melted in the shadows, wanting no part in fixing the damage his taunts had caused.

Tears flooded her eyes and slid down her cheeks. She didn't bother to hide them or sweep them aside.

"I just wanted—" She hiccupped and couldn't finish.

"Shh." Roan dropped to his knees in front of his crying queen. He cupped her face. Her tears filled his ugly twisted hands. "Don't cry for me. I have made my peace." His voice broke, brittle and damaged he tried to go on, tried to reassure her. "Knowing you has lightened the curse. You showed me love."

She threw her arms around him. Her face buried against his neck. Not used to being touched as a goblin, he was paralyzed and not sure what to do. The man remembered. He wrapped his arms around her and smoothed his hands down her back while she wept for a goblin who could never love her back. Her body shook. The gouges in his heart became fissures. His heart was tearing apart over Eliza's grief. The metal tore itself into shrapnel that cut into his flesh. He couldn't breathe without making fresh wounds.

And Roan forgot what he was.

He kissed her cheek and when she lifted her face, he kissed her lips. She responded, her eyes closed, her fingers through his hair. He couldn't love her, but she owned his soul and always would. It was no longer his to surrender. But Eliza owned a fragment so small; would she recognize what she held?

The metal shards broke free from his chest. He doubled over, sure the curse was taking his life for cheating it of a soul. He placed his hand over his heart like he could stop the split.

"Don't fade. Roan, stay with me." Her hands were on his face, over his chest. They danced like panicked birds.

The star expanded and went supernova, exploding in a destructive brilliance. The only thing destroyed was the dark abyss that had been ready to swallow him whole. The heat seared his lungs, his skin burned and peeled. The frozen muscle in his chest contracted.

His nails dug through the woolen tunic and into his skin. Then it happened again, the awful tightening that spread splinters and razors through his arteries. A heartbeat.

Roan lifted his head and drew a breath. Part of him was missing. The ice-burn of the Shadowlands, the weight in his chest. Eliza sat back on her heels, her mouth open. Was he human, or goblin? Had the curse spat him out? He lifted his other hand, too afraid to take the one off his chest in case the painful beating of his heart stopped. The hand in front of his face was flesh colored and the nails white.

She reached out to touch his hand. Her fingers traced his palm. He placed her hand over his chest so she could feel his heart beneath her hand. As the muscle became accustomed to working, the pain eased.

"What happened?"

"You broke my heart, and the curse." He couldn't look away from the hazel-eyed woman who'd cared enough to carve out his heart. He was trapped in her eyes and never wanted to leave. Eliza was his air, his soul, his heart.

A male cry from the garden broke the spell that held them on their knees. "Le Roi est mort!"

Roan's first human smile in the Fixed Realm in nearly two thousand years tightened his cheeks. Eliza smiled back. She leaned in and whispered, "Vive le Roi."

He cradled her face. Their lips touched. This kiss was different. Lust boiled through his blood but it was tempered with something more powerful.

Love.

It was his love for Eliza that enabled his golden heart to break. He wasn't fool enough to question how that was possible.

Her fingers brushed the day-old stubble as if he might vanish. "You're human. You're here." Eliza's smile faltered and her hand fell away. "You're free."

Roan caught her wrist and kissed her fingertips. "There is no freedom without you."

Without Eliza, the world would be as dull and dead as the Shadowlands. Doubt clouded her eyes, tarnishing the flecks of gold.

"You have the whole word to explore."

She was pulling away from him. His lips grew cold without her kisses. His heart wouldn't beat if she left him alone in the Fixed Realm. His place here was with Eliza, by her side.

Roan reached into the leather pouch on his belt and pulled out the silk-wrapped object.

"There's nothing I haven't seen or stolen." From the cloth slipped a silver ring. The black diamond entwined in vines glittered in the candlelight.

She drew in a breath at the sight of her ring in his palm. "You don't need a queen."

"No I don't." He was no longer a king, but without Eliza he was nothing. He held out the ring once given to her to protect and to mark. "Marry me, Eliza."

She placed her palm over his heart. "You said once that all you could love was gold."

The light wool tunic was an impenetrable barrier when all he wanted was to feel her touch against human flesh. "I didn't know what it was to love a woman. You made every day I passed in the Shadowlands worthwhile. I love you, Eliza."

He held her hand. This time he selected the ring finger on her left hand. The ring didn't bind to her skin. She was free to remove it. To reject him.

Eliza stared at her hand. Her tremors passed into his fingers like he held a tiny bird in his palm. Would she stay or fly away?

She looked up with tears in her eyes but a smile on her lips. She threw her arms around his neck.

"Yes."

Chapter 20

THE CHURCH WAS SILENT. NO MUSIC PLAYED. NO RIBBONS or flowers decorated the aisle. No people filled the pews. The biggest church in Perth was being used for the smallest wedding. Eliza stopped in the entrance and smoothed the black wedding dress that had scandalized the bridal boutique. It didn't matter what she wore as long as Roan was waiting for her at the altar.

Amanda and Brigit stood to one side, two men in suits on the other. Amanda fiddled with her hair and smiled at one of the men on the other side. Talking without words. He responded with a tilt of his head, his long hair hiding his face.

Where was Roan?

Brigit waved. And the other man turned.

Eliza's breath caught, her heart stuttered, but she met his gaze. It was all she could do not to gather up her skirts and run down the aisle into his arms. Roan was almost unrecognizable. He wore the suit like it had been made for him, not bought in a rush to use the booked church. But the biggest change was the loss of the dreadlocks.

Gone.

His hair was cropped close to his scalp. Her eyes prickled. The music that had filled her nights would never play again.

She walked down the overly long aisle. Not the slow, measured pace a bride should use as if reluctant to go to her future husband. Without the demands of society expectations she did what she wanted—she walked too fast. Roan's gaze never left her. His blue eyes burned with the fire of a desert sky at dawn. She was breathless when she reached the altar. Her blood surged, coloring her cheeks.

She was getting married.

Roan took her hands and kissed her cheek. Her toes curled in her shoes.

"You cut your hair." She ran her fingers over the short strands, already missing the tails of hair.

"It was time." From his pocket he pulled out a necklace made of gold and amber beads. Two strands woven together as one.

She bent her head as he fastened it around her neck. The gold he could never give her in the Shadowlands. It was beautiful, but she felt the weight of history and this was just a fraction of the beads he'd worn in his hair.

"It was a heavy burden." She touched the necklace. Every bead was a little different, a different story told by each one. She was sure he knew which ones she now wore.

"But worth it." His knuckles caressed her cheek. He leaned in to kiss her.

The priest coughed. "Shall we start, Mr. King?"

Roan straightened. "Yes."

The priest gave her a look that suggested she wasn't worthy to be standing in the house of God. What kind of woman swaps grooms at the last minute? Eliza straightened her back.

A woman who dared to dream.

The priest began to read, not the elaborate service that had been planned by Steve, but straight from the prayer book.

"If there is any reason why you may not lawfully marry, confess it now." The priest paused for longer than necessary.

To her side Brigit scuffed her feet like she knew their secret and was struggling to keep it to herself. One day she would tell Amanda and Brigit everything. But Roan passed in modern society; he had a birth certificate and a passport. His bank, Birch Trustees, had taken care of his future. Money couldn't buy humanity, but it could buy the documents.

Not getting the answer he wanted, the priest continued through the consent. "Roan, will you take Eliza as your wife? Will you love her, honor her, and protect her for as long as you both shall live?"

Roan held her hand. His grip was firm and cool. He glanced at her as he spoke. "I will."

"Eliza, will you take Roan as your husband? Will you love him, honor him, and protect him for as long as you both shall live?"

A smile formed, and she almost missed her cue. "I will."

They turned to face each other.

"Take her right hand with yours," the priest told Roan.

Roan took both her hands. Orders still grated on his skin. The inability to carry weapons had him reaching and finding nothing. A sword lay under their pillows. How long would it take for the Shadowlands to stop haunting Roan?

"I, Roan, take you, Eliza, to be my wife. You're the

light in my dark. My hope that never died. Without you there is no life. My soul is yours. My sword is at your feet."

Dai was still paying enough attention to the service to hand Roan the ring.

Roan slid the plain platinum band onto her finger. It sat perfectly next to the ornate, black diamond ring. "To this I pledge you my word."

The hairs on the back of her neck pulled tight as if they were being watched by unseen eyes. For a moment the overwhelming quiet stole her voice. She took a breath before saying her vows.

"I, Eliza, take you, Roan, to be my husband." The air in the church thickened. She had to swallow before she could go on. "You're my wish made true. The strength that helped me fight my demons. With you I can dream. My love is yours. My heart is in your hands."

Brigit dropped the ring and it bounced three times, ringing through the church like a solitary bell. Amanda gasped. Laughter tightened Eliza's throat, and she glanced at Roan. He wasn't hiding his smile. Brigit placed the ring in her hand and mouthed *sorry*.

Eliza placed the ring on Roan's finger. The small, black diamond was almost lost in the wide band. "To this I pledge you my word."

Thunder rolled through the church. The air became metallic, sharp like a storm was about to break within the church. Roan and Dai looked up at the vaulted ceiling. For a heartbeat the church was full. Then the past let go and made room for the future. The priest muttered a prayer to God. Dai spoke in Decangli.

Roan nodded. "And so it is. The vows are accepted."

Ice rippled down her back. They didn't need any paperwork to be witnessed and signed when the gods had accepted their words.

The priest spoke just loud enough to be heard. "Those who God has joined let not man put asunder." He closed the prayer book silently and stepped back with his eyes on Roan as if he were the devil incarnate. "Kiss your bride."

And be gone was left unspoken. If the priest knew the truth, he would damn them both.

Eliza stepped toward Roan. The beads around her neck danced to their own tune. The music would never leave her. His lips brushed hers. A perfectly chaste kiss, suitable for priests and children to observe. But not what she wanted from her husband. She sighed and leaned into his arms.

They had survived the nightmare and created a dream. Her one and only wish was to live happily ever after with her king.

A wish Roan was more than happy to fulfill.

Read on for an excerpt from the next book
in the Shadowlands series

KISS OF THE GOBLIN PRINCE

by Shona Husk

Chapter 1

THERE WERE NO DECORATIONS IN THE CHURCH, NO FAMILY OR friends filling the pews. Amanda paused and glanced at the altar where Eliza's new mystery man waited with his brother. This was very different from the wedding that had been planned by Eliza's ex-fiancé Steve. This one hadn't been planned at all. Eliza and Roan were just making use of the church reservation. She took a breath and forced a smile. Eliza wanted this and even though Amanda thought Eliza was rushing to marry a man she hardly knew, she had to be happy for her. And Eliza seemed happy, happier than she'd been for years.

"She's on her way," Amanda called out as she walked down the aisle with her daughter, Brigit, at her side. The slim-fitting black-and-white bridesmaid dress restricted each step—well, that and the heels. She couldn't remember the last time she'd gotten dressed up. When she'd gotten married it had been in a registry office. That seemed so long ago now she could've been another person. She *had* been another person back then. Young and carefree. Her life had changed so fast. Widowed three months later. She glanced at Brigit, the only part of her husband she had left.

At least Brigit wasn't hampered by her dress. Instead it was the responsibility of carrying the ring Eliza was going to give Roan that slowed Brigit. She walked very carefully clutching the it as if it were going to jump out of her fist. From her other hand hung the black-and-white little bag made especially to match the dress. But it wasn't for show. Inside was Brigit's inhaler. She couldn't go out without it. Anything could set off a fatal asthma attack.

Please not today. Brigit had been looking forward to the wedding for months—she didn't care that Eliza wasn't marrying Steve; instead she'd been fascinated about Roan.

But it was Dai who captured Amanda's attention. He stood to one side, his long hair loose but not scruffy. The hair and black suit were at odds with how she'd thought he'd look. She'd been told he was a scholar. When she'd been at college, none of her professors had looked like him. He was too…too something she didn't want to label.

Dai turned his head and caught her gaze. His eyes were dark and mesmerizing. Her heart gave a solid thump, as if beating for the first time in years. Her smile widened before she could stop her lips from moving, and then a slow, creeping heat colored her cheeks. Dai gave her a small nod and a smile that made her feel like she was the one walking up the aisle.

Get a grip. It was a wedding and she was just in a happy, romantic mood because of Eliza. She was living vicariously through her. Being in love was exciting… even if Eliza was rushing to the altar with a man she'd known for only a heartbeat.

Wonder what Dai thinks of the quick wedding. She'd have to ask him later. And also take the opportunity to find out a bit more about the King brothers—for Eliza's sake.

She and Brigit took their places on the other side of the altar with the scowling priest looking on. He obviously didn't approve of the late change of groom. Brigit opened her hand for the third time to check on the ring.

"You'll do great," Amanda reassured her.

Brigit nodded and looked at the men on the other side. She frowned and asked, "Why does Roan's brother still have long hair?"

Her little voice echoed in the empty church. Amanda wilted on the inside—there was no way Dai could've missed the comment.

"I don't know," Amanda whispered with an awkward smile stuck on her lips.

Dai didn't need to cut his hair. It suited him, softened what otherwise might have been a fierce expression, with dark blue eyes someone could drown in.

Dai's gaze landed on Brigit, his face neutral as he spoke to his brother in another language—Welsh maybe from the soft lilts. Amanda held her breath, ready to leap to Brigit's defense, waiting for him to either laugh or scowl at her daughter. He did neither.

"To answer your question, little one—I like it long," he said in English with an unidentifiable accent.

Amanda sighed. At least he wasn't a children-shouldn't-be-heard type of academic. When she realized she was checking out how nicely the suit fit his body, she looked quickly away and studied the stained glass window before he could notice she was looking, again.

It was one thing to look at Dai and wonder what he looked like beneath his clothes, but another to act on it. She glanced at Brigit. Unlike Eliza, Amanda couldn't take risks and leaps of faith.

As she watched her sister-in-law walk down the aisle, Amanda realized she was jealous. Not pea-green, but enough that she knew what she didn't have, and what she'd lost. Matt should've been here watching his sister marry, watching his daughter grow up. Part of her had died with him and the rest had forgotten how to live as she'd poured her attention into Brigit and her battle for survival.

She didn't hear the words of the vows, only the echo of the words she'd promised years ago in a registry office. Her finger touched the wedding band Matt had given her. His was at home, barely scratched after only three months of use.

A tiny chime rang through the church. She gasped as she realized Brigit had dropped the ring and was scrambling to retrieve it as it spun on the stone floor.

Eliza let out a small laugh.

A peel of thunder rolled over the roof. Dai glanced up as if he could see something no one else could. He spoke in Welsh and his brother nodded.

"And so it is. The vows are accepted," Roan said in English

Accepted by whom? A trickle of ice traced down Amanda's spine, the church suddenly cold. Who were these men? Did Eliza truly know? And if she did, what was she hiding and why?

Amanda turned away when Roan and Eliza kissed, unable to fight the rising disquiet. She couldn't even remember what it felt like to be kissed by a man. Her gaze landed on Dai. He was watching her. The moment they realized, they both looked away as if they'd found something else suddenly absorbing.

"It's like in Cinderella." Brigit was grinning at the idea that her favorite fairy tale could come true.

Amanda stroked her daughter's hair and hoped that Brigit would be saved the heartache she'd experienced. It was a relief to step outside into the warmth of the winter sun. The sky was clear, and while the sun was bright, it lacked the heat to take away the chill. She shivered as gooseflesh rose on her arms.

"Here." Dai offered her his jacket, leaving him only a shirt and waistcoat against the cool weather.

She hesitated, not sure she wanted to take anything from him when she knew nothing about him. But that would be churlish and today wasn't about her.

"Thank you. Are you sure you won't be cold?"

He shook his head, his dark hair spilling over his shoulders. "This is practically summer."

"Of course." He was used to freezing Welsh winters and snow. He was going to find an Australian summer rather hot.

She draped the jacket around her shoulders, the lining still warm from his body. For a heartbeat she let herself be enveloped in his warmth and scent. Her body responded, craving his touch. It had been so long since she'd been close to any man.

If she could, would she? If Brigit never knew, did it matter? And how would she manage to date? She'd have to ask Eliza to babysit and then Eliza would ask a hundred questions...Eliza wouldn't want to babysit when she could be spending time with her new husband. Amanda twisted the ring on her finger, then stopped, horrified at what she'd been thinking. Could she really betray the man she loved for a moment of pleasure?

Brigit counted out jumps and hops on the pavement, entertaining herself while they waited for the cars. Her handbag swung from her wrist. Amanda wanted to ask Brigit to stop, but bit her tongue. She couldn't wrap her daughter up in cotton wool and force her to sit still in case she had an asthma attack—no matter how tempting the idea.

Her gaze slid sideways, but Dai had his back turned to her and was studying the church. He probably wasn't interested in her anyway. What man wanted an instant family? And if they did, it made her suspicious. Roan and Eliza were talking softly, their hands linked as if nothing could separate them.

That was what she missed the most. Having someone there. Someone she could count on. Someone to hold her. She closed her eyes and took a deep breath. For just a moment she let her imagination wander. What would it be like to be held by someone other than Matt? To have more than just Dai's jacket around her? She shivered as if cold fingers traced the nape of her neck.

"The cars are here." Brigit grabbed her hand.

Complicated. She opened her eyes. Dating was complicated without a fragile child that required constant attention.

The two black Jags parked out front. Eliza had told them to be back in half an hour, but the wedding had taken less than that. On the way to the church, the guys had been in one and the girls in the other. Now Roan and Eliza would take one, which left Amanda and Dai and Brigit with the other.

Dai held open the car door and Brigit slid into the backseat. Amanda followed, carefully swinging her legs

in, knees together. *Stupid dress*. Then he closed the door
and got in front. Out of the cool air, Amanda took off his
jacket and laid it on the seat, even though she wanted to
keep it wrapped around her.

She licked her lips. She had a hundred questions she
wanted to ask, but quizzing him in the car probably
wasn't the best idea as Brigit listened to everything.
And just because the chauffeur was silent didn't mean
he didn't gossip. After the media fiasco with Steve's
fraud, the last thing Eliza needed was questions about
her new husband. So Amanda leaned back and gazed
out the window. *Later*.

But maybe she was just making an excuse to spend
more time with Dai later.

The chauffeur drove back through the city and
stopped at the gourmet pizza shop not far from Eliza's
house. Dai went in and picked up the order. There was no
fancy reception, just pizza and champagne. She watched
as he walked back to the car, her fingers brushing his
jacket. He didn't move like someone who'd spent his
life behind a desk. There was a grace that only athletes
and people who understood their body acquired. There
was more to his life than study.

But it was much easier to label her attraction as
curiosity and to ignore the tightening in her belly. She
touched the ring on her finger; she'd never taken it off.
Couldn't. Yet Dai had caught her attention. She tried to
ignore the fragile sensation but it grew anyway, tightening her breath and making her light-headed like a
teenager in lust.

That's all this was. Simple lust. And she was only
overheating because she hadn't been with a man since

her husband. Dai got back into the car and gave her a small smile as if he knew exactly what she was thinking. Just because she was thinking about what he'd look like with less clothes didn't mean she would act on it. She forced herself to focus out the window. She didn't have time to indulge, or even dabble, in lust, and Eliza's new brother-in-law was definitely the wrong person.

With the pizza almost gone and an empty bottle of champagne sitting in the middle of the dining table, everyone was eased back in their chairs. Pizza tasted better when it hadn't been stolen and brought back to the Shadowlands. Dai's lips curved. Everything tasted better when not eaten in the Shadowlands. He finished his champagne and flexed his fingers against the glass. He'd never expected to be eating in the Fixed Realm again—as a man. But then he'd never expected to live again as a man. For too many centuries he'd thought either the curse or a blade would claim him. Despite his years of magical study he'd never have guessed the cure would've been as simple as love.

Then again, loving a goblin was never simple.

Coming Spring 2012

Acknowledgments

A lot of peopled helped shape this novel. I'd like to thank BN and TH for their advice on the police and legal work; the WINK girls for making sure I got the story out of my head and onto the page—a cross-genre critique group is worth their weight in gold; JD Cregan for his knowledge of story spine and structure; my family for being themselves. And my editor, Leah, for loving my goblins as much as I do.

About the Author

A civil designer by day and an author by night, Shona Husk lives in Western Australia at the edge of the Indian Ocean. Blessed with a lively imagination, she spent most of her childhood making up stories. As an adult she discovered romance novels and hasn't looked back. Drawing on history and myth, she writes about heroes who are armed and dangerous but have a heart of gold—sometimes literally.

The Eternal Guardians series...

TEMPTED

by *Elisabeth Naughton*

Isadora is missing. The words pound through his head like a frantic drumbeat. For her own protection, Demetrius did all he could to avoid the fragile princess, his soul mate. And now she's gone—kidnapped. To get her back, he'll have to go to the black place in his soul he's always shunned.

As daemons ravage the human realm and his loyalty to the Guardians is put to the ultimate test, Demetrius realizes that Isadora is stronger than anyone thought. And finally letting her into his heart may be the only way to save them both.

"ELISABETH NAUGHTON COMBINES DYNAMIC DIALOGUE AND SIZZLING ROMANCE WITH A WICKED COOL WORLD. DO NOT MISS THIS SERIES."

—*New York Times* bestselling author Larissa Ione

978-1-4022-6046-9 • $7.99 U.S./£5.99 UK

The Amoveo Legacy

UNLEASHED

BY SARA HUMPHREYS

WHAT IF YOU SUDDENLY DISCOVERED
YOUR OWN POWERS WERE BEYOND
ANYTHING YOU'D EVER IMAGINED…

Samantha Logan's childhood home had always been a
haven, but everything changed while she was away. She has
a gorgeous new neighbor, Malcolm, who introduces her
to the amazing world of the dream-walking, shapeshifting
Amoveo clans…but what leaves her reeling with disbelief is
when he tells her she's one of them…

And shock turns to terror as Samantha falls prey to the
deadly enemy determined to destroy the Amoveo, and the
only chance she has to come into her true powers is to trust
in Malcolm to show her the way…

*Get swept away into Sara Humphreys's glorious
world and breathtaking love story…*

978-1-4022-5843-5 • $6.99 U.S./£4.99 UK

No Proper Lady

ISABEL COOPER

"HIGH-STAKES MAGICAL ADVENTURE WITH WONDERFUL CHARACTERS AND A SEXY ROMANCE."
—Susanna Fraser, author of *The Sergeant's Lady*

England, 1888. The trees are green, the birds are singing, and no one has any idea that in a few hundred years, demons will destroy it all. Joan plans to keep it that way. All she has to do is take out the dark magician responsible—before he summons the demons in the first place. But as a rough-around-the-edges assassin from that bleak future, she'll have to learn how to fit into polite Victorian society to get close to her target.

Simon Grenville has his own reasons for wanting to destroy Alex Reynell. The man used to be his best friend—until his practice of the dark arts almost killed Simon's sister. The beautiful half-naked stranger Simon meets in the woods may be the perfect instrument for his revenge. It will just take a little time to teach her the necessary etiquette and assemble a proper wardrobe. But as each day passes, Simon is less sure he wants Joan anywhere near Reynell. Because no spell in the world will save his future if she isn't in it.

978-1-4022-5952-4 • $6.99 U.S./£4.99 UK

The Storm That Is
STERLING

LISA RENEE JONES

HE'S HER BEST WEAPON...

Sterling Jeter has remarkable powers as the result of a secret experiment to create a breed of super soldiers. Now he has to use everything he's got to help beautiful, brilliant Rebecca Burns, the only astrobiologist alive who can save humanity from a super-enhanced, deadly street drug.

Sterling and Rebecca's teenage romance was interrupted, and now they're virtually strangers. But the heat and attraction are still there, and even entrapment by an evil enemy can't stop them from picking up their mutual passion right where they left off...

PRAISE FOR *THE LEGEND OF MICHAEL:*

"JONES LAUNCHES A NEW SERIES WITH THIS THRILLING STORY OF LOVE AND DETERMINATION IN A SOCIETY ON THE BRINK OF WAR... READERS WILL BE HOOKED."
—*RT Book Reviews*, 4 Stars

"AWESOME SERIES...PLENTY OF ACTION AND ROMANCE TO KEEP YOU GLUED TO YOUR SEAT... AN AUTO-BUY FOR ME."
—*Night Owl Romance*, Reviewer Top Pick

978-1-4022-5159-7 • $6.99 U.S./£4.99 UK

HEART *of the* HIGHLAND WOLF

BY TERRY SPEAR

IT'S A MATTER OF PRIDE…
AND A MATTER OF PLEASURE…

EACH HOLDS A SECRET THEY CAN'T POSSIBLY OVERCOME ALONE…

Julia Wildthorn is sneaking into Argent Castle to steal an ancient relic, but reluctant laird Ian MacNeill may be the key to unlocking the one answer she really wants discovered…

From brilliant storyteller Terry Spear, modern day werewolves meet the rugged Highlands of Scotland, where instinct meets tradition and clan loyalties give a whole new meaning to danger…

Experience for yourself the sensual, action-packed, critically acclaimed worlds of Terry Spear, author of a *Publishers Weekly* Best Book of the Year:

"Crackles with mystery, adventure, violence, and passion."
—LIBRARY JOURNAL

"A thrilling, engaging, wonderful ride." —SERIOUSLY REVIEWED

"Romance, adventure, and a paranormal twist…If you like your werewolf stories with a bit of a bite, then pick this series up now."
—NIGHT OWL ROMANCE (REVIEWER TOP PICK)

"Full of action, adventure, suspense, and romance…one of the best werewolf stories I've read!" —FALLEN ANGEL REVIEWS

978-1-4022-4552-7 • $7.99 U.S./£4.99 UK

DREAMING *of the* WOLF

BY TERRY SPEAR

HE'LL PROTECT HER
OR DIE TRYING…

A FIERCE HUNTER…

Alicia Greiston is a no-nonsense bounty hunter determined to bring a ring of mobsters to justice. Her dogged pursuit of the crime family has forced her to avoid relationships—any man would only become a target for retribution. Luckily, Jake Silver is more than a man, and his instincts are telling him to stop at nothing to protect her.

However, the mob isn't entirely human either, and soon Alicia must flee for her life. When Alicia and Jake's passion begins to spill over into their dreams, Jake learns he will have to do more than defend her—he'll have to show his mate the way of the wolf.

"Riveting and entertaining…makes one want to devour all of the rest of Terry Spear's books." —FRESH FICTION

"Sensual, passionate, and very well written…another winner of a story." —THE LONG AND THE SHORT OF IT

"A must read…the chemistry is sizzling." —ROMFAN REVIEWS

"Full of nail-biting suspense, sexy scenes, and plenty of hot alphas… Spear knows how to keep her readers riveted."
—LOVE PASSION ROMANCE

DECEMBER 2012

978-1-4022-4555-8 • $7.99 U.S./£5.99 UK

DEMONS
Prefer Blondes

SIDNEY AYERS

Killer new haircut? $50... Creepy Antique Chest? $100...
Unleashing Hell on Earth? Priceless!

A BAD DAY FOR A DEMON

Rafe Deleon is a senior demon and he resents like hell his
assignment to Earth to retrieve the Chest of the Damned
before it falls into the wrong hands. But then he meets
beautiful, intriguing succubus Lucy Gregory, and she's
just unleashed a whole load of trouble...

REALLY SUCKS FOR A SUCCUBUS

Lucy's chic suburban beauty salon has suddenly become
the Underworld's center of mass chaos and destruction.
The only good thing in a day rapidly going down the tubes
is the arrival of a gorgeous demon who's adamant that he
can help her...

But Lucy has quite a few deeply unpleasant—not to mention
deadly and hateful—surprises ahead of her, and surely
there's never been a worse time to try out a new boyfriend...

978-1-4022-5174-0 • $6.99 U.S./£4.99 UK

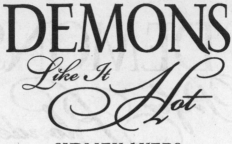

DEMONS
Like It Hot

SIDNEY AYERS

If you can't stand the heat,
get out of hell's kitchen.

A RECIPE FOR DISASTER...

Matthias Ambrose is a demon mercenary who never took sides, until his attraction to the spunky caterer he was hired to kidnap leads him to almost botch a job for the first time in eight hundred years. Now he must protect her from his former clients, but even an ice-cold demon like Matthias struggles to resist her fiery charms.

OR THE PERFECT INGREDIENTS FOR PASSION...

Completely engrossed with planning menus and prepping recipes for her shot at cooking show fame, star caterer Serah SanGermano refuses to believe she's on a fast track to Hades. But how's she supposed to stick to the kitchen if she can't stand the heat of her gorgeous demonic bodyguard?

As a diabolical plot to destroy humanity unfolds and all hell breaks loose in Serah's kitchen, she and Matthias find themselves knee-deep in demons and up to their eyeballs in love...

DECEMBER 2011

978-1-4022-5177-1 • $6.99 U.S./£4.99 UK

TOUCH IF YOU DARE

STEPHANIE ROWE

HE'S JUST ABOUT THE HOTTEST
WARRIOR SHE'S EVER SEEN…

Reina Fleming really appreciates a man who's on a mission—especially when he's a badass warrior doing his best to impress her. And Jarvis is charmed by the way Reina's magic touch can soothe his dark side.

But when Jarvis's attention puts her job, her home, and her family in danger, Reina has to decide whether love is worth the price…

Enter the nonstop, action-packed world of
Stephanie Rowe's love stories—you'll never
think of the manly arts in the same way again.

"ROWE IS A PARANORMAL STAR!"

—J. R. Ward, #1 *New York Times* bestselling author
of Black Dagger Brotherhood Series

978-1-4022-4196-3 • $6.99 U.S./£4.99 UK

HOLD ME IF YOU CAN

STEPHANIE ROWE

ESCAPING HELL WAS THE EASY PART...

Nigel Aquarian finally escaped from hell—now he wants to go back. After losing his best strategy for controlling his all-consuming rage, he'll need to find something—or someone—to keep his inner demons under control long enough to strike back at the maniacal witch who has captured his comrades.

NOT KILLING EACH OTHER'S GOING TO BE THE REAL CHALLENGE...

Enter Natalie Fleming. She is supposed to be able to bend anyone to her will, but since her own brush with death, she's been just a little off. The only way she can kick-start her powers is by giving free rein to her sensual side, and while that didn't go so well last time, the tortured warrior who needs her help is making quite a convincing case for losing control...

When these two fiery, passionate souls cross paths, they discover they are each other's best chance to defeat the hell that haunts them...if, of course, they don't destroy each other first.

JANUARY 2012

978-1-4022-4197-0 • $6.99 U.S./£4.99 UK